I SEE THE FACE

Praise for Shahidul Zahir

It's good to read works outside the sphere of the Anglophone and the European, not because we perform a duty by doing so, but because, as with these arresting novellas by Shahidul Zahir, they amplify our sense of what fiction can do. Zahir's world is close, sometimes violent, but never claustrophobic. It enables discovery, even love, showing us the curiously moving ways in which human beings assign value to small things, including their own lives. – AMIT CHAUDHURI

In these novellas the political is the personal is the intimate is the lyrical is the ironic is the universal. Perhaps it would be best if you were to read these books which will leave you with unforgettable images of a jamdani of skulls and a flock of sarus cranes as harbingers of a nation in the throes of birth. – JERRY PINTO

Celebrating
30 Years of Publishing
in India

Zahir's writing is propelled by an alertness to the inner lives of objects, animals, the landscape, and marginalized people as they collide against the obscene lies created by those in power. Haunting and apocalyptic, his fiction may be about the recent past, but it reads like a literature of the future. – SIDDHARTHA DEB

Zahir, through this prose, has the ability to make the readers revisit and re-evaluate some of the most important truths of life. – DEVAPRIYA SANYAL, *Sunday Standard*

Short, pithy, compact ... unsettling the present and casting a dark shadow on the future. – RAKHSHANDA JALIL, *The Wire*

A rare gift ... Zahir synthesises hard-hitting social realism with a surge of surrealist paranoia to forge a style that keeps the reader on tenterhooks. – SOMAK GHOSHAL, *Mint*

Translating a work of this literary value is challenging. It becomes even more difficult when much of its power is associated with nuances of language and local culture. The translation succeeds spectacularly in this regard. The descriptions of places cast a spell that leaves you wide-eyed, like a child listening to stories of faraway places. – DIPANJAN SINHA, *The Hindu*

SHAHIDUL ZAHIR

I SEE THE FACE

A NOVEL

TRANSLATED FROM
THE BENGALI BY V. RAMASWAMY

HARPERPERENNIAL
An Imprint of HarperCollins *Publishers*

First published in English in India by Harper Perennial 2023
An imprint of HarperCollins *Publishers*
4th Floor, Tower A, Building No. 10, DLF Cyber City,
DLF Phase II, Gurugram, Haryana – 122002
www.harpercollins.co.in

2 4 6 8 10 9 7 5 3 1

P-ISBN: 978-93-5629-407-3
E-ISBN: 978-93-5629-408-0

Typeset in 11.5/16.2 Adobe Caslon Pro at
Manipal Technologies Limited, Manipal

Printed and bound at
Replika Press Pvt. Ltd.

FSC
www.fsc.org
MIX
Paper from
responsible sources
FSC® C016779

This book is produced from independently certified FSC® paper to ensure responsible forest management.

For Mr G.M. Khan

It would not be appropriate for the author to explain *I See the Face*; nevertheless, it is necessary to clarify a couple of things. First, the names of some individuals and places associated with the Christian faith in Bangladesh, as well as some related information, used in this novel have been taken from: *Banglapedia,* published by the Bangladesh Asiatic Society; *Bangadeshe Khristodhormo O Khrishtiyo Somproday* (Christianity and the Christian Community in Bengal), by Louis Prabhat Sarkar, published by Lord Jesus Church, Kolkata; and the collection of volumes, *Bhakti Pushpo* (Flowers of Faith), published by Protibeshi Prokashoni, Dhaka. However, in regard to the use of individuals' names, historical chronology has not been followed. The excerpts from Christian hymns used in the narrative are taken from Louis Prabhat Sarkar's book. Second, while some other names from the present which are used in the book may match those of actual persons, all the incidents and associated descriptions narrated in this are, needless to say, entirely imaginary.

S. Zahir
Dhaka
February 2006

pour elle
si je lui vois encore

Perhaps Chan Miya of Ghost Lane had been nourished by monkey's milk as an infant, because if you ever met someone like, say, Mamun and Mahmud's Ma, Mrs Zobeida Rahman, who was witness to that, at her residence in No. 25, and if the conversation turned to the subject of Chan Miya, she never forgot to say, '*O toh bandorer dudh khaichhilo.* But he was raised on monkey's milk,' and if anyone ever cast doubt on that, she would definitely get into an argument and, if necessary, quarrel. For instance, take Fakhrul Alam Ledu, he was Mamun's childhood friend, they were both first-year Intermediate students; let's say he went to Mamun's house one day to meet him, but maybe Mamun was not at home then, something like that could definitely have happened, Ledu might have gone there, and Mamun may well not have been at home then, and so it would be a most normal thing for Mamun's Ma to meet Fakhrul Alam Ledu when she emerged from her room. And after that, if Mamun's Ma said, 'Since you're here, come, have a cup of tea,' and if Fakhrul Alam Ledu agreed, then in that case, the situation would have been created for some stray conversation between Ledu and Mamun's Ma as they sat together in the house; the subject of Chan Miya could have come up in the course of this conversation, and if Fakhrul Alam Ledu expressed any doubts in that connection, Mamun and Mahmud's Ma would definitely have told him, 'You know nothing!'

But why wasn't Mamun ul Hye, aka Mamun, at home? And so Fakhrul Alam Ledu asked Mamun's Ma, 'Where's Mamun, where's he gone?' Perhaps Mamun's Ma knew where he had gone, or maybe she didn't know, perhaps she said, 'I don't know where he's gone,' or perhaps she said, 'He went to fetch sawdust.' Mrs Zobeida Rahman used a sawdust-fired stove in her kitchen.

Perhaps one day, because Mamun's school was closed, he left home with an empty wheat sack – the same one which his Ma had lengthened by stitching another sack on to it – and proceeded towards the timber yard in Nayabazar. Perhaps he walked down Twin Bridge and Lalchan Mokim Lane and then made his way through Malitola, and presented himself at The New Chondroghona Saw Mill & Timber Depot, perhaps it was raining that day and the sawmill had closed in the evening after running all day, and after reaching there and bargaining with some employee or sawyer about the price of sawdust, when a price of three taka for a sack was finally agreed upon, he descended into the pit of sawdust at the base of the siris tree in the sawmill. The dust from the wood sawn all day had accumulated in the pit, so upon descending into this pit and seeing the mountain of sawdust there, perhaps a kind of elation came over Mamun, like it did over Ali Baba of yore, and perhaps on account of being rapt, or perhaps for some other reason, he somehow got buried under a mound of sawdust while trying to fill his sack, and since the employees of the mill didn't notice it, he remained concealed like that. That night, four five-ton trucks belonging to Abdul Wodood Chowdhury, the brother of the sawmill owner, Abdul Mabud Chowdhury, were parked in front of The New Chondroghona Saw Mill & Timber Depot, and a group of coolies, or porters, who were ready in advance carried baskets of sawdust from the pit and emptied them over some white sacks that were already inside, thus concealing them. The coolies asked the drivers of the trucks, 'What's going today?' But the drivers of the trucks didn't reply, they frowned and looked deadpan as they sat with a lordly air, their hands on the steering wheels, but nothing was lost thereby, because these coolies were extremely intelligent, they reckoned, 'It's fertilizer, going to Burma.' Or perhaps these coolies weren't intelligent, but be that as it may, the problem that should have arisen in this regard, irrespective of whether the coolies were intelligent or otherwise, did arise, and Mamun Miya left Dhaka for Chittagong along with the fertilizer and sawdust. This is how it happened: while these intelligent, or stupid, coolies were loading their baskets with sawdust, they certainly found him; perhaps he was lying unconscious within a mound of sawdust when they discovered him, but given that they were unable to turn the lights on while working, and therefore it was dark inside the mill, they bundled the curled-up, unconscious Mamun into a basket and threw him into one of the trucks, but it did occur to them that perhaps it was a piece of wood, it wasn't far-fetched on their part to think so, after all they were coolies who were the offspring of coolies, and so they thought that whatever lay within sawdust couldn't be anything other than wood, perhaps it was something expensive, like teak or beech, it could also be siris or gorjon, or some sundry tree, like kadam or chhatim, or perhaps just any kind of wood. Or perhaps they didn't think along those lines, perhaps they were not so stupid, and when they were using their hands to load the sawdust into their baskets and found Mamun ul Hye lying there, they realized, notwithstanding the darkness, that it was a human and not a block of wood, because they found that it had two arms, two legs and a head, and these coolies knew that it was humans who had two arms and two legs and a head, and so they got scared, it occurred to them that perhaps this was a corpse, and then they displayed their intelligence: without saying a word, they carried Mamun in a basket and dumped him into one of the trucks, because they thought that if they tried to report this matter now it was they who would get in trouble with the police, who would ask them a thousand and one questions, perhaps they'd kick and punch them too, so it was best to dispatch the object found in the mill owner's sawdust in the lorry belonging to his brother!

Perhaps Mamun was unconscious as he lay in the sawdust, and so when the lorry left for Chittagong late at night, he wasn't aware of anything; and because it had been raining that day, the trucks had tarpaulin covers, and whenever these trucks departed from Nayabazar, they went down the road beside Dholaikhal, turned at the Jatrabari crossroads and got on the road to Chittagong. It's difficult to say where exactly the trucks would have gone to unload the goods that day, the stuff might have been loaded on a trawler or a sampan in Chittagong at either the Firingibajar or Sadarghat docks, or at the foot of the Kalurghat bridge, but before that the trucks fell into the clutches of the police mobile squad near Chouddogram, in Cumilla District, and although the police were able to halt three trucks, one truck didn't stop, and amidst the fluster, the veteran driver quickly turned into some side road and escaped. But perhaps the truck driver got scared, and so he took the truck directly to Satkania where the export merchant Abdul Wodood's village house was, or perhaps the truck went to Firingibajar or Sadarghat, and when the merchant's employees there heard about the trucks having been chased by the police, they decided that the goods ought to be taken to the village house. So in this way, Mamun Miya arrived, together with the consignment of urea to be smuggled, at Abdul Wodood Chowdhury's house in Boyaliyapara, in the Satkania locality of Chittagong District, and after that he encountered Asmantara Hoore Jannat; and so one day

Mamun ul Hye's Ma narrated to Fakhrul Alam Ledu the story of Chan Miya, and told him, 'Just go and ask Chan Miya's Ma, Khoimon, who suckled him.' Perhaps that was because there were monkeys in the moholla during Chan Miya's infancy, and those monkeys could be seen on the roofs and walls of the houses in the moholla, with their brown backs, whitish bellies and red backsides; they used to walk along walls or lie on the parapet of some house with their tails dangling. Perhaps there were one, or two, or many, female monkeys in this troop of monkeys then, with the baby monkeys clinging to the breasts of the female monkeys and swaying between their legs. Perhaps Chan Miya had drunk the milk of some she-monkey like that when he was an infant, when his Ma, Mochhammot* Khoimon Begum, aka Khoimon, left him unattended at home, latching the door from outside, and proceeded from her house on No. 36 to the house of Nurani Bilkis, aka Upoma Begum, at No. 37, and requested her, *'Aafa, amare ek kaap chini dhar daen.* Aapa, please lend me a cup of sugar.'

Nurani Bilkis's husband, Fajlur Rahman, ran a ration shop in Raysha Bazar and so there were huge quantities of sugar, rice and wheat in his house, but she simply glared at Khoimon Begum; perhaps Moyna Miya was

---

* 'Mochhammot' is the way 'Mosammat' is pronounced in Puran Dhaka, the old quarter of the city of Dhaka. It is an honorific; used at the beginning of a Muslim woman's name, it says that she is a follower of Prophet Mohammad. In abbreviation, it is written as 'Mst'.

alive then, or maybe he wasn't, because Moyna Miya went missing in 1971; he used to sell taro stems and gourds of different kinds in Thatari Bazar, he was a vegetable seller there; so, on hearing Khoimon's request, Nurani Bilkis glared at her, she observed how comely Khoimon was, and so she got annoyed again, and she thought that a missing vegetable seller's wife, who, like the proverbial washerman's dog, belonged neither at home nor at the jetty, oughtn't to be so comely, and so she said, '*Ekdin ahosh tyaler laiga, ekdin ahosh chinir laiga – khali chaya mainga khach, ki tui!* You come one day for oil, you come the next day for sugar – you just go around begging for food, what's this?'

Perhaps Khoimon felt ashamed, and replied, 'Please give it to me, I swear I'll return it as soon as I draw my rations next week!'

But Nurani Bilkis was not moved by such talk, she kept Khoimon waiting, she thought that Khoimon would get frustrated and perhaps leave after some time; but she didn't leave, she squatted in the kitchen and waited silently, holding a porcelain cup with a broken handle. Nurani Bilkis carried on with her cooking, she poured out the rice starch, tempered the dal, after which she went inside on the pretext of some important task, and then returned with a busy air, and all the while Khoimon kept sitting there, and so Nurani Bilkis addressed her again, 'What's wrong with you?'

Khoimon proffered the cup in her hand and said, 'I told you, I'll return it!'

Nurani Bilkis felt utterly helpless, she got angry, and after that she turned despondent when she realized that there was no way she could drive out this coarse, shameless and greedy woman; she said, 'Go and get my wheat ground.'

Khoimon agreed, 'I'll do that.'

Nurani Bilkis was adamant, 'No, go now and get it ground first, you'll get the sugar after that.'

Khoimon told her that the mill wasn't open in the afternoon and that she'd get the wheat ground when the shop opened in the evening; so there was nothing Nurani Bilkis could do, and she was compelled to give Khoimon the sugar. Returning home with the sugar that day, Khoimon saw that the door was unlatched and a troop of monkeys was jostling inside the room. Perhaps the monkeys had entered the room with a purpose, and if they had found bananas or radishes inside they would have carried those away; but they had found Khoimon's pot of cooked rice, so they brought the rice down from the shelf and began to eat it up, but perhaps the infant Chan Miya woke up and began bawling then, and so the monkeys were in a terrible fix, they were afraid that people might arrive there hearing Chan Miya's screams – and that's when the incident of a female monkey suckling Chan Miya occurred. Perhaps there was a mother monkey in the troop of these thieving monkeys, and perhaps she was very clever, or maybe she had turned soft-hearted on account of being a baby's mother, and so she then advanced and thrust a hairy nipple into Chan

Miya's mouth, and sucking noisily at the teat, Chan Miya drank the monkey's milk and fell asleep. When Khoimon went later in the evening to Nurani Bilkis's residence to get the wheat ground, perhaps she herself narrated this tale, and said, 'When I returned home I saw that there was a troop of monkeys inside the room, and they had brought the rice pot down and were eating that, and a baby monkey was playing with my boy'; or perhaps the monkeys hadn't unlatched the door and entered the room on that first day, perhaps Khoimon had made a mistake, or simply made it up; perhaps when she returned from Nurani Bilkis Upoma's place with the sugar, she had seen one, or two, or maybe five monkeys sitting quietly atop a wall near her house, and perhaps the female monkey with a baby was also among them, and that day Khoimon observed that the female monkey's eyes looked ashen and melancholy as she gazed into the room through the window grille, perhaps they were teary. Seeing this, Khoimon's heart missed a beat, and she said to herself, what's this, what are so many monkeys doing here, and then rushing inside the room she saw to her relief that Chan Miya was lying spreadeagled on his back, sleeping; after that, Khoimon went in the evening to pick up the wheat to be ground, and observing her, Nurani Bilkis exclaimed, 'Why have you come so late?'

Khoimon replied, 'Give me two measures of wheat flour!'

Nurani Bilkis turned breathless with rage when she heard that, and she retorted wheezingly, 'You're a crooked one indeed, when I gave you sugar in the morning, you said you'd get the wheat ground, and now you ask for two measures of wheat flour! You needn't do anything, go away!'

Khoimon said, 'I'll return it,' but Nurani Bilkis didn't feel like talking any more, she said, 'Just go, you're simply greedy!'

Khoimon went to the wheat mill in Banagram Lane and returned after getting five or seven seers of wheat ground, and Nurani Bilkis came with an old, lidless, medium-sized can of Robinson's Barley and said, 'Wait, let me measure it.'

Khoimon began to walk away, she said, 'You measure it, I'm off!'

When Khoimon then neared her house, she saw that the door was latched, but there were monkeys sitting quietly on the wall; seeing the monkeys, Khoimon's heart once again trembled with fear, she wondered, what's this, it seems whenever I'm not at home the monkeys come and sit here, and after that, when she unlatched the door and entered the room, she saw that, like before, Chan Miya was lying on his back on the cot, fast asleep. But even afterwards, when Khoimon observed the monkeys, initially Khoimon didn't have any suspicions as such, she was only a little scared, after all a monkey was a violent creature, a wild animal, what if it jumped and bit the baby; and when Nurani Bilkis Upoma said that Khoimon was very greedy, it was apt, perhaps Khoimon really was greedy, but it was difficult to say why this was so, perhaps this was something she was born with, perhaps the matter of this disposition expressed itself soon after her birth, when she was an infant, perhaps she sucked the nipples of her mother Jorimon's fat, swollen breasts continuously for seven or ten days until they were sore, and perhaps Jorimon said, '*Eita kemun maiya hoilo, Allah, rakkos niki!* Allah, what kind of girl is this, is she an ogress or what!'

But perhaps it wasn't so, perhaps Khoimon was only a tiny, bundle-like, innocent and cuddly girl; and her father, Abdul Jalil, and brother, Rashidul, went around carrying her in the crook of their arms and indulged every whim of hers, and after that, when she grew up, they said, '*Tui boro hoya geli ga, haay Khoda, awkhone tawre loya amra ki kori!* You've gone and grown up, O God, what are we to do with you now!'

Khoimon was plaiting her hair then; she heard Abdul Jalil, she heard Rashidul, and perhaps she said, '*Ja mone loy koro!* Do whatever you want!'

Abdul Jalil then pulled her into his arms, '*Tui amar ma hawch na?* Aren't you my precious?'

Khoimon thought that she was indeed Abdul Jalil's precious, and she replied, '*Hoi toh.* Of course I am!'

After that she grew up some more, her hips swelled and she developed breasts, and then Abdul Jalil again said, 'You've grown up, girl, oh what am I to do with you,' but this time, Khoimon didn't speak; perhaps Abdul Jalil drew her close once again, placed his arms around her shoulders and said, 'Aren't you my precious?' Khoimon was silent once again, and realization then dawned on Abdul Jalil, so at night he said to his wife, Jorimon, '*Maiya dekhi chup maira gechhe, kotha jigai, kunu ra kore na.* I observed our girl's turned silent, I asked her something but she didn't say anything at all.'

Then, on Jorimon's advice, Abdul Jalil and Rashidul set out to find a boy for Khoimon, they searched here, there and everywhere, they searched in the north and in the south, and then, after all that searching, they found Moyna Miya in Thatari Bazar. Someone said, perhaps it was Babul Miya, 'There's a boy, he's handsome and tall, just like a prince, he must be from somewhere like Bikrampur, he has a shop in Thatari Bazar, go and meet him.'

Hearing Babul's recommendation, Abdul Jalil was eager, although the boy was only a shopkeeper; and perhaps after that Jorimon too was pleased to hear about it from Abdul Jalil, and after that one night, when Jorimon told Khoimon about Moyna Miya, Khoimon trembled, she felt feverish, she saw a merchant's son, like from the film *Arun, Barun O Kiranmala*, standing before her, and then she felt drowsy. But it occurred to Khoimon that she wasn't going to marry some shopkeeper even if he was a prince or the son of a merchant, she would rather marry a peon or a watchman in some office, or a school clerk. Nevertheless, they went one day to meet Moyna Miya, perhaps Babul Miya accompanied them; they found Moyna Miya when they advanced a bit towards Kaptan Bazar after going past Thatari Bazar, he sat waiting for customers on the pavement with a basket of potatoes, pointed gourds, and two or four or ten large-sized ash gourds smeared with lime. Abdul Jalil realized that he had been deceived, Moyna Miya was like flotsam, and there was no question of marrying his daughter to him; Jorimon too was of the same view, she said, '*Babul bhaiye emun thokbaji korlo!* How could Babul Bhai cheat us like this!'

But Khoimon felt dejected then, she couldn't fathom why this man had to be a vegetable seller and sit with a basket of wretched ash gourds in the market, waiting for useless customers, why was Moyna Miya not a watchman or a peon or a school clerk instead of a vegetable seller, and thinking about that made her lose her appetite, she slept poorly, and she had dark circles around her large eyes! Then one day, her Ma observed that her daughter's plight was dire, so she said, 'Hey Khoi, what's happened to you?'

But Khoi didn't say anything. Perhaps Abdul Jalil and Jorimon realized what the matter was, they said, 'Just you see, we'll bring such a fine boy for you!' They set out in all directions in search of a groom, but it was difficult to find a good match for the daughter of the paan-and-biri seller, Abdul Jalil, until finally Babul Miya arrived once again; matchmaking wasn't his profession, he did it out of love; he looked for Abdul Jalil and spoke to him about Khoimon's marriage, he said, 'Moyna Miya is a good boy, he's an independent vendor, what's wrong with that, what's the problem with selling ash gourds, at least he isn't a thief, maybe he sits with a basket beside the street, but he'll certainly not be sitting there for long, his circumstances will surely improve, if he sells a basketful of thirty ash gourds at seven or eight taka each, perhaps he makes a profit of two taka a day, if he spends eight annas for his meals, he'll make a taka-and-a-half each day, that's forty-five taka a month and five hundred and forty taka a year – a lot of money – and then by bribing the market committee perhaps he'll find some place in a niche inside the vegetable market very soon, after that perhaps he'll even have a permanent shop in the vegetable market, and perhaps thereafter he'll set up a provisions store or a ration shop – that could well happen, who can say, tell me, can't that happen, after all, how many people are born rich!' Abdul Jalil listened to all this talk, but he didn't seem interested as far as Moyna Miya was concerned, a vegetable seller was merely a vegetable seller, how could he have any savings? Perhaps he was a pauper; Babul Miya then spoke about Humayun Kabir, he lived in South Moishundi and ran a ration shop in Shah Shaheb Lane, he wore gold buttons on his punjabi, 'He's a fine boy, he'll be a good match for Khoimon.' Abdul Jalil then considered the matter at length with Jorimon, they discussed and analysed in detail what might transpire and what might not, and then they spoke to Khoimon about the matter, but Khoimon was in a quandary when she heard them; she thought that Humayun Kabir was a far better name than Moyna Miya, or maybe it was Moyna Miya that was a better name – the name of a bird, the mynah; but she felt dejected at the fact that Humayun Kabir was the owner of a ration shop, she couldn't understand why vegetable sellers and ration shop owners were the only matches that could be found for her! Nevertheless, Khoimon accompanied her parents one afternoon to the ration shop in Shah Shaheb Lane to meet Humayun Kabir; perhaps Humayun Kabir didn't realize the reason for the group's visit, and he asked, '*Apnera koithon aichhen?* What brings you here?'

Abdul Jalil then made up a lot of things, and perhaps he was successful in making Humayun Kabir ill at ease with his irrelevant talk, or perhaps he wasn't able to fool him and Humayun Kabir figured out the matter; be that as it may, whether Humayun Kabir understood or not, they had seen what they had come for, and they didn't like Humayun Kabir. Although he was the owner of a ration shop, the man was too old, he hardly had any hair on his head, and on making enquiries, Abdul Jalil found out that Humayun Kabir was looking for a girl for his third marriage, both his previous wives had died but they had borne him no children and so, even though he was a widower, he was free of any encumbrances. Babul Miya tried to reason with him. 'What's wrong with him?' he asked. But even if Abdul Jalil was in two minds about the matter, it was a real wrench for Jorimon's maternal feelings, after all it was her beloved daughter, so she again remarked, 'Babul Bhai did this to us? He's brought a boy who's a doddering widower!'

But even after that, the matter of Humayun Kabir's being the proprietor of a ration shop was of great relevance, they could not disregard the fact that the girl would live in comfort if she married him, and perhaps Jorimon then spoke to Khoimon about this, but Khoimon remained silent; a day went by, two days went by, and on the fifth day, Jorimon became restless, she called her daughter and asked her, '*Tui kawta koch na kyala?* Why don't you say anything?'

Khoimon then said, 'I'll marry Moyna Miya, make the arrangements.'

But in this country, a girl couldn't get married merely by consenting; before this, Khoimon had gone with her parents and brother to see Moyna Miya, now it was Moyna Miya who came to their residence in Ghost Lane to see her. Moyna Miya arrived one evening at their two-roomed premises on No. 36 Ghost Lane, he came alone, or perhaps the matchmaker, Babul Miya, accompanied him; so that evening, Khoimon Begum entered the outer room wearing a sari, the ghomta drawn over her head, and sat down on a vacant wooden stool, and through the gap in her ghomta she studied Moyna Miya closely in the light of the hurricane lamp; her regret knew no bounds. Moyna Miya was dark-skinned, but he had a sharp nose, his eyes were like two pebbles submerged in a limpid pool and his arms were muscular; once again it occurred to Khoimon that this man sold vegetables, that he sat like a simpleton on the edge of the road with ash gourds – how amazing! At night, Khoimon vividly recalled Moyna Miya's youthful body, and her sleeplessness worsened; Jorimon and Abdul Jalil then hoped that they would come to know Moyna Miya's decision very soon, but Moyna Miya didn't say anything. Didn't he like Khoimon? Had they lost him? Abdul Jalil then rushed to Babul Miya, 'Babul Bhai, have you heard anything yet!'

Perhaps Babul Miya too was waiting for Moyna to tell him something, but Moyna Miya hadn't spoken to him either, and so Babul Miya himself went one day to meet Moyna Miya at Thatari Bazar and asked him, '*Ki re? Maiya deikha aili, kichhu koch na!* What's up? You saw the girl, why aren't you saying anything!'

Moyna Miya then told him that he hadn't been able to see anything of Khoimon's ghomta-covered face in the dim light of the hurricane lamp, so how would he know what the girl looked like and whether he liked her or not! Abdul Jalil and Jorimon heard about this, as did Rashidul; Khoimon was her parents' beloved daughter and her brother's much-adored sister, they got angry when there was mention of showing the girl again to the vegetable seller, that wretched lowly chap, they said, '*Amago maiya rastay kuraya paichhi nihi, baare baare dekhamu!* Did we pick up our girl from the street that we'll show her again and again!'

They turned down the proposal of showing the girl again and thought that they had thereby saved her from a calamitous and grave humiliation; perhaps Jorimon then told Khoimon about all this one evening or night, perhaps Jorimon was applying coconut oil to her daughter's hair and plaiting it, she made a single thick plait that hung over her back, with a red satin ribbon flower at the top, and said, 'He says he couldn't see her properly, the donkey! Is our child some orphan who came floating on the river that we'll show her again!' Because when Fakhrul Alam Ledu went to Mamun's house looking for him, he didn't find Mamun, so he then asked Mamun's Ma, Mrs Zobeida Rahman, 'Where's Mamun gone? Where's he gallivanting!' Perhaps Mamun had gone to the residence of Mrs Mary J. Clark, the Anglo-Indian teacher of Silverdale Kindergarten School, or of Miss D'Costa – perhaps it was to Mrs Clark's residence only, because it was she who loved and indulged her students, and so they knew her house too. Perhaps it was to her house that Mamun had gone, because her daughter, Julie Florence, who was like a talking Barbie doll, was there, perhaps Mamun hadn't said anything to Fakhrul Alam Ledu, perhaps he regularly made secret visits to Mrs Clark's home in the lane in Tikatuli where the Women's Education Institute was located, perhaps he sat quietly with Julie in the hazy light of dusk, perhaps Julie Florence Clark gazed at the darkness outside while Mamun looked at the pictures hanging on the walls; or perhaps they talked, and looking at a picture on the wall, Mamun asked her, 'Which mosque is this?' And Julie Florence then laughed and said, 'It's not a mosque, it's a church, it's St Peter's Basilica, the church of St Peter in the Vatican.'

'*Vatican kun jaygay*? Where's the Vatican?'

'Why do you say *kun jaygay*? The Vatican is in Rome, in Italy.'

'Where's Italy?'

'Italy is in Europe.'

'Where's Europe?'

Julie Florence thought that Mamun was joking with her, so she said, 'I don't know where it is.'

'Wherever it might be, do you feel like going to Europe?'

'I do, *yes, I would like to go, but my Mom is trying to go to Australia.*'

Mamun Miya then silently gazed at the pictures again; he recalled that on the day he first came all by himself to Mrs Clark's house, he wanted to flirt a bit with Anglo-Indian girls, after all this was a Muslim country, it didn't really matter if one did a bit of all that here with them, and so that day when he saw Julie wearing a dotted sleeveless frock with a floral pattern, he felt breathless as he observed Julie's budding breasts, exposed arms, knees and legs, and the small crucifix on the thin sterling silver chain around her neck. He thought that Julie Florence wasn't human, she was a fairy, she would fly away that very instant to

Rome or to Australia, he felt a great desire to put his arms around Julie Florence and give her a kiss; he said, 'You're great, Julie,' but the girl was very shrewd, she sat beside the door, far away from Mamun, on a cane-bottomed chair, she didn't sit close to him, she pretended not to understand what he was saying as well, because she knew such talk was like a trapdoor and that as soon as you went through it you were done for. Mamun Miya then said to her, '*Tumi awto doore boshe thako kyala? Kachhe aisha bosho!* Why do you sit so far away? Come and sit near me!'

But although Julie Florence was fourteen years old, the feminine entity within her made her as alert as a doe in the realm of a tiger, so she asked him, '*Apne kyala bolen kaeno?* Why do you say *kyala* for why?'

It occurred to Mamun that perhaps Julie was fooling around a bit with him, he liked this banter; he said, '*Kyala komuna kyala?* Why shouldn't I say *kyala*?'

'Say *kaeno*. Not *kyala*. Say *kaeno bolbo na*.'

'All right, I'll say *kaeno*. But why do you people want to go away to Australia?'

Julie Florence didn't really have a clear idea, it was her mother, Mrs Mary Joyce Clark who wanted to go. Her father, Robert Francis Clark, and her brother, Joseph Eugene, too wanted to go. But why did they want to go?

'Why do you want to leave the country and go away? *Kyala*?'

Julie Florence thought she didn't know the answer, or maybe she did; perhaps there was nothing for them to do in this country; her father, Bob, was the garden supervisor at the British Council, he managed the gardeners in the grounds, planted grass, had it mowed, he had the gardeners cultivate flowers according to the season, and then returning home to the lane where the Women's Education Institute was located, he told stories about all this ludicrous work of his to his wife and children, about chrysanthemum seeds that were to be brought from Holland this monsoon, about a famous story by John Steinbeck about this flower, and he lamented, 'If only tulips could be made to bloom in this country!' Perhaps the girl Julie listened to his stories with interest, and although she was young in years, she was concerned about her father, about how the man was trying to protect himself from the feeling that his life was useless, perhaps it occurred to her that, in truth, if tulips could grow in this country then her father would definitely have made tulips bloom in the garden of the British Council on Fuller Road, and perhaps then Steve, Mr Steven H. Arnold, the Director of the British Council in Dhaka, would see the flowers one day and stop, extend two fingers and touch a bud and say, 'Hey, Bob, how fabulous, I see you've grown yellow tulips from Amsterdam here! Bravo!'

Perhaps Robert Clark would then smile and reply, 'It's nothing great, sir, if only there was some more dew, you'd see the kind of tulips I could have grown in this very country!'

But that wasn't to be; here, in this country, there were only cosmos and dahlia, and there were yellow marigolds, of course, there was kolaboti too; Robert said that when Steven had newly arrived in Dhaka after his transfer from Nairobi, he grew very fond of the white kolaboti flowers of the rainy season. But how long could a person like the same thing? If only there was a bit more dew in this country, if only the winter was a bit longer and colder, then perhaps Robert Francis Clark's life would have been different; Julie Florence felt sad for him, but Joseph couldn't bear to hear his father, he'd say, 'Why do you talk such rubbish, what difference does it make to a gardener, nothing, *kuchh nahi*, you're a useless man, Dad, take it easy and enjoy your futility!'

Perhaps Julie understood Joseph's point too; Joseph Eugene Clark worked in the Bangladesh Government Press in Tejgaon, he was a mistri, a mechanic; the compositors and machinemen salaamed him, and when the Heidelberg or the Honar treadle machine, or the Yamaha double demy or double crown flat machine manufactured in Japan, were out of order, he repaired them. He received a monthly salary – the gross monthly salary was 1,350 taka, according to the national salary scale in 1985, but he had some additional earnings as well – he got a share of the money for buying spare parts – and private parties too arrived after office hours to get his services, machinemen came and took him to Bongshal or Bangla Bazar perhaps to the Alexander Machine Press in Nawabpur – '*Iktu deikha daen, ostad, roller niya bahut jhamelay achhi.* Just take a look, chief, I'm in a fix with the rollers' – the proprietor was happy if Joseph mistri laid his hands on the machine, perhaps the machine was too; but Julie Florence thought that her mother wasn't happy, and that her mother couldn't get over the fact that, although she was a teacher in the Silverdale Kindergarten School, her husband was the chief of the gardeners, and her only son was a printing machine mistri! For all these reasons, her mother was distraught, nothing was achieved in life, and as Julie Florence grew older, she realized that her mother's uneasiness about her coming of age also increased, but nothing could halt her maturation, her skirts, frocks and panties kept getting smaller, it occurred to her that alongside her bodily growth she felt somewhat disoriented too, she wondered what would happen now, she was going to become an adult in this country – what was to happen to her now in this country, with this body! Then the young Mamun Miya arrived like a fox in their Women's Education Institute lane, hoping a piece of meat would fall by chance from a crow's beak, perhaps Julie Florence understood the matter, or perhaps she did not understand it very clearly, yet she felt a strange, unspecified sense of alarm, perhaps she felt a bit confused when she looked at Mamun Miya's face, perhaps she wondered why Mamun Miya said this. Didn't Mamun Miya know why they wanted to go away to Australia? She said, 'I don't know why I want to go away, my Mom is the one who wants to go, I don't know why she wants to, maybe she doesn't like it here!'

'Do you want to go? Why?'

Julie Florence got upset when Mamun Miya said that, perhaps she hadn't encountered such behaviour before in her young life, she looked at Mamun Miya's face and said, 'What are you saying? Won't I go? If Mom goes, of course I'll go – where else will I be?'

Did Mamun ul Hye then start weeping in the semi-darkness of dusk? Perhaps he didn't cry but was melancholy, and he gave up the idea of forcefully or semi-forcefully kissing Julie Florence in the darkness, he thought how beautiful this daughter of Teacher Mary was, and why wasn't there a place for her to stay in this country, so he said, '*Tumi jaayo na, Julie, tumi ekta phul pori, tumi Australia jaayo na, ei deshe thako, tumi gele ga amader ki hobe, amader phul baganer ki hobe bolo?* Don't go, Julie, you are a flower fairy, don't go away to Australia, stay in this country, what'll become of us if you leave, what'll happen to our flower gardens, tell me?'

Fakhrul Alam Ledu guessed what the matter was, because he wasn't at all as much of a fool as people thought him to be, so he said to Mamun, 'Do you go often to Teacher's house?'

'What's it to you if I go?'

'Are you after Julie Florence? Have you kissed her?'

'I haven't been able to yet, but I want to.'

'I'd like to as well.'

'*Mandarpola! Maira phalamu tawre, bhadro ekta meyere niya tumi bodmaishi chinta koro!* You son of a swine! I'll kill you, you dare have wicked thoughts about a decent girl!'

'*Tumi ki koro, haramjada bandor?* And what do you do, you bastard monkey? If you keep on going to Teacher's house, I'll tell her that you're hovering around to do mischief!'

But Ledu's words had no effect, Mamun knew that Ledu was saying these things just like that; and so Fakhrul Alam Ledu went again to Mamun's house and found that he wasn't at home, and when he encountered his Ma, he said, 'Tell me where he's gone, Khala!'

Not bringing up the subject of Chan Miya this time, Mrs Zobeida Rahman said, 'What was the name of your teacher?'

Ledu understood, he asked, 'Has he gone to Teacher's house?'

'Yes, your teacher has a daughter, he's gone to meet her.'

'Who told you that?'

Perhaps it was from Mamun that his Ma had heard that, and Mrs Zobeida Rahman had then told him, 'I don't like girls like that, they lie in wait with their mouths agape, to swallow men – like Chan Miya's mother, Khoimon – and shrewd girls like that have only devious motives in mind'; but why did Zobeida Begum say all that? Because Khoimon perhaps eventually had to resort to guile in order to marry Moyna Miya, the vegetable seller in Thatari Bazar; she was perhaps sixteen or seventeen then, because girls were married early then, or perhaps she was older, twenty or twenty-two, but in Zobeida Rahman's words, 'She was too old, no one liked her when they saw her.' And regardless of whether she was sixteen or seventeen or twenty or twenty-two, after Moyna Miya came to view her, he said that he hadn't been able to see her; Moyna Miya may have been up to some mischief, after all, does anyone say something like that after seeing a girl? How amazing! Consequently, Khoimon's parents' ire was justified, but however angry and full of bluster they appeared to be, Khoimon's days just didn't seem to pass, her nights seemed unending, there were dark circles, like at the bottom of a cooking pot, under her large eyes, and she thought that perhaps Moyna Miya was actually being naughty, that perhaps he had seen her just fine and perhaps he simply wanted to see her once more. So after her Ma, Jorimon, said, 'We're not so cheap, we don't show our daughter again and again,' she turned speechless when she looked at Khoimon's face, and she asked, 'What's happened to you, Khoi?'

Khoi replied, 'If he wants to see me, call him again!'

Jorimon then told Abdul Jalil about this, who told Babul Miya, and the worth of Moyna Miya, who sat on the road in Thatari Bazar with vegetables adorning his basket, could be gauged in this Bengali land, but Moyna Miya wasn't demanding any more, if he was, then Khoimon Begum would have wept, or perhaps she would have gone to Thatari Bazar and asked him, 'Why are you doing this?' But he did not make any further demands, he only wanted to see Khoimon once more, and so he arrived again at her house in Ghost Lane. That is when the incident took place, and perhaps it was because of this that Mrs Zobeida Rahman said so many things about her, because perhaps the incident had been prearranged, and Khoimon had organized it together with the moholla kids; or perhaps it hadn't been prearranged, perhaps it was merely a coincidence. That evening, while Moyna Miya, who was clad in a shirt and trousers and wearing plastic shoes, walked down the lane adjoining the temple, and Khoimon once again lit a kerosene lamp in the outer room of the house on No. 36 and waited like a female spider – a black widow that had spun a wide web to catch prey, and was sitting still in the centre. And so Moyna Miya advanced; he passed the house on No. 25, and perhaps it was the rainy season then, so he got the heavy fragrance of kamini flowers wafting from inside that house, and after that he walked by the house on No. 32, and he saw that on either side of the paved terrace in front of the house was a platform on which a tiger made of cement sat with its head raised; after that, when he arrived in front of the house on No. 36, a bunch of kids suddenly came running from who knows where, raising an uproar, and just then a dog too landed up from somewhere, and the end of the stocky, well-rounded dog's tail was cut; as Moyna Miya was about to enter through the gate of Khoimon's house, the kids set the dog upon him – stretching their arms and pointing towards Moyna Miya, they screamed, 'Shoo, Tommy, shoo, shoo!'

Springing up threateningly, the dog then sought to jump upon Moyna Miya, so he began to run in fear, and entering the house he went into the room where Khoimon Begum, having just lit a hurricane lamp, was waiting. But Moyna Miya's misfortunes didn't end even after he was in the room, he stumbled over the threshold and fell with a crash on the cot, and after that when he gathered himself and his eyes adjusted to the room's dimness, he saw in the weak light of the hurricane lamp that his body was pressed over Khoimon's – perhaps she reprimanded him then, '*Ki koren, shoren!* What are you doing, get off me!'

Or perhaps she gazed at Moyna Miya's aquiline nose and small chin as he pressed down on her and said, '*Amare niki apne dekhen naika, awkhone deikha lawn, abar koyen na je harikol battir aloy chokkhe dekhen naika kichhu!* I believe you couldn't see me last time, see me now, and don't say again that you couldn't see anything in the dim light of the hurricane lamp!'

It's difficult to say what Moyna Miya did then, perhaps he fondled Khoimon's tender, young body and she felt as if she had lost her moorings, perhaps Khoimon said,

'Please marry me, Moyna Miya, after you buy vegetables from Shyam Bazar, I'll sort and wash and clean them, you won't have to do anything, you just rest awhile, have a paan, smoke a biri, puff on your hookah, and after that I'll wind a gamchha around for your head and lift the basket up for you to carry to the market, and if even that's difficult for you, if you find it too heavy, I'll carry the basket on my head and walk behind you while you lead the way, I'll lay out and arrange your shop and then return home, and once there, I'll cook rice for you, make a curry for you, I'll make whatever you feel like eating, and when you finish the vending you'll eat lunch, I'll sit close to you with a palm-leaf fan, so please marry me'; or perhaps Khoimon didn't lose her moorings and Moyna Miya hurriedly got off Khoimon's body and went and sat on a corner of the cot and said, 'The kids are so terrible, they set a dog upon me!'

'Did you get frightened?'

'No, why would I get frightened? The kids are simply monsters!'

Khoimon left the room and returned with a bowl of rice payesh prepared by Jorimon, she brought a glass of sherbet made with Rooh Afza, and Moyna Miya had the payesh, making a clinking sound as his spoon scraped against the porcelain bowl, he drank the sherbet making a glugging sound, and Khoimon watched him eat; she then moved her face forward, close to the light from the hurricane lamp placed on the table, and gazed at him, her eyes said, 'Look at me,' her face said, 'Look at me,' her bent, hazy figure said, 'Look at me again, Moyna Miya!' Perhaps Moyna Miya gazed at her once, and then when he exited after eating the kheer, he told Babul Miya, 'Make arrangements for the wedding, and ask the girl's father what he'll give me,' and when Mamun's Ma, Mrs Zobeida Rahman, told Fakhrul Alam Ledu these things as well, Ledu asked her, 'How do you know this?'

'Hey, wouldn't I know? Don't we live in the same moholla!'

So Khoimon got married to Moyna Miya, and perhaps this took place before the Liberation War of 1971, because when war broke out on the night of the 25th of March, Chan Miya was probably in Khoimon's womb, maybe she had come to full term, and so when everyone in the moholla fled towards Cumilla or Jinjira out of fear of the Pakistani army, it wasn't possible for Khoimon to leave home. When the moholla was completely deserted, Jorimon became terribly anxious, Abdul Jalil too became perturbed; then, rather than have all of them remain in the moholla and die, Jorimon stayed at home with her daughter, while Abdul Jalil went with his son and his son-in-law and took shelter in Jorimon's uncle's or aunt's house in the village of Chorail in Jinjira. The people who had fled Dhaka were trapped in Jinjira by the Pakistani army like mice caught in a crevice; and once the women, men, elderly folk and children from Dhaka gathered there, the army launched an operation, and after Abdul Jalil ran through the paddy fields in Jinjira with his son and son-in-law, he spotted a single-storeyed building at one end of a field, the building was enclosed by walls on all four sides, with a wooden door on one side which was latched on the inside. It then occurred to Abdul Jalil and his companions that it was not possible for them to run any more, they had exhausted almost all the strength in their bodies, and if they continued running through the fields in this way they would be spotted by the Pakistani army and be shot at and killed. And so they went and banged on the door in the boundary wall of the house, but no one opened the door, so they banged on the door again, and still no one came, and they then called out in a hushed tone, 'Help, open the door!'

When the door wasn't opened even then, Rashidul climbed over the wall, he had to do that because their lives were at stake, and when he entered the compound and unlatched the door, Abdul Jalil and Moyna Miya entered, and they saw that the door of the house inside was ajar. They walked up to the door and peeped inside, and they saw a tall, bearded man dressed in a long, white shirt that reached his knees sitting on a mat spread out on the floor with his back resting against the wall, thumbing prayer beads with his eyes shut, he seemed to be meditating – only two of his fingers moved. They were astonished to see this man, they were afraid to disturb his meditation by speaking or entering the room, they did not spot anyone else inside or outside in the compound, and so they found themselves in another kind of danger. They shut the door of the compound and crouched in one corner of the courtyard, and all three of them muttered prayers; a long time went by, and then they heard the indistinct sound of people's uproar coming from afar, they kept their ears peeled, the clamour steadily drew closer and then they could make out the words amid the commotion, they heard the people chanting the slogan, 'Pakistan zindabad,' and Abdul Jalil and his companions realized that perhaps the Pakistani army was advancing this way, and that the people were doing it out of fear after having spotted the soldiers! The sound of the people proclaiming their love for Pakistan became clearer and clearer until it was very close, it made their blood run cold; they rushed inside the house even as they squatted, and seeing them, the tall man in the long shirt stood up, his right hand was slightly raised, and a tasbir, a set of brown-coloured prayer beads, hung precariously from it, he became terribly agitated and restless, and without stopping to find out who Abdul Jalil and his two companions were, he said, 'You people stay here, I'm going'; he then exited the house, climbed over the rear wall and left. There was nothing they could do, they gave up the thought of climbing over the rear wall and fleeing like this man, the three of them went inside and sat down on the mat with their backs resting against the wall, they recited prayers and blessings; Abdul Jalil put his hand into the pocket of his punjabi, took out a skullcap and put it on, and after that some more time went by; they kept thinking that perhaps the danger from the army had passed, and they became drowsy after all the anxiety and exhaustion, and then, as they slumbered, they thought they could hear someone knocking on a door somewhere! When they woke up, they listened carefully and were then certain that someone was banging the outer door of the house very loudly, they had no option, Rashidul or Moyna Miya, perhaps it was Rashidul, went and opened the door and saw soldiers in khaki uniforms, holding Chinese automatic rifles, standing in front of him, they pushed the door and entered the compound, and one of them asked, '*Yeh kya darwesh ka makaan hai? Kahan hai tumhara darwesh?* Is this the darwesh's house? Where's your darwesh?'

It's difficult to say what Rashidul made of that, in fear he pointed to the house and said, '*Ei, ei.* There, there…'

That afternoon, when the army men went and stood at the door of the room, they saw the bearded and skullcap-wearing Abdul Jalil sitting inside, resting his back against the wall, and they asked, '*Aap darwesh hain kya?* Are you the darwesh?'

Seeing the soldiers, Abdul Jalil stood up, and when the soldiers saw that, they felt ill at ease, the same soldier then spoke again, perhaps he was the leader of this squad of four or five soldiers, and when he said, '*Aap baithiye ji, aap buzurg hain, aap baithiye*. Please sit, sir, you're an elder, please sit,' Abdul Jalil sat down, and Rashidul and Moyna Miya sensed an opportunity to run away but there were two soldiers standing at the door of the building and looking outside, and so it was not possible for them to escape, they remained standing, that's all they could do. But gradually they realized something, and perhaps Abdul Jalil too, who was by now bathed in perspiration out of mortal terror, realized the same to some extent; the man who had climbed over the wall and fled was perhaps regarded as a darwesh by the people of the area, the Pakistani soldiers had heard about him from the local people, and arriving here and seeing Abdul Jalil now, they felt ill at ease, his long white beard and the skullcap on his head had created an illusion in their minds – and even after seeing Abdul Jalil's dirty punjabi and even dirtier lungi, the truth of the matter didn't become clear to them – so Abdul Jalil sat down on the mat once again, and indicating the empty space on the mat with his hand, he said, '*Aapnera boshen*. Please sit down.' It was certain that they had no clue as to what Abdul Jalil said, but since he had pointed to the mat, their leader, perhaps he was a lance naik or a naib subedar named Khamisu Khan or Shahbaz Khan or Bachcha Khan from the Baloch or Punjab or Sindh regiment, nodded, '*Nahi, nahi, hum log nahi baithenge, aapke yahan kya pani hai, hum pani pee sakte hain?* No, no, we won't sit, do you have water here, could we drink some water?'

Thus it became evident that the throats of the Pakistani soldiers, who were fed up with killing people, had become parched, and that they had come to the darwesh's house to drink water, and so Abdul Jalil called out, 'Rashidul, Moyna Miya, come here!'

Rashidul and Moyna pushed past the soldiers and went and stood in the room inside, trembling like two captured convicts, and Abdul Jalil said to them, 'They want to drink water, go and bring water for them.'

Rashidul and Moyna Miya figured out that they would lose their lives if they weren't able to provide water to the Pakistani soldiers, so they went into another room inside and found an aluminium jug and two or three glasses there, but there was no water in the jug or anywhere else in the room, so they put the glasses down on the mat and went outside with the jug, they decided that if they found water, they would return, and if they didn't, they would leave Abdul Jalil behind and flee. But they found a hand pump at the rear of the house, and Moyna Miya worked the handle of the pump and filled the jug with water, and then Rashidul went to the rear wall and stood on his toes and looked over it, and he saw that a short distance away from the wall, the ground sloped down and met the paddy field, and the darwesh's bullet-ridden, lifeless body lay haphazardly on the slope, face down; but when Babul Miya fixed Khoimon's marriage, Abdul Jalil and Jorimon were incensed upon hearing the boy's dowry demand, they said, '*Eita kemun pola, koy jigan amare ki dibo*. What kind of fellow is this, he says ask them what they'll give me,' and they were certain that the boy wasn't a decent sort, he was taking advantage of them, and so they once again said that their girl was not so cheap that she had to be married off to a vegetable seller by paying a dowry, '*Dimu na biya maiyar*. We'd rather not get the girl married.'

But Khoimon was not as agitated, she said, 'Ask him what he wants, give him whatever he wants!'

Moyna Miya demanded half of their house, and Khoimon was in tears when she heard that, she cried and cried, there was no end to her crying, and she wondered what kind of man was this, he was merely a vegetable seller, not a watchman in any office, nor a peon, not even a school clerk, he was a pauper, and he wanted half of a house built on a katha of land in the city of Dhaka! When Khoimon couldn't stop crying, Babul Miya arrived, he thought over the matter, and he had no doubt that the village boy was extremely imprudent, he could have asked for the money to set up a provisions store, he could have asked for the earnest money to start some other business, but instead of doing that he had straightaway made a bid for their vitals, and so Babul Miya spoke once again about Humayun Kabir, and hearing him say that, Khoimon stopped crying at once, and she said to her Ma, 'Give him what he wants, give him whatever's my share, after all it'll remain mine!'

Abdul Jalil and Jorimon finally agreed to that, Rashidul didn't object, and on the wedding day itself Abdul Jalil wiped his tears and put his zigzag signature at the bottom of the transfer deed made out on a sheet of white, foolscap paper, and Moyna Miya uttered 'kabool', meaning 'I agree to the marriage', only after that. This was how Mst. Khoimon got married, and on the nuptial night, the first thing she asked Moyna Miya was, 'How could you do something like that!'

'What did I do?'

'Why did you ask for the house to be transferred in your name in order to marry me?'

'You set a dog upon me, so I took the house.'

Perhaps Khoimon wondered whether the man was a soothsayer, how had he found out that she had done that! Or perhaps she was surprised and wondered what the man was saying, what dog, why would she set a dog upon him, amazing!

She asked, 'Why would I set a dog upon you?'

'I know you did!'

But perhaps Moyna Miya was yet to learn about Khoimon, and so when he entered the bedroom that night, Khoimon realized there was a sheet of paper in his punjabi pocket, and she thought that it must be the transfer deed for half of the house, the man didn't even have a place to keep that piece of paper and such a man had done this deed! Be that as it may, perhaps Abdul Jalil said, '*Maiyar mukher dike takaya korlam.* I did it for my daughter's sake; perhaps Jorimon had a heavy heart, but still thought, 'We had a duty to get our daughter married!' It seemed then that perhaps Moyna Miya said a bit too much to Khoimon on the wedding night because the demand for property transfer by the vegetable seller Moyna Miya was indeed something excessive, and for that reason, or because of stress owing to the wedding, it was a sad Khoimon, wearing a red Banarasi or some other red sari, who was sitting on the nuptial bed, perhaps the look on Abdul Jalil's face while signing on the house transfer deed too upset her greatly – yet even after all that, she was waiting for something joyful. But she didn't like it when Moyna Miya accused her of setting a dog upon him, and when the night advanced a bit and Moyna Miya was busy preparing for the first intercourse, Khoimon was silent at first, and then she said, 'What do you have in your punjabi pocket, it's making a rustling sound?'

Moyna Miya didn't say anything, so Khoimon once again said, 'Why don't you take the paper out and put it on the table?'

Having lost his senses in his state of arousal, Moyna Miya did just that, he took out the thick sheet of paper kept folded in his pocket and placed it on the table beside the bed, and then after he finished his business he lay on his side or on his back and Khoimon hurriedly got up and did various things: she poured water from the jug placed on the table and drank it, she poured some for Moyna Miya too and gave it to him, and as she did that she caused an accident, the jug wobbled and fell on its side, the water in it spilled on the table and soaked the deed of Moyna Miya's suddenly acquired house; Moyna Miya asked, 'What happened?'

Khoimon didn't reply, and perhaps Moyna Miya was tired, so he too kept quiet, and after that they fell asleep or didn't sleep, and a long time later Moyna Miya again asked, 'What happened?' And then Khoimon said that the water in the jug had spilled on the table, and perhaps even then Moyna Miya didn't realize what had happened. Moyna Miya got out of bed after a considerable while and he saw Khoimon sleeping on the cot, curled up next to the wall, and then as he turned up the wick of the hurricane lamp and was about to leave the room to piss, he noticed that the land title lying on the table, made out by his father-in-law, was drenched and destroyed! His heart almost stopped beating, and when he raised the wick of the lantern some more and tried to pick up the document, it tore because it had been drenched with water for so long; he screamed, and after that he carefully unfolded the document and laid it out on the table and observed it, perhaps the ink in Abdul Jalil's pen wasn't permanent either, perhaps it was the Hero Royal Washable Blue ink, and so all the writing had been washed away by the water, nothing remained except for some blue smudges! Moyna Miya, the boy from Bikrampur, the tall, dark-skinned, sharp-nosed vegetable seller sobbed uncontrollably; of course Khoimon was woken up by his crying, she hurriedly sat up on the cot and asked, 'What are you doing? What are you up to?' And then everyone in the next room woke up and entered, they saw the new groom drowning in tears on the nuptial night; but Moyna Miya was unable to say anything, so Khoimon then consoled him, '*Apne kainden na emun koira, ekta kagoj gechhe, aar ekta leikha dibone!* Don't cry like this, one piece of paper was lost, I'll get another one made!' And consequently, it seemed there was a reason behind Zobeida Rahman's exasperation with Khoimon, but again perhaps it could be said that Khoimon hadn't really done anything cunning, that was how things transpired and she had nothing to do with it – although it was very difficult to prove this. However, if Khoimon was indeed cunning, it wasn't possible to figure out how Mamun's Ma was harmed by that, of course when Chan Miya organized the monkey brigade in the moholla many years later, it seemed then that even before figuring it out logically Zobeida Rahman had a gut feeling about some things – what the monkeys would do to her one day – although the matters were perhaps not very clear to her. And it seemed that badmouthing Khoimon was her sole preoccupation, perhaps she said to Fakhrul Alam Ledu or to someone else, 'Just see how cunning the woman is, since she doesn't have the time to take care of the boy, how cleverly she got a band of wild animals to do it. *"Khaat tawra, ami aram kori!* You lot work, let me relax!"'; and so a monkey suckled Chan Miya, put him to sleep and kept watch over him while that wretched woman gallivanted in the moholla! This was perhaps true, or perhaps it wasn't, because it wasn't possible to get so much done by wild monkeys, but hadn't Khoimon herself said all this to Nurani Bilkis Upoma? Although Nurani Bilkis got annoyed from time to time, it was she who Khoimon was fond of, whenever she got the chance she went from her residence on No. 36 to Nurani Bilkis's residence on No. 37, and said, 'Aapa, give me something or the other!'

That day, Nurani Bilkis was in a pleasant state of mind and body, she asked, 'What shall I give you? I'll give you a cup of sugar, take it.'

'What will I do with sugar? I've drawn my sugar ration.'

'Then take a bowl of curry, I've cooked khoilsa fish with eggplant.'

But it was observed that Khoimon was not as greedy as she was thought to be, she said that she didn't want the curry.

'Then what do you want?'

'Give me a sari.'

Nurani Bilkis got really angry then.

'You want a sari, do you know what the price of a sari is?'

'Give me an old one.'

Nurani Bilkis's anger then abated somewhat.

You always leave your boy at home, aren't you scared?'

'I'm scared of the monkeys, but what can I do, after all I have to go out.'

Perhaps Khoimon also told Nurani Bilkis why she was scared of the monkeys, or perhaps she didn't say all that and only said some things while remaining silent about others, perhaps she also made up some things. She said that one day she returned home from somewhere, perhaps it was from Upoma Begum's residence, and she observed a row of monkeys sitting on the wall in front of her house, seeing her returning they continued lazily plucking lice from one another, this happened for three or four days in succession, she was terribly scared, and she observed that there was also a female monkey with a baby in the band of monkeys, and this female monkey gazed strangely from between the rods of the open window of the room at Chan Miya who was lying on the cot inside, 'Seeing that, my heart froze,' she said. After that, she cut up an old sari and made a curtain which she put up at the window; she said that when she had to go somewhere nearby, she didn't feel like leaving her son behind and locking the door, that made her unhappy – so she only latched the door before leaving. But on account of the depredations of the monkeys, perhaps nothing was gained by putting up a curtain at the window, monkeys were monkeys after all, they removed the curtain; when

Khoimon subsequently began shutting the window, the monkeys exceeded themselves, after all they didn't have much sense, one day when the monkeys went to sit on the wall and scratch each other and saw that the window of Khoimon's room was shut, they were unhappy, and that was when the mother monkey showed them the way; the band of monkeys opened the latch on the door, entered the room and sat there, they brought down the pot of rice from atop the shelf and ate the rice, the baby monkey slipped off its mother's bosom and jumped around, and so Chan Miya, who was lying on a piss-soaked kantha, woke up and the baby monkey began playing with him. The reclining female monkey watched them playing, then she suckled her baby, and when Chan Miya began bawling, this female monkey inserted her nipple into his mouth; although Fakhrul Alam Ledu maintained that this was not possible, it didn't matter, why would people heed what he said? If Khoimon said the monkeys sat atop the wall of her residence and kept watch over Chan Miya, then, if they could do that, why on earth wouldn't they be able to enter the room and feed him as well! Perhaps Khoimon did not know about all these events, perhaps she didn't want her son to be suckled by a monkey, but if Mrs Zobeida Rahman didn't believe that, she was justified in doing so. Perhaps she told Fakhrul Alam or somebody else that it wasn't just the matter of suckling, that Khoimon actually left the entire task of raising of her son to the monkeys of the moholla while she was busy with her business of making and selling paper packets, and the proof of this was that after Chan Miya was born, when the milk in her breasts dried up despite her being healthy and robust, she began buying milk from milkmen, who came regularly from Dayaganj or from the water tank at Twin Bridge to deliver milk, but as soon as she observed the monkeys and especially the suckling one, the idea grew in her head and she somehow managed to make the female monkey comply and stopped buying milk from the milkmen, and nourished by the freely given milk of the female monkey, Chan Miya kept growing; second, Khoimon observed that the monkeys were a nuisance, the female monkey kept gazing sadly at the little baby inside the room, and seeing that she was perturbed, Khoimon put up a curtain at the window, and later she also shut the window, but she kept the door shut in such a way that the monkeys could open the latch and enter the room, and Zobeida Rahman opined, '*Kemun chalak maiyalok, Alla!* Allah, what a shrewd woman!'

It was difficult to say with certainty whether or not Chan Miya had been suckled by a monkey, but perhaps after his name came to be associated a lot with monkeys, it was towards them that he inclined, and then the matter was not favourable for Zobeida Rahman as the monkeys kept coming to the roof of her house and shitting there! But perhaps there was nothing Khoimon could do, her reasoning was not so weak, if she had to go somewhere far, she did take Chan Miya along, but if it was close by, her maternal instincts could well be averse to locking up her boy, and if the monkeys seized that opportunity to do something, it would not be correct to call her shrewd or cunning or a scoundrel on that account.

Consequently, perhaps Khoimon latched the door of her house and went to Nurani Bilkis's place, and on her way she saw the troop of monkeys sitting in a long line on the wall, she paused for a while near the monkeys, she gazed at the female monkey with the kid, perhaps the monkeys felt uncomfortable seeing her gazing at them, they scratched themselves with their long arms, they blinked repeatedly, turned their faces and looked away. After that, Khoimon went and presented herself before Nurani Bilkis and said, '*Ahoner sumoy deklam bandorgula line diya amar ghorer samne deowaler upore boya roichhe, amare deikha chokh pitpitay!* As I was coming, I saw the monkeys sitting in a line on the wall in front of my house, they blinked when they saw me!'

'You left your son behind, aren't you afraid?'

'What can I do? Actually I think the monkeys aren't bad.'

'Just you see, they'll carry your son away!'

Nurani Bilkis merely voiced her fear, but it was later learnt that whatever a person thinks can also come to pass if there is a conducive environment; and in this instance the situation was indeed conducive, Khoimon became increasingly daring in regard to the monkeys and thus became inattentive, and the infant Chan Miya too perhaps grew fond of the baby monkey, and so one day, the female monkey carried him along. When Khoimon realized what had happened, there was nothing she could do, or perhaps by then she was no longer alarmed by this behaviour of the monkeys, she tried to keep mum about the matter but it was Nurani Bilkis who found out first, because some time during one night when Nurani Bilkis Upoma opened the door of her room and went outside to take a shit, it seemed to her that a small child was crying somewhere nearby; at first she thought that perhaps the sound was coming from Khoimon's place, but after that she realized that the sound of crying was coming from the roof of a nearby building, she felt a bit perturbed then, but when she heard the sound of crying again on her way back to her room, she stopped by the well and heard the chattering of the monkeys and felt extremely scared, she thought, 'Oh Allah, the monkeys haven't taken the careless, inattentive woman's boy, have they!' She then went and stood on a raised brick base next to the wall of Khoimon's house and called out to her; hearing her name being called in the middle of the night, Khoimon woke up, and when she opened the window and peeped out, Nurani Bilkis said to her, 'The monkeys have taken Chan Miya!' Khoimon was startled, and she blurted out, 'What on earth are you saying!'

'What can I say! As I stood at by the well, I heard a baby crying on a roof!'

'Go to sleep, it's not my baby.'

Nurani Bilkis went home, what else could she do other than go back, the boy's mother didn't care, 'Who is she to me anyway,' she thought; yet she felt ill at ease, she thought she could hear the sound of a human baby crying for a long time from somewhere nearby, she thought that it must surely be Chan Miya, that perhaps his mother, Khoimon, was lying, oh dear, perhaps the monkeys took him away every now and then with their troop, and Khoimon too slept without a care knowing no harm would come to him! Perhaps Mrs Zobeida Rahman didn't hear the sound of a human baby crying in the monkeys' den, she didn't need to, because in such matters wasn't it enough that one person heard it? And so she said, 'If the monkeys take along with their troop the baby of a mother who has him suckled by a monkey, then what's so surprising about that? There's nothing to be surprised about, it's definitely possible'; perhaps she said to Fakhrul Alam Ledu, '*Bandorer doodto khaichhei, bandore awre loya gechhilo ga!* He wasn't just suckled on monkeys' milk, they monkeys took him away too!'

Although Fakhrul Alam Ledu didn't believe that, nevertheless it occurred to him that it might be true, and why shouldn't it? Because Ledu recalled that after he was admitted to the Silverdale KG, the first day he went to school, wearing the school uniform – a white shirt with a tie, maroon-coloured shorts, and Bata 'naughty boy' shoes – he saw that there were two others from Ghost Lane in his KG-1 class, one of them was Mamun, his dear friend, and the other one was Chan Miya, but he could never figure out the nature of his relationship with him. When Ledu heard Mamun's Ma's words, he remembered Chan Miya and he thought that Chan Miya could be a boy suckled by a monkey, because he recalled that he had never come across such a disorderly human child. Perhaps Chan Miya too knew what Mrs Zobeida Rahman said, perhaps he grew up being suckled by a monkey when he lived in Khoimon's house, and after that when he was three or four years old, perhaps someone asked him for the first time, 'You drink monkey's milk, are you a monkey?' And so that day, for the first time, his child's heart fell into confusion, perhaps he felt ashamed and scared on account of having drunk monkey's milk while living among humans, or felt so because he was living among humans after having been suckled on monkey's milk – perhaps that was why he later returned to the monkeys. But however fat Fakhrul Alam Ledu might be, and however much his front teeth protruded, or however straightforward he might seem, he was not at all an idiot, and that was why when Mamun's Ma later told him one day that Mamun was not at home, Ledu then ventured past Baldha Garden and presented himself at Teacher Mary's house in the lane that housed the

Women's Education Institute; Julie Florence opened the door and said, 'Hi Ledu Bhai, it's good that you've come, your friend is waiting for you!' Following Julie up the stairs then, Ledu arrived at the flat on the first floor and found Mamun ul Hye gazing at a picture on the wall; he noticed Ledu and asked Julie, 'Is this a mosque, Julie?'

Perhaps the little girl Julie was wearing a red dress, and hearing Mamun's query she replied, 'It's not a mosque, it's a church!'

'Where is this?'

'In the Vatican, in Rome.'

'Where's Rome?'

But could such talk at all advance with the nuisance of a Ledu in the room? It couldn't. Mamun ul Hye was very unhappy, he thought that Ledu was a prize idiot: my dear, when you know full well that I've come to Teacher's house, where's the need for you to come, leave me alone, let me talk to her in my own fashion, and you can come some other day and talk to her in your own fashion; but no, you have to come and be a big fat fly in my ointment! However, Ledu didn't fathom all that, what was the harm in both of them meeting Julie? He placed his big fat hand on Julie's head and asked, 'Where's Teacher? What's she doing? Why don't you call her!'

Perhaps Julie Florence then went and fetched her mother, and Mrs Mary Joyce Clark emerged from her bedroom and came and sat down in the living room, she removed her spectacles and looked at the boys, her facial muscles were slack and a part of her hair had turned white; perhaps she looked in their direction and smiled wearily, and asked Ledu, 'How are you Fakhrul? Doing well?' Perhaps she asked Mamun, 'Mamun Miya, what's your news?'

Perhaps Ledu felt heartbroken seeing her tired face, 'Why have you become like this, Teacher, you were so beautiful' – but he didn't say any such thing, he just kept gazing at her, and after that, he replied, 'I'm fine, Teacher,' as did Mamun; or perhaps Julie didn't even fetch her because her exhausted mother was asleep then, or wasn't, and she sat still and muttered something under her breath, but Julie said, 'Mom is sleeping.'

Ledu then laid a heavy arm once again on Julie's shoulder, but he placed it so lightly that Julie felt as if a parakeet's feather had dropped on her shoulder, and she looked at Ledu, who then said, 'Won't you give us some tea, we were Teacher's most favourite students, get us some biscuits along with the tea!'

Julie Florence was unruffled as regards being hospitable, perhaps there were no biscuits and suchlike at home either, she sat at a little distance from these two former students of her mother, and then suddenly for some reason she said, 'Mom liked Monkey Boy the most! Where is he?' Perhaps Ledu wondered, why is this girl asking about Monkey Boy? Why? The subject of the name given to Khoimon's son thus arose, because after the return from Jinjira in 1971, chased by the Pakistani army, in June–July, or in August, it was time for Khoimon's child to be born, she felt as if her belly was about to burst open, fluid had accumulated at her feet which were swollen, but Abdul Jalil asked, 'Is it time now? Can't it wait a few days more?' Jorimon said, 'Not now! Wait for a few days.' But Khoimon's body couldn't wait any longer, perhaps the razakar leader, Abdul Goni, came in the morning or in the evening, and asked, 'Hey Moyna Miya, why doesn't your wife step out of the house?'

Moyna Miya retorted, 'Why are you asking me this?'

'Oh, just like that!'

Abdul Jalil's whole family was seized by terror then, and there seemed the likelihood of Chan Miya's name being Bijoy (Victory) Miya, or Swadhin (Independent) Ali, although Moyna Miya had already scorched that possibility, but after all, the razakars didn't know that, and so they tucked their lathis at their sides and walked up and down the moholla, their job was to gather information about the moholla folk; and then one day, they landed up at Abdul Jalil's house, and spotting them, Jorimon emerged from inside and stood in the veranda, and perhaps Khoimon sat inside and gazed at the razakars through the window, because after all, Khoimon was Khoimon even if she was possessed by the weight of her womb, it occurred to her that she ought to keep a watch over her Ma, even though she felt reluctant as well as afraid to step outside – and then while Abdul Goni was talking to Jorimon, he turned his head and spotted Khoimon through the gap in the window. Because Khoimon was sitting inside, Abdul Goni could not see her full figure, he could only see her face, perhaps Khoimon's face hadn't yet begun to swell up, perhaps the razakar Abdul Goni was distracted on seeing the olive-complexioned face of, in the words of Mrs Zobeida Begum, 'Khoimon the great expert', and so she saw through the look on Abdul Goni's face as she sat by the window – after all, which woman can't see through the look on a man's face? Abdul Goni was aware of what else the Pakistani soldiers stomped around the country doing besides killing people, he thought that Pakistani soldiers would arrive in the moholla very soon, they would go from house to house, set homes on fire, and then they would do what they had to do, and having gone around this moholla for a few days, it suddenly struck Abdul Goni that the woman sitting by the window didn't have a chance! But once Abdul Goni learnt about Rashidul, he realized that the old woman had lied to him, someone from this house had definitely joined the Liberation War, because the moment a count of the family members was made one would find that there was one man missing, so where was that person? No! He had to have joined the Liberation War! Abdul Goni arrived again with his squad and stood in the courtyard of Khoimon's house, and Jorimon was helpless.

'What's your son's name?'

'Rashidul.'

Khoimon too was certainly visible at the window then, perhaps she was ready and waiting, or perhaps when Abdul Goni asked about Rashidul, she thought, let me go and sit for a while beside the window – but this was a deadly move indeed! Because as soon as Abdul Goni saw Khoimon, he changed tack, he dropped the subject of Rashidul and asked Jorimon, 'What's your daughter's name?'

'Khoimon.'

Abdul Goni thought that Khoimon had intentionally sat by the window, showing her face, and so he felt emboldened, and he said, 'Call your daughter, I want to ask her something.'

Khoimon heard everything, and from her perch beside the window she asked, 'Tell me what you want to know,' and perhaps Abdul Goni fell into confusion and asked, 'Is your name Khoimon?'

'*Amar maay amar naam koy naika apnere? Apne ki boyra, hunen na kaane?* Didn't my Ma just tell you my name? Are you deaf? Can't you hear?'

Abdul Goni panicked momentarily.

'She told me, but I still asked.'

The razakar Abdul Goni had lost face in front of his squad, and he tried to save face now by whatever means and get out of there, and so he had to say something more; he asked, 'So your brother's gone to Nawabganj to your aunt's house? Nawabganj – that's close to Jinjira?'

'Yes.'

'Is your aunt your Ma's own sister?'

'Yes. Her own.'

Abdul Goni left with his squad, and after that, word of his encounter with Khoimon reached the ears of Moulana Abu Bakr, who sent for Abdul Goni that day or the following day asking him to meet him at his house, and perhaps a woman's visage was ever-present in Abdul Goni's mind, for when he told Moulana Abu Bakr that he didn't think the people of Ghost Lane were so bad, that they were quite nice, didn't he say that with Khoimon in mind? Perhaps so, and perhaps he explained to his razakar army too that these were not bad folk, so what was the point in making unnecessary trouble? And perhaps the intelligent members of his razakar army assented to that, but when Julie Florence asked where Monkey Boy was, Fakhrul Alam Ledu knew who she was referring to, Mamun ul Hye did too, yet they had a kind of puzzled look on their faces; after that Mamun said, 'No idea – lost perhaps!'

Ledu then pondered over the matter and realized that perhaps he really didn't know, although they lived in the same moholla, he had not seen Chan Miya for a very long time – he was the boy who had been suckled by a monkey! Or perhaps Ledu thought that this wasn't correct, but nevertheless it occurred to him that perhaps Chan Miya really had been suckled by a monkey, because after all wasn't he *Monkey Boy*? Perhaps from his very infancy

Chan Miya too knew this, and so he was embarrassed, and perhaps by and by everyone else learnt this about him, for that matter even their KG-1 teacher, Mrs Clark. Perhaps Mrs Clark developed a special attachment towards Chan Miya for that reason, a fondness, perhaps she thought, '*Poor child*,' because Ledu was of the view that this woman was simply a repository of love; and all the children in the class went for an outing to Baldha garden with this woman who was as pretty as a picture – for a class picnic – and when they approached the water trough inside Baldha Garden, the naughty children said to Chan Miya, 'If you look into the water, you'll see a monkey looking back at you!'

Consequently, whether out of fear or for some other reason, Chan Miya went near the trough and steeled himself, he didn't look into the water – perhaps in the city of Dhaka, it was only here, in Baldha Garden, that there were goldfish then – and when Teacher told him, 'Look, Chan Miya, goldfish!', Chan Miya felt at a loss, he turned his face up towards the sky and the first sighting of goldfish in his life failed to happen. When some boys then tried to force him, he emitted a loud, piercing scream, moved away from the trough and stood with his back pressed against the wall of the garden, and that was when Mary Joyce laid out her heart, she advanced and cupped little Chan Miya's face in her hands and said, 'Oh my boy! It's okay, it's okay!' But people failed to understand what the infant or boy Chan Miya's Ma, Khoimon, had in mind when she admitted him to Silverdale KG School, they reflected that perhaps she only did that imitating others, or perhaps she had done this calculatingly; Khoimon certainly couldn't afford to send her son to a school which charged twenty-five taka a month as fees, she could have had him admitted to the government's free primary school in Narinda, but no, she had him admitted to Silverdale – how would one explain this excess? Mrs Zobeida Rahman later said that Khoimon certainly had been calculating, because she was such a shrewd woman that she didn't do even the simplest of tasks without artifice, and it wasn't even as if proof of that hadn't been found. Then when Chan Miya went for the class picnic to Baldha Garden with the KG-1 teacher, Mary Joyce, she noticed him, and when Chan Miya stood with his back pressed against the wall, whether out of fear or driven by some other emotion, Mary became alarmed looking at the frightened but at the same time piercing and bright eyes, and when she cupped his face in her hands and asked, 'Why are you afraid, sweetie?', Chan Miya simply wept, and his warm tears wet Mary Joyce's palms that day.

'Sweetie' – meaning, Chan Miya didn't know what he was afraid of because he was just a little boy, his body was as light, tender and fragile as a freshly sprouted sprig of a tree, his mind was as unreserved as a newly dug pond, crystal clear and free of weeds. But perhaps he quickly learnt the secret and the language of society and the world, and consequently thorny shrubs suddenly began to grow in the depths of the waters of his mind, the shadow of the life beyond the banks fell on them – unless that was the case, what was the explanation for his behaviour in Baldha Garden? Perhaps Mrs Zobeida Rahman knew about this incident, perhaps Mamun had told her, and so one day, a long time later, when Mamun and Fakhrul Alam Ledu were studying in St Joseph or St Gregory, Mrs Zobeida Rahman remarked that it was all Chan Miya's cunning, wasn't his Ma terribly cunning too? So what was the problem in her son becoming cunning! Mrs Zobeida Rahman's reasoning was that Khoimon did all these wily acts in order to charm Mary Joyce, even though perhaps she wasn't entirely successful in that task; because after all, Mary Joyce wasn't a monkey, one who would lovingly take care of someone else's boy all day, feed him, clothe him, but notwithstanding that, perhaps on account of her nature, Mary Joyce fell under his spell, like the female monkey with a kid. It's difficult to figure out the reason for this, one doesn't love a child just because it is lovely, there was no dearth of lovely children in the world, perhaps Mamun was lovely too, that's what his Ma said, perhaps Ledu too had looked lovely when he was little; but ignoring the fifteen or twenty children in the class, Mary Joyce became ardent about Chan Miya, the son of Mst. Khoimon, a nobody – that simply wasn't done! And what *was* the secret of Chan Miya's allure? Mrs Zobeida Rahman said that it was Khoimon's sheer roguishness that lay behind this, she had been stricken seeing the handsomeness of a vegetable seller on the street, and the two of them had then played a game, and on the wedding night, she poured water and destroyed the title deed of the vegetable seller Moyna Miya's property; when Moyna Miya wept, she reassured him that another deed could be made out later. But Moyna Miya hadn't seen through Khoimon, that 'later' never seemed to arrive, and he pressed her on this matter, 'Tell your father to get another deed made.'

Khoimon replied, 'I'll tell him, but why are you being so pushy?'

Upon hearing Khoimon's retort, Moyna Miya was quiet for a long time, and after that, when he declared, '*Amar songe chalaki korle morba.* If you try to be cunning with me, you'll die,' perhaps Khoimon was afraid, because she didn't know much about such village folk, she kept gazing at her husband, his tall body was dark-skinned but sleek, the bodies of city folk were not like this, fair-skinned people in the city were not really fair-skinned, and dark-skinned folk weren't really dark-skinned; but this dark-skinned vegetable seller was indeed dark-skinned, and he was handsome – so her attitude softened, and she said, 'Don't worry, you'll get it!' Or perhaps Khoimon had some other plan in mind; nonetheless, Moyna Miya thought that perhaps Khoimon was not lying, but he could not forget about the incident of the dog being set upon him either, and however much Khoimon denied it, he realized that she knew roguery; because the day following the day she said to Babul Miya, 'Go and fix the wedding,' he didn't set up his shop at the regular spot in Thatari Bazar, but went instead to Ghost Lane to sell vegetables, carrying the vegetable basket on his head – he had a scheme in his head then – and when he arrived at Ghost Lane, he shouted out, 'Vegetables, vegetables, here's vegetables!'

The womenfolk from the houses called him, 'Hey, what vegetables do you have? Do you have snake gourd?'

Moyna Miya didn't have snake gourd, he walked ahead; perhaps Parween Sultana from the house with the tiger gate then emerged and called out to him, 'Hey, vegetable seller, do you have papaya?'

He didn't have papaya either, so once again he walked on, shouting, 'Vegetables, vegetables'; Showkat's sister, Johura, then came out, 'Hey, Vegetables, come here.'

Moyna Miya did not go there, he kept walking; perhaps Johura thought that the vegetable seller ignored her because she was young! Moyna Miya then encountered Tulu-Bulu and Dulal on the street, he recognized them, they were playing 'king' or dandagulli in the lane; Moyna Miya waited till one round was over, and then asked Tulu or Bulu or Dulal, '*Tumra notun manush paile kutta chunyaya deo naki?* When you spot a newcomer, do you set a dog upon him or what?'

The play-weary children were taken aback when they heard him, they couldn't figure out what this man was saying, but perhaps after that they recalled the incident and they said, 'We did that once, someone told us to do that.'

'Who told you?'

'Khoimon.'

'That rogue of a woman!'

The boys pondered, it occurred to them that Khoimon was indeed a rogue, but perhaps not entirely one; on the nuptial night, when Moyna Miya asked Khoimon about the matter of the dog being set on him, Khoimon thought it was just a shot in the dark, but perhaps after that Moyna Miya said a bit too much, because Khoimon was nothing if not Khoimon, and so the title deed made out for half the house slipped out of his hands, and he never got it back; however, he was able to name the boy born of Khoimon's womb Chan Miya, as he wished; Khoimon accepted that. When Mrs Zobeida Rahman spoke about this Mst. Khoimon, she had a sneer on her face, it wasn't clear whether that was out of contempt or something else, but the fact is she couldn't stand the sight of Khoimon, and Fakhrul Alam Ledu had no doubts whatsoever about that. Perhaps at first this contempt was unexpressed, because it was difficult to find any logical reason for the people of the house on No. 36 to get into a fight with the people of No. 25, by that token Khoimon should have had a squabble with Nurani Begum Upoma of No. 37, or with Raziya Banu of No. 35, or with Sharmeen Yasmin of 35/1, from the family that occupied part of Khoimon's house and divided the property soon after independence; but no, jumping across so many houses, it was with Mrs Zobeida Rahman that Khoimon's relations soured – astonishing, or perhaps there was nothing to be astonished about because there was no real basis for who in the world one loved or had contempt for. Perhaps even when Mrs Zobeida Rahman was a student at a Bangla Bazar school and lived in her father's house on No. 62, in the lane with the mosque, her aversion to Khoimon revealed itself, even though everything in life was in her favour. The house that belonged to Khoimon's family was the smallest and most dilapidated one in the moholla, with all its plaster peeled off, her father was an illiterate paan-and-biri seller, her Ma was nothing but a labouring woman, her brother a worthless hoodlum who had nothing by way of education, and after that she married a vegetable seller! Mrs Zobeida Rahman's situation was quite good in comparison, she was a woman who had studied till class eight in Bangla Bazar Girls High School, she used to walk past the people of the moholla in her turquoise-coloured uniform, the people of the moholla were witness to that, her marriage too was to someone in the moholla, her father owned a biscuit factory, and her father-in-law had a scrap metal shop in Dolaikhal, her husband, Golam Rahman, had passed Intermediate Arts from Salimullah College, he was a clerk in a food godown in Kalta Bazar – she was not badly off in any way, and yet she was at odds with Khoimon. Perhaps it had begun even before her marriage, perhaps one day – when Dolaikhal was actually a canal, and one could cross the murky-as-shit water by boat to proceed towards Raysha Bazar or Patla Khan Lane – Zobeida Begum was going to her school; when she reached the Gudara jetty, near Lalmohan Saha Street, a dinghy full of passengers was about to leave from that bank, Zobeida Begum then ran and boarded the boat, and the boat rocked, and the boatman then shouted at her and asked her to get off. Perhaps Zobeida Begum had an examination that day, perhaps she would get into trouble if she was late, so she refused to get off the boat, but because the boat was already packed, the boatman too refused to take her; Zobeida Rahman then spotted Khoimon in the crowd of passengers, she was going somewhere, one couldn't figure out whether she was in a hurry or not, but Zobeida certainly thought that an idle girl who didn't go to school couldn't be in any hurry, she could easily take the next boat, how would it inconvenience her if she went by the next boat! But why would Khoimon agree to that? When Zobeida Begum asked her to get off, she refused, and asked, 'Why?'

'*Pore aay, chhemri, ja naam, amar schoole jaon lagbo!* Take the next one, girl, get off, I need to get to school!'

Khoimon then pounced on Zobeida Begum like an enraged bull, the boat tipped over as both of them scuffled, and so all the passengers fell into the foul water; it became evident then that perhaps Zobeida Begum was in no tearing hurry, because after getting drenched in the water, the two of them walked back home. Perhaps even after that Zobeida Begum decided to forget about it, and perhaps because Khoimon was younger than her, she later wanted to patch up with her, and wanting to chat with her when she encountered her on the street, she asked, 'Where are you going?'

'I'm going to my aunt's place.'

But Khoimon was indeed bad-natured, she lost her head when she was angry, she had no idea what she did then, and so this attempt at a conciliation didn't go very far; perhaps Zobeida was sitting at home then after failing twice in class eight, and in the rainy season, or some season, the jhulan or swing festival had begun in Chandrakanta Basak's house, and after installing the two images of Radha and Krishna swathed in flowers and vines on a swing made of a stage-like wooden platform, they ululated as they pulled a string and moved the swing. The moholla folk went in groups to watch the jhulan, perhaps Zobeida Begum went one day and found Khoimon there, she was chattering away with Chandrakanta's daughter, Purnolakshmi; Zobeida Begum then ate the prasad handed out by Mayarani and asked Purnolakshmi, 'What's up, Purno, what are you doing?'

'I'm talking.'

'What are you talking about so much?'

Khoimon began to get angry then, *'Kyala amar lawge kotha kawown jaay na? Khali tumi kotha koya paro – kelech eighte duibar fail dichhaw!* Why can't I talk? Is it only you who can talk – you who failed twice in class eight!'

But Zobeida Begum didn't let her off, 'And you're a zero,' she said, 'you can't even write your name, you say *kelech* for class, you beggar!'

Khoimon's face turned red when she was called a beggar, at first it seemed that she would burst into tears, but she didn't do that and instead attacked Zobeida, *'Amare kow fokinni, nijer cheharata dekhchhaw? Chakrani bedi!* You call me a beggar, but have you seen your own face? You servant girl!'

But despite being called a servant, it was Zobeida Begum who got married first, she left her residence in her father's house on No. 62 and moved to her father-in-law's house on No. 25, and meanwhile, despite Khoimon's good health and attractive looks, it was only in her case that no match could be found, and then a vegetable seller was found; after returning from Jinjira in 1971, this vegetable seller, Moyna Miya stopped working and lay in bed all day in his father-in-law's house, he said that he was afraid to go to the market. Then, either before the razakars arrived or after that, youths from the moholla began going off to join the Liberation War, Rashidul left, Zobeida Begum's Intermediate Arts graduate husband, Golam Rahman, left, but Moyna Miya didn't move an inch, he remained in the moholla; perhaps he really was afraid of the war; and when Mamun's Ma, Mrs Zobeida Rahman, told Fakhrul Alam Ledu that Mamun had gone to fetch sawdust for the stove, perhaps Mamun ul Hye had just arrived at The New Chondraghona Saw Mill & Timber Depot, with a gunny sack at his side. The coolie and labourers at the sawmill were all dunderheads, although they were also well versed in cunning; perhaps the coolies and labourers at this sawmill were already acquainted with Mamun Miya since he went there every month and a half or two months, and after haggling over the price of a sackful, left with one and a half or two sackfuls of sawdust in the pair of sacks joined together by his Ma; they didn't mind that because everyone did it. But this day – perhaps it was raining or perhaps it wasn't, perhaps the dry Sharat season following the rains had begun – he arrived there, and seeing him, the labourers at the sawmill, especially the coolies, whispered to one another, they wondered whether this wasn't the boy they had dispatched fifteen days, or a month, or two months ago, in a lorry loaded with sawdust. The foolish, or shrewd, porters from The New Chondraghona Saw Mill & Timber Depot then complicated the matter, and despite the strict prohibition imposed by the proprietor in this regard, something got into the heads of these porters – perhaps their names were Idris, Maqbool and Sridhar Das – and they became restless, they were rendered weak once again on account of a little bit of conscience, and they wondered,

'Oh dear, whose child is that?' And then they – perhaps it was Idris and Maqbool – went to Ghost Lane and looked for Mamun's house. They walked around asking people at random, and then finally they arrived at the foot of the flowering kamini tree in the courtyard of the house on No. 25 and called out.

Mamun's Ma, Mrs Zobeida Rahman, thought that this was definitely a conspiracy, because when her son was at home, if someone came there and said, 'Your son is not your son,' how would it feel, how would it be then! That day, the two ghost-like figures from The New Chondraghona Saw Mill & Timber Depot arrived and called out from under the kamini tree, 'Is anyone at home?' Mamun's Ma was inside, she thought it must be the post, the postal peon in the khaki-coloured uniform from the Wari sub–post office came to their house all the time, he would arrive with a postcard or perhaps an envelope and call out most courteously, and hearing that call the folks at home knew for certain that this was the postal peon, it was only postal peons who were so courteous; but when Zobeida Rahman emerged from the house upon hearing the coolies from the sawmill calling out, she saw that there were two men who had called out like the postal peon, but they were not postal peons. Be that as it may, when Zobeida Begum saw the two fellows standing under the tree, she thought that perhaps they were the nightwatchmen, or something else, the fasting season was coming, and then would come Eid al-Fitr, perhaps they had come with a plea for bakshish. But Idris and Maqbool had definitely not come for bakshish, they were workers at the sawmill, they knew nothing about bakshish and suchlike, and when they asked, 'Isn't this where Mamun lives?', Zobeida Begum became flustered, who were they, what did these fellows want? And she replied, 'Yes, why?'

That day, Idris and Maqbool subsequently advanced from under the tree towards Mamun's Ma who was standing in the veranda, and when they said in low whispers that her lost son Mamun had been dispatched by lorry together with the sawdust from the sawmill, Mamun's Ma was utterly dumbfounded. What were these people saying!

'What are you saying?' she exclaimed.

But these men, that is to say Idris and Maqbool, were in turn taken aback by Mamun's Ma's behaviour, they could not figure out what was going on, this was not the reaction of a mother of the boy who was lost; faced with this strange dilemma, they fell silent, they had no clue what they ought to do, it occurred to them that they had only landed in trouble after having come to do good, but they did insist that what they said was true.

'Don't you use a sawdust-fired stove?'

'Why wouldn't I use it?'

'Hadn't your son gone to Nayabazar fifteen days or a month ago to fetch sawdust?'

'He may have. But he fetched sawdust just yesterday.'

'Your son didn't return after that!'

Zobeida Begum became perturbed now: who was it then that returned with the sawdust yesterday? She asked them, 'You're saying that my boy Mamun didn't return with the sawdust?'

These two workers from the sawmill then said that there was no way Mamun Miya wasn't lost, he was definitely lost, because they recognized their customers, they recognized Mamun Miya too, and they knew that fifteen days or a month ago he had been dispatched with a load of sawdust in the proprietor's lorry. After that, when they said that if she went to the sawmill even now to enquire, perhaps she would find out something about Mamun Miya, Zobeida Begum thought that these two donkeys were under some misapprehension; she asked, 'Then who returned with the sawdust?'

'*Apner pola ashe nai, taare joldi khunjen!* It wasn't your son who returned, look for him at once!'

'Who are you people?'

'We are nobody, but please go right away and look for Mamun, go and ask the proprietor of the sawmill, you won't find him later.'

Zobeida Begum couldn't help but be alarmed, she made a hue and cry but she could find no one who would say, 'Hey, look for Mamun, bring him here,' and so word of the matter spread; one or two women from the moholla arrived and joined the fray, and when they learnt about

Zobeida Begum's dilemma, they could not figure out what the real problem was, Zobeida Begum told them that two chaps from Nayabazar had come and told her that fifteen or twenty days or a month back, Mamun had not returned home after having gone to buy sawdust, and that the one who had returned with the sawdust – was not Mamun! These women from the moholla thought it was all very strange, they had never heard something like this in all their lives, they asked, '*Apne Aafa china parlen na, Mamune je Mamun na apne buja parlen na?* Aapa, couldn't you recognize him? Couldn't you make out that the one you thought was Mamun wasn't Mamun?'

'No, I couldn't!'

These women then suspected that perhaps Mamun had really not returned after having gone to buy sawdust, that perhaps no one had brought back sawdust or suchlike, perhaps Zobeida Begum had forgotten, perhaps she was using sawdust purchased two months back as fuel, and merely assumed that Mamun had returned with the sawdust; they then told her, 'Think carefully, Aapa, did Mamun really return, or did he not return, you're simply assuming that he returned with the sawdust, perhaps he didn't actually return!'

Even a strong-willed woman like Zobeida Begum fell into disarray; she wondered, so then did Mamun really not come back after going to fetch sawdust? But she got back her mental clarity at once, and in order to clear all doubts, she went inside and saw that there was a newly filled sack of sawdust in the kitchen veranda – if someone had gone to bring sawdust, he had definitely returned with sawdust! It became clear to the two women from the moholla too that someone had indeed returned with a sack of sawdust. The question now was: who was it?

If Mamun was indeed lost, then who was it that had returned with the sawdust? Who was he? Who?

Mamun's Ma became agitated, perhaps Mamun's younger brother, Mahmud, returned home, perhaps his father, Golam Rahman, returned too and they could not figure out what Zobeida Begum said, but finding the real, or false, Mamun became imperative right then; they found a group of boys near the Christian cemetery at one end of Tipu Sultan Road, the boys were occupied with their game of 'seven tiles' using pieces of broken roof tiles and a tennis ball, perhaps Mamun was concealing himself somewhere nearby for fear of being hit by the ball, because he suddenly emerged and his father caught hold of him. When Mamun was taken back home, he had no idea what he had done and what punishment he was about to receive, but he sensed that something was coming, and if he fell into Ma's hands, she wouldn't let him off lightly! After he was handed over to Zobeida Begum, she examined him in various ways, she went to another room and called out his name and observed whether or not he responded properly, she asked him about school, 'Which class are you in?' And hearing this question,

Mamun panicked, but there was nothing Zobeida Begum could do, she had to do all this in order to be certain about Mamun's identity, and finally, when she said, 'Let me see your birthmark,' Mamun rolled up his shorts and showed the black wart on his left thigh. Zobeida Begum could not disbelieve all these proofs; she thought that this Mamun was indeed Mamun, not fake, two dolts from the sawmill had arrived and told her utter nonsense and made her lose her head; she said, 'Go and play,' and like a bird that had been freed from its cage, Mamun flew off in a trice. But Zobeida Rahman did certainly wonder what was really going on. Why did those two people arrive and say what they did? But who would provide her the answer to this question? And so she forgot about this incident; but meanwhile, very far away, in Satkania, in Chittagong, the rabbit tied to a rope held in Asmantara Hoore Jannat's hand grew in size, he forgot about what had happened in the sawmill, and his name and address were only faint memories. And so, on another evening, fifteen or twenty years later, Asmantara's rabbit arrived and presented himself under the old kamini tree, and he said that his name was Mamun Miya, that he had got lost many years ago, and Zobeida Begum was confronted with the old subject after a long time, and she wondered, what was all this actually? Perhaps it was difficult to provide an answer to what all this actually was, but the reason for this complexity was that, despite being shrewd, the coolies of the sawmill were essentially what they were; they had dispatched a boy together with the sawdust, all right, if a boy went to fetch sawdust, he could well be dispatched together with the sawdust, but oh dear, they had better keep quiet about it; however, that was not to be, their tongues would definitely wag, and so they again whispered among themselves about the identity of the boy who had been smuggled away in the lorry, and these coolies of the sawmill were unanimous that all these people were almost permanent customers, the porters may also have been acquainted with Mamun Miya before the incident, he was a boy from Ghost Lane in South Moishundi – he was definitely Mamun Miya; after that, when word of the conversation between these workers of the sawmill reached the ears of Abdul Mabud Chowdhury, he told these dunderheads to be silent and telephoned his younger brother, Abdul Wodood Chowdhury, and informed him about Mamun Miya having been smuggled away together with the sawdust, but Abdul Wodood Chowdhury couldn't really understand the matter, he said, '*Aain awner hawta naw bujidde!* I can't follow what you're saying!'

Abdul Mabud Chowdhury explained the matter to him, that the coolies had loaded a dead or half-dead boy in the lorry together with the sawdust, his name was Mamun, and he was a boy from Ghost Lane, in Narinda, Dhaka; Wodood Chowdhury then began to worry, he couldn't figure out whether or not the boy was in one of the lorries seized by the police, he phoned his employees in various places and found out that the lorry had gone in the direction of Satkania, perhaps it had reached already, or would shortly.

The day Mamun Miya was in the process of being smuggled inside the sawdust, Asmantara Hoore Jannat had been badgering her Ma, Dolly Akhtar, terribly all morning, perhaps she began forsaking her Ma even before she was born, as she lay in the womb; giving birth to a child was never something new or difficult or complicated for Dolly Akhtar, when it was time, she sent word to her neighbour, Ambiya's Ma, and shut her door, and several times she finished her business even before Ambiya's Ma could arrive, perhaps when Ambiya's Ma subsequently turned up, she waited for the placenta to come out, and when it did, she cut the umbilical cord with a blade, washed and cleaned the baby, put fresh clothes on Dolly, helped her up from the floor and put her on the cot, placed the baby on Dolly's bosom, and then cleaned the room, and finally carried the bloody placenta, Dolly Akhtar's soiled clothes, the kantha that had been spread on the floor and the blood-soaked swab to the wall on the eastern side of the pond behind the Chowdhurys' homestead, dug a hole in the ground there and buried them. When she had her first child many years ago, Dolly Akhtar was happy it was a boy, because she thought that if she had a daughter now, there would be nothing for anyone to say; perhaps Abdul Ali Chowdhury was alive then; after his elder son,

Abdul Mabud, left for Chittagong city and then settled down in Dhaka, he knew no happiness, but he was glad that when Wodood Chowdhury got married he left his wife in Satkania itself; after that when Dolly Akhtar had a son, his contentment knew no bounds, and he whispered the azan into his grandson's right ear, concluding with 'Allahu Akbar, Allahu Akbar', and named him Abdul Qader Chowdhury; his grandson grew up, and Abdul Ali Chowdhury dandled him on his knee, saying *'O dada, o dada!'* Fifteen months later, Dolly Akhtar had her second child, also a boy; Ambiya's Ma arrived and saw that Dolly Akhtar had once again finished the business of delivery, so she cleaned the newborn and his mother and laid them on the cot; perhaps old Abdul Ali returned then after a stroll in Satkania Bazar, and reaching home he learnt that he now had another grandson; he exclaimed, 'Alhamdulillah,' and he whispered the azan in the baby's right ear and named him Mohsin Ali Chowdhury. Then, having given birth to two sons in succession, Dolly Akhtar was in the family way again, and this time too she thought that if it was a girl now there would be nothing to fear, but fifteen months after Mohsin, Dolly Akhtar had another son and Abdul Ali named him Nurul Haq Chowdhury. When Dolly Akhtar became pregnant for the fourth time, she really wished it was a daughter, 'Give me a baby girl, dear God!' she yearned, perhaps she wept when she sat to pray and raised her hands in supplication, perhaps old Abdul Ali too wished for a girl, but their prayers were not answered, it was a boy again, and Abdul Ali named him Raisuddin Chowdhury. Dolly Akhtar was depressed, she went around asking anyone and everyone why she couldn't have a daughter, '*Odi Ambiyar Ma, aanr bekgun morod poya, antthe khushi naw lar, aanr ekguya maiyafoya naw hoy kiya!* Hey Ambiya's Ma, they're all boys, how can I be happy when I can't even have a single daughter!' Ambiya's Ma pondered over the matter, at first she thought something like this was nothing out of the ordinary, after all, a lot of women had no daughters, just like a lot of women never had sons; and when Dolly Akhtar again asked her why she couldn't have a daughter, she explained that to Dolly Akhtar, and then something came over her, a thought arose in her head, and she said that perhaps this was a kind of disease! But Dolly Akhtar didn't like that idea, she was a girl who had studied till class nine in Satkania Girls School, she knew this wasn't any disease; however, she tied amulets all around her waist, but when she had a fifth son fourteen or fifteen months later, she broke down; however, old Abdul Ali was still happy, after all, every child was Allah's gift, and he named his grandson Shahjahan Ali Chowdhury. Dolly Akhtar then remembered what Ambiya's Ma had said, but she was certain that the illiterate Ambiya's Ma knew nothing, and that she talked too much for no reason, but nonetheless she was depressed, and she became perturbed and stricken with doubt, and then she became pregnant for the sixth time.

She was melancholy all the time, she suffered the thought that despite being a woman there was no place for a girl in her womb, she lost her appetite, and she was afflicted with insomnia, she had to visit the doctor time and again, or else folks at home went and fetched the doctor. Doctor Mojahar examined her, he took out his instrument and measured her blood pressure, he pushed down her lower eyelids and examined her eyes, and he said, '*Awner obostha toh gom nawoy babi, haowahaidyo thikmoto naw khaan faanlar!* You don't look well, bhabi, you aren't eating properly!'

When there was no improvement in Dolly Akhtar's condition, Abdul Wodood Chowdhury went again to Doctor Mojahar, but there was nothing the doctor could do, he dropped in again at Wodood Chowdhury's house, examined Dolly Akhtar and took his leave, and Abdul Wodood Miya went to the Mirzakhil mazaar across the Dolu river, got two more amulets from the pir gracing the shrine, and slung them around Dolly Akhtar's neck. After that, when the time came Dolly Akhtar didn't take very long on this occasion either, but because she was weak, she fainted after sending word to Ambiya's Ma and lay unconscious on the mat, Ambiya's Ma arrived then and when Dolly Akhtar returned to her senses, she saw two infants on her bosom, Ambiya's Ma had cut their umbilical cords, cleaned them and wrapped them in kanthas, she said, 'One baby's a girl and one a boy – it's Allah's will!' Dolly Akhtar was dumbfounded, but perhaps she thought that this could well happen, why not, don't people have twins unknowingly? But because of Dolly Akhtar's doubts, similar doubts entered Abdul Wodood's mind, and he sent for Doctor Mojahar; as soon as the doctor got word, he hurried there, but when he heard what Abdul Wodood had to say, it was as if he had been struck dumb, he could simply not figure out the meaning of what they said, he wondered why they did this. They didn't like it if there was no girl, and when there was one, they said so much – amazing! Be that as it may, the only MBBS doctor in the bazar in Satkania was of the same opinion in this matter: there was no reason for it not to happen, there could definitely be two when one was under the impression that there was only one, it could be three as well. Abdul Ali Miya then named his grandson number six Abdul Wahab Chowdhury, and after some thought, the newborn girl was named Asmantara Hoore Jannat.

Following Doctor Mojahar's elaborate explanation, Dolly Akhtar no longer had any doubt that it was possible for Abdul Wahab and Hoore Jannat to be born together from her womb; but still, her mind cavilled with regard to Asmantara – why did she have this doubt about her? Was it because she had never imagined that she would or could have a daughter! And so after she regained consciousness, when Ambiya's Ma told her about a boy and a girl being born, it seemed she wasn't happy, she kept thinking that it wasn't possible, that it was a set-up, but when she saw two babies looking like lumps of soft clay on her bosom, she realized it wasn't a lie; but even after that, her doubts did not leave her. Dolly Akhtar later tried to recall that when she had looked for the first time at the two babies, she thought that beside the newly born Abdul Wahab, the girl looked somewhat older, she seemed tidier; perhaps she said so to Ambiya's Ma, and she thought that Ambiya's Ma seemed to become alarmed at her words, or perhaps she actually thought wrong, Ambiya's Ma responded to her by saying, 'Don't say that, the girl was born earlier!' Dolly Akhtar thought that Ambiya's Ma's reasoning was weak, it was the girl's severed umbilical cord that looked more healed to her, the boy's cord was absolutely fresh – was such a thing possible? It was to Ambiya's Ma that Dolly Akhtar Begum again directed her query, and hearing her, Ambiya's Ma once again seemed to fall from the sky, she said, '*In gom nawoy babi, awne maiya poya chailende, Allay awnere maiya poya diiyye, awne in hawta puchhallawdde kiya?* This is not right, bhabi, you wanted a daughter and Allah's given you one, why are you asking me this?'

Dolly Akhtar then felt ashamed of herself, she sought forgiveness from Allah, 'Forgive me, God,' she wept, and after a long time she looked properly at her newborn girl, she drew her face, uncovered her breast and thrust her nipple into her mouth; but Dolly Akhtar observed that the girl only held the nipple in her mouth, she didn't suck at it. At first Dolly Akhtar thought that it was nothing, she thought that perhaps Asmantara had fallen asleep with her eyes open, but then she realized that the baby wasn't asleep – she observed everything with wide eyes. Dolly Akhtar became a bit alarmed then, she thought that perhaps the girl's tummy was full, she wasn't interested in feeding; but after that, either at noon, or late in the afternoon, or at dusk, when she tried to feed her again, Asmantara Hoore Jannat just held the nipple in her mouth, she didn't suck at it. Dolly Akhtar then got scared, she raised a commotion, and hearing her screeches, everyone at home rushed there; perhaps Abdul Wodood was at home, he arrived, his old father Abdul Ali Chowdhury arrived, and Ambiya's Ma arrived from next door; everyone was astounded to hear what she said, what was she saying, that the girl hadn't fed since morning! Dolly Akhtar attempted to feed the girl again to demonstrate to Ambiya's Ma, she uncovered her breast and thrust the nipple into the girl's mouth, but there was no response from Asmantara, and Ambiya's Ma exclaimed that she had never seen something like this in her life. And so there were doubts regarding the girl's survival, they wondered if, having arrived uninvited on earth, she felt ashamed; had she decided to not feed and die out of a sense of hurt? Or had she begun to fast as soon as she was born? Or could it be that she was angry on account of Dolly Akhtar's lingering doubts and her behaviour? Like a fool, Ambiya's Ma conveyed that to Dolly Akhtar, 'The little girl might be angry with you!'

Of course, Dolly Akhtar didn't believe what Ambiya's Ma said, it wasn't possible for the girl to be angry so soon after popping out of the womb, but when the baby went without feeding for twenty-four hours and didn't cry in all that time, wailing and weeping began in Abdul Ali Chowdhury's house; it was Dolly Akhtar who wept the most, and that was when Ambiya's Ma arrived again, and she brought with her cow's milk in a china bowl. Ambiya's Ma found Dolly Akhtar inside her room, the baby girl had her mother's nipple in her mouth and stared blankly, like a lifeless person, and Dolly Akhtar's slightly dimpled but nonetheless radiantly fair-skinned breast seemed like an upside-down, unwanted, leftover fruit, and all the while, the owner of the breast, Dolly Akhtar, sat and wept. Ambiya's Ma pulled Asmantara away from Dolly Akhtar, lay her down in her own lap, and using a teaspoon, fed the cow's milk from the bowl to her, and then the two of them observed with astonishment that the girl eagerly drank the cow's milk. Perhaps Dolly Akhtar had brought her weeping to a close, but seeing Asmantara drinking milk now from Ambiya's Ma's hands, she began wailing, her exposed, rejected mammary trembled feverishly at her outburst, it seemed Asmantara was proving that she hadn't come so easy, and that she would not like there to be any neglect; that day, once Ambiya's Ma had fed Asmantara the milk, Dolly Akhtar took the girl to her bosom, saying, 'Give her, give her to me.'

Doctor Mojahar was again consulted, but he could not fathom why one of the two babies couldn't feed when the other could, so he came to Wodood Chowdhury's place, and when he examined the baby's mouth he found a red sore inside; he advised that if she was fed cow's milk for a few days, the sore in the mouth would also heal, and the baby would be able to suckle and feed after that. And that was what happened, for three or four days Dolly Akhtar pressed her baby against her bosom and fed her cow's milk with a spoon, she burnt borax, mixed it with honey and applied it on the mouth sore, and when she cooed to her baby, '*Aanr shona aanr manik, aanr lawge awne goswa koirawgonde na, odi goswa koirawgende na!* My treasure, my gem, don't be angry with me, you were angry with me weren't you?', Dolly Akhtar observed that the baby was asleep with her eyes shut, and when she undid the buttons on her blouse and put the nipple of her breast into her mouth, Asmantara Hoore Jannat's eyes remained shut but she sucked at it noisily, and the baby then seemed to be a kind of gourd, or pumpkin, or melon that had sprung up on the plant of Dolly Akhtar's body – and now Dolly Akhtar wanted to weep with joy; and Asmantara Hoore Jannat was born in order to meet the rabbit that was concealed within the sawdust that had been transported together with the smuggled fertilizer, but Mamun ul Hye's Ma, Mrs Zobeida Rahman, of the house on No. 25 in Ghost Lane, said it was all pretence, and sitting in her house, when she told Fakhrul Alam Ledu that Mamun had gone to visit the daughter of their skirt-clad, Anglo-Indian teacher at her residence, then, although she grimaced when she said that, Ledu thought that Zobeida Rahman said it with a subtle expression of secret joy at this success on her son's part. Fakhrul Alam Ledu recalled that when they were admitted to Mrs Rokeya Anwar's Silverdale KG School, among the students in their KG-1 class, Chan Miya was the one who was most out of place, and perhaps that was why their class teacher, the exceedingly beautiful woman, Mary Joyce Clark – who signed on the progress report as 'MJ Clark' – became very fond of Chan Miya, but Chan Miya was also a good student. Once their KG-1 classes began, one day Mary Joyce Clark opened *At Home – Book 1* and taught them 'Jack and Jill', and it was observed that it was Chan Miya who memorized the poem before anyone else, 'Jack and Jill / Went up the hill…' and so on; two girls in the class, Nargis and Iffat, gazed at him with wide eyes, and Mary Clark went up to him, put her hand on his skinny shoulder and patted him gently and said, '*You are brilliant, Chhan Miya!*'

Mamun, Ledu and Abhijit observed all this as they sat in class, the teacher called Chan Miya brilliant, she said, 'lovely', but there was nothing they could do in KG-1, they couldn't brandish a fist at Chan Miya in Mrs Clark's class, and later, they forgot about the matter. But nevertheless, it seemed that Mrs Clark didn't forget Chan

Miya; two years later they went to class two where Miss Rosalyn D'Costa was their class teacher, and when Mary Clark sometimes came to D'Costa's class and enquired, 'How are my children doing?', Ledu, Mamun and Abhijit then thought that perhaps it was Chan Miya that Mrs Clark was actually asking about, and Miss D'Costa smiled weakly at her words and said, 'They're getting along, not bad!' After the final exams, it was play time, and then came the prize-giving ceremony; a girl from KG-2, perhaps it was Khaleda or Tabassum, received a bundle wrapped in coloured paper, and she read the note written in English attached to that: 'Give it to a friend whose shoes are the dirtiest.' The little girl wandered around with the package, she couldn't decide whose shoes were the most soiled, and after that maybe she targeted Chan Miya, and Mrs Clark noticed that and hurried to Chan Miya and wiped his shoes clean, and so the girl had to wander around some more to find a shabbily clad boy, and perhaps the girl Julie was then under the pandal, perhaps she had been observing the affair, and when she asked her mother, 'Mom, who was he?', her mother replied, 'He is Monkey Boy'; of course, Mamun and Ledu later remembered that they hadn't seen their favourite teacher and her daughter, Julie Florence, in a long time, perhaps they went to Shah Saheb Lane and enrolled in St Joseph School after they left Silverdale KG School, and when they made a mistake in the arithmetic class there, Brother Tom bent them over his knee and hit them with a wooden ruler on their backsides, Brother Daniel made them stay back almost every day in the detention class for not doing the homework, he wrote down their roll numbers in his notebook, and they had to attend the detention class in the evening, after school hours; they wrote out a sentence written on the blackboard – like 'Man is known by the company he keeps' – as many times as the punishment awarded to them, fifty, or a hundred, or two hundred times, and then they tore off the pages and handed them in. But here, in this school, they discovered basketball and cricket, they discovered the railway line nearby, and the path leading from the rear gate of the school, along Monir Hossain Lane, to the Dayaganj railway bridge where they could hang out, and so for a long time they forgot about Mrs Mary Clark and her daughter, Julie. Later, when St Joseph School moved to Asad Gate, basketball and cricket began to lose significance in the lives of Mamun ul Hye and Fakhrul Alam Ledu, and it suddenly occurred to them that they hadn't met their Teacher in years. Then, perhaps late one night, desire was awakened in Mamun's breast, and he then telephoned Ledu and said, 'Let's go and visit Teacher.'

'We can go.'

They then remembered Julie Florence's birthday – 21 September; when they were in KG-1, Teacher had taken all the children to her residence for the first time on Julie

Florence's birthday; after that, they went up to a new class every year, but Teacher did not forget Mamun, Ledu and Chan Miya from among her former students, she always invited them home on Julie Florence's birthday. They attended the birthday celebrations wearing their school uniforms, and sang 'Happy birthday to you' along with the other children there, Julie cut a white cake, and when the big paper piñata with a fat belly that hung from the ceiling fan was burst open with a stick, countless bits of coloured paper rained down, and along with that were colour pencils, toffees in tinsel foil, and loose change. What an uproar there was then, Mamun ul Hye got three toffees while Ledu got two, and Chan Miya found a twenty-five paisa coin. They were then studying in class two, and they had become quite big, Julie too had grown from a child to a girl, or was in the process of doing so, seeing her in a white nylon frock that day, Mamun ul Hye and Fakhrul Alam Ledu gaped at her, and after that when the cake was cut and divided into slices, they had their share, they chewed the toffees they got from the piñata, Mamun ul Hye polished off two of the three toffees he had got, and persuaded Chan Miya to buy the remaining one; of course, he regretted this later, because although Chan Miya hadn't been able to collect a single toffee, he gave Julie Florence the one he purchased from Mamun ul Hye, and Julie unwrapped its tinsel foil, put it into her mouth and sucked at it, and Ledu, Mamun and Abhijit thought, isn't the boy a shrewd one! But that day, the matter didn't end there, Chan Miya picked up the slice of cake on his plate and ate it, and offered his banana to Julie, as if to say 'Have it,' and Julie took the banana and ate it too. And so, after a long time, when Mrs Clark said to Julie one day, 'Beware of man and banana,' it was already too late, but at the birthday party that day they then saw Teacher come dressed in a long frock with a flowery design, and pose with Julie for a picture; Bob, in a black coat, white shirt and black bow tie came and stood on one side, he had a smoking pipe in his hand, and then the children came up to have a picture taken with them, but they did not notice that Chan Miya wasn't in the crowd, and so, after Mamun ul Hye woke up in the dead of night one day, he and Ledu went on Julie Florence's birthday and presented themselves in the lane with the Women's Education Institute and found to their astonishment that, even after all these years, Teacher continued to live in the same house. Later, while sitting in Mrs Clark's drawing room and looking at the pictures hanging on the wall, Mamun asked Julie, 'You people continued living in this house for so long? The whole world's changed, but you stayed in the same place?'

'Where would we go?'

'After all, tenants regularly change their premises.'

'Who knows, we have a problem, we are not like others, we can't be like others!'

Mamun ul Hye then gazed at Julie, 'Why can't you, why not?'

'Because we can't!'

'But why?'

'Because I am not like you!'

Mamun gazed at her again, Julie was not like him, but why wasn't she? Perhaps he understood, perhaps he didn't; however, Abdul Wodood Chowdhury's people discovered Mamun once the truck loaded with smuggled fertilizer reached Satkania, they found him lying within the sawdust when they began removing the sacks towards the end of the night, and they saw that he was alive but perhaps still unconscious, and then they recalled that the boy's name was Mamun; they took him, together with the sacks of fertilizer, to a tin shed beside the pond in the compound and kept him there.

Come morning, the junior or intermediate officer from the Satkania police station arrived with a lathi in his hand, perhaps Abdul Wodood Chowdhury had not yet reached there after leaving Chittagong, or perhaps he had come very early in the morning in his Toyota Corona and learnt that Mamun had been discovered within the sawdust, and so when the officer showed up later and asked him, 'Merchant saheb, how are you?', Abdul Wodood Chowdhury understood the matter, he said, 'I'm fine, not bad, come inside,' and took this junior or intermediate officer inside the house and made him sit down on the velvet sofa in his living room.

The officer sat down, he had tea and refreshments, and then he said, 'I heard a truck arrived at night, what was in it?'

'I brought sawdust in that!'

'What will you do with sawdust?'

'You see, I'm setting up an ice factory here, I brought the sawdust for the factory.'

With a little bit of thought, the officer figured out that sawdust could be needed if an ice factory was set up, fine; but he then asked something else, 'Was there a boy in the sawdust?' But was that possible? It wasn't possible, and Abdul Wodood Chowdhury said that, after all, a boy was not a ball that fits in one's hand that he can be found within the sawdust, you can't find even a human baby in the sawdust – no, it wasn't a human baby which was in the sawdust from his brother's sawmill that was brought from Dhaka, but a large rabbit, perhaps when the truck was going along a mountainside, then perhaps somewhere near Sitakund or Pahartali, the creature somehow climbed into the truck. The officer then smoked a Benson & Hedges cigarette and thought that it could well be, it wasn't impossible, a rabbit could well clamber up into a truck in such mountainous or semi-mountainous places, and when he took his leave and left, Dolly Akhtar and the other women and children in the house learnt about the rabbit. Asmantara Hoore Jannat was perhaps three or four years old then, she became excited when she heard about the rabbit, '*Aain khorkosh deikkom, Amma aanre khorkosh aani daow.* I want to see the rabbit, Amma, fetch me the rabbit,' she said.

The servants of the house explained to her that the rabbit was a very nasty animal, it bit you, it stank and was a menace, but Asmantara refused to listen, so then Dolly Akhtar had to turn her attention to the matter because she hadn't forgotten the misadventure around her newborn daughter drinking her milk, and so, accompanied by the servants, she went to the locked door of the tin shed by the pond and had it opened and saw that a boy was lying inside amidst rows of sacks. Dolly Akhtar was astonished, 'Hey Abuilya, where's the rabbit? Who is this little boy here?' she asked, and the servants of the house had to divulge everything to her, perhaps they had heard about it all from Abdul Wodood, and then perhaps Mamun Miya began returning to his senses; he opened his eyes and looked, and there was Dolly Akhtar, looking dumbfounded, standing in front of him, and he saw Asmantara; Dolly Akhtar bent a bit towards him and asked, 'What's your name?'

But the boy only stared back at her blankly when she asked him that, and then the servants of the house told her that his name was Mamun Miya, and that's when Mamun learnt that his house was in Narinda, in Dhaka, in Ghost Lane. But on that day, when the servants said that his name was Mamun Miya, Asmantara refused to accept that, she began screaming, 'No, it's a rabbit, it's a rabbit!'

Abdul Wodood Chowdhury's servants then had no option then but to bodily pick up Mamun Miya from where he lay on the ground, tie a rope around his neck, and hand him over to Asmantara, and so Mamun Miya became Asmantara's rabbit; because Chan Miya was born in the year '71, perhaps in the month of June, on the 12th of June, perhaps he was a Gemini boy, or in July, on the 12th or 22nd of July, a Cancer, or perhaps he was born in December, a Sagittarius or Capricorn boy, and therefore his name could perhaps have been Bijoy Miya, denoting victory – be that as it may, in 1971, Khoimon waited under extremely difficult and dangerous circumstances for her offspring and freedom. When the Pakistani army began killing Bengalis, her belly turned round like a bundle, the soles of her feet became swollen, and like a distraught pregnant cat, she shuffled around inside their house like a shadow – and then the razakars showed up, or perhaps the razakars came before that. The commander of the razakars, Abdul Goni – commanders of the razakars always have the name Abdul Goni – went on a tour of the moholla one day with a lathi in his hand, and stopped at Khoimon's residence, and while he was talking to Khoimon's Ma, he saw Khoimon inside through a gap in the window, and asked, 'Is that your daughter?' Perhaps amidst the darkness of the room, Khoimon's pride at her imminent motherhood gave her face the appearance of some rain-drenched flower or leaf, perhaps it looked like a wet, black, eroded seat made of oak on the bank of a brimming pond, Abdul Goni couldn't say what happened to him, but perhaps his razakar heart wailed in lament, what would be this woman's plight once the soldiers arrived! He told Jorimon, '*Apne kawn je apner pola muktibahini te jaay naika, taile apner pola koi gelo, taartoh ekta thiktaak hishab deown lagbo, naki kawn? Ghorer bhitore oita apner maiya naki, hyare daken, jigai.* You said that your son has not gone off to fight the Liberation War, so then you need to give a proper explanation for where he's gone, isn't it, tell me? Is that your daughter inside the house, call her here, let me question her'; and Jorimon was then in a bind, 'You are like my son, dear, my daughter's in the family way!'

'Call her, let me speak to her!'

Khoimon then emerged and stood in the veranda, her belly, bulging like a washerman's clothes bundle, looked as if it was about to burst open, and gazing at her face, Abdul Goni asked, 'How many months has it been?'

Jorimon was terrified, but Khoimon retorted, '*Apne ki jigaiben jigan.* Ask me what you want,' and Abdul Goni went up to her, perhaps it was dusk then, and so a gust of the uncertain dusk wind turned wayward with the anchal of Khoimon's sari, excessively so, buffeting it, whooshing all the while; Abdul Goni and his razakars could not figure out why the wind suddenly turned so crazy, they were at a loss, and gaping at Khoimon's sari, they thought that something was flying, and they asked, '*Ki udaan?* What's that you're flying?'

'*Ki udamu? Apnera hainja bela aya dikdari shuru korlen kyala!* What will I fly? Why have you come at dusk and started pestering us!'

Abdul Goni left with his squad that day, he was excited, he couldn't figure out the meaning of the wind's sport with Khoimon; and when at night Moyna Miya heard about the incident, he thought that they were now done for at the hands of the razakars. He then went looking for his father-in-law, Abdul Jalil, and found him, perhaps Abdul Jalil was then sitting with Abdur Rahim Byapari inside the house with the tiger gate, turning the dial of the three-band National Panasonic transistor radio and listening to BBC or Free Bangladesh Radio – 'Pakistani soldiers dumbfounded by the severe pounding they are receiving at the hands of the Mukti Bahini, the Bangladesh liberation force' – Moyna Miya then called him, and when he took him home and asked him, 'Abba, what should we do now?', Abdul Jalil got very annoyed, he retorted, '*Ki korba, boisha boisha khao.* What will you do, just sit and eat,' and it seemed Moyna Miya couldn't exactly understand what Abdul Jalil was actually saying – had he given him some instruction, or had he abused him? At night, when his wife plopped down like a balloon beside him on the cot, he thought that he ought to think of a name for his child, and he said so to Khoimon. She could not figure out why Moyna Miya was suddenly impatient to name the child in her womb right now, she reassured him, 'Why are you so scared, the razakars won't come again, don't be scared.' But perhaps Moyna Miya hadn't been scared, perhaps it had simply occurred to him that it was best to give a name, and he then told her about his conversation with Abdul Jalil, 'I asked him what we ought to do, and he said "Just sit and eat", why did he say that?' Khoimon could not understand what the matter was, she was silent, perhaps she fell asleep, but Moyna Miya knew that she wasn't asleep, she was merely pretending, and so for the first time he revealed the details of the incident at Jinjira, 'You know your father's a darwesh,' and from the depths of her slumber Khoimon replied, 'I know'; perhaps the razakars reported the incident at Khoimon's house to the chairman of the South Moishundi Peace Committee, Moulana Abu Bakr, or perhaps Abdul Goni waited some more, and at night when Khoimon wanted to fall asleep close to Moyna Miya, he kept her awake, he told her, *'Pola hoile naam rakhum Chan Miya!* If it's a boy, I'll name him Chan Miya!' It was difficult for Khoimon to assent to this name, and although Abdul Goni went around Ghost Lane with his band and they visited this house and that house, it was the incident in the house of the paan-and-biri seller, Abdul Jalil, that pricked his conscience like a thorn, and after that, one day Jorimon again observed Abdul Goni standing all by himself in the courtyard, near the veranda, so she emerged from inside and asked him, 'You?'

Abdul Goni didn't know what he wanted, he said, 'I came to meet your son, Rashidul, is he at home today, or isn't he?' But Rashidul was certainly not at home, there was no question of that, and so Khoimon, with her even more swollen belly, went and sat beside the window like before; looking through the gaps in the window grille, Abdul Goni observed that sunlight had fallen diagonally on one side of her face, the shadow under her eyes was such that it looked like she was wearing a fine veil, and from behind this chiffon veil her face was visible, and yet invisible, and Abdul Goni then said, 'Call your daughter, let me speak to her!'

For the second or the third time, in the afternoon, or later, in the evening, Khoimon stepped out of the house and came and stood in the veranda, she moved her sari anchal over her bulging belly to cover her modesty, and when she said, 'Were you asking about Rashidul?', Abdul Goni changed the subject and asked, 'What's the meaning of your name?'

Khoimon was in a fix, she couldn't quite fathom what Abdul Goni's intentions were, and Abdul Goni then advanced a bit towards the veranda, and looking at the weighed-down woman, he asked, 'What kind of name is Khoimon, what does it mean?' Khoimon's worn-out anchal then began to flutter in an angry gust, and Abdul Goni felt as if he was caught in a rogue wind; his body seemed light all of a sudden, it swayed, he thought he would float away somewhere, and so he stretched his hand to retain his balance, and then it occurred to him that Khoimon was definitely flying something, and when he got back his balance and asked, 'What are you flying?', Khoimon retorted, 'What will I fly? Don't bother us. Go away now!'

Abdul Goni remained standing there, and he asked again, 'What is it that you fly?'

The anchal of Khoimon's sari kept fluttering, she held on to her sari with both hands and replied, 'I don't fly anything at all.'

'You certainly fly something, as soon as you see me the anchal of your sari seems to fly off; tell me what you fly!'

Then Khoimon turned impatient, she planted the anchal over her shoulder and said, 'I fly the flag,' which frightened Jorimon, 'What are you saying?' And so Moyna Miya went at night with his father-in-law to the house with the tiger gate and listened to the programme on BBC, or Free Bangladesh Radio, Swapna Roy's songs played on Rahim Byapari's radio – '*Ek sagor rokter binimoye.* In exchange for an ocean of blood' – and then Abdul Goni, who was standing below Khoimon's veranda, was caught in a gust of wind, he thought that the wind would veritably blow him away, he then raised his arms high, the .303 rifle held in his right hand was pointed upwards; lifting his face up to the sky, he seemed to dance like one in a trance, he saw that the sky had turned red and the crazy wind was now spiralling upwards; and then when he accidentally pressed the trigger of his rifle, there was an ear-splitting bang, and it was observed that the force of the recoil of the rifle butt had felled Abdul Goni and he lay flat on his back on the earth, amidst the dust and sand. Jorimon almost fainted at the incident, she fetched water in a jug, splashed some on his face and brought him back to his senses, and with Khoimon's help, she pulled him to his feet, and she asked him, '*Byatha paichho ni, baba?* You didn't get hurt, did you, dear?' Abdul Goni then brushed the water off himself, he observed that Khoimon had gone inside and was sitting in a queenly pose beside the window, and gazing at the striped Khoimon through the gaps between the window grille, he was unable to imagine what he would do now, and so he said, 'I didn't get hurt, call your daughter, let me ask her something.' When Khoimon once again came to the veranda, he asked, 'What flag do you fly? Tell me what flag you fly! You're playing the fool, are you? You dare play the fool with razakars?' Jorimon got scared then, but Khoimon's head was as hot as a griddle, she got into a rage at Abdul Goni's words, 'Why do you ask the same thing again and again?'

'You didn't answer me, which flag do you fly – independent Bangladesh's?'

Khoimon was silent.

'Pakistan's?'

'*Pakistaner potaka udai na amra!* We don't hoist the flag of Pakistan!'

It wasn't just Abdul Goni who was astonished, even Jorimon was at a complete loss when she heard what Khoimon said, she brought a crumpled, medium-sized green-and-white flag from some corner of the house, held it high in front of Abdul Goni and said, 'We went and bought the Pakistani flag, we'll hoist it on the 14th of August!' But this didn't seem to penetrate Abdul Goni's ears, it was as if he was oblivious to Jorimon, right then it was only Khoimon, swollen like a pufferfish, who occupied his consciousness – if only she was not with child – and Khoimon said, 'You can leave now!'

The night programme at the house with the tiger gate was turning adventurous then, the situation in the country was extremely dire, one lived with the presence of the Peace Committee and the razakars in the moholla, this was not the time for doing things out of habit, but it had become like an addiction for Abdul Jalil, and even after the razakars' ludicrous conflict with Khoimon, he continued to think, 'After all what can happen?' But he hadn't actually understood the matter, and so the razakars raided Rahim Byapari's house and apprehended them; when they were sitting in the darkness behind the house, beside the pond, preoccupied with listening to the radio, the razakars carried out this operation of theirs; perhaps Moulana Abu Bakr borrowed additional razakars from Banagram, and that day three people were apprehended while they were listening to Free Bangladesh Radio – Abdul Jalil, Moyna Miya, and Gazi Gofran of the house on No. 20 – while Abdul Rahim Byapari and some others fled. There was no news of Abdul Jalil and Moyna Miya after that, perhaps the razakars then visited Abdul Jalil's house and informed the women, and when Jorimon, stricken with grief, didn't emerge from the house, Khoimon did, and stood on the veranda once again, and because the veranda lay along the alleyway between two houses, the wind seemed to come through a tunnel and strike the veranda with great force, and Abdul Goni stood speechless, gazing at Khoimon's billowing anchal.

'You asked me what I flew, isn't it?'

'What do you fly?'

'I fly the flag of Pakistan, please let my father go, let my husband go.'

Did Abdul Goni still think Khoimon's face was like the drenched branch of a tree? He said that they had no information about Abdul Jalil and Moyna Miya, they did not participate in the operation that day, it was the soldiers; he said, '*Ke ki felag uday dekhumne, apne khalas koira lawn!* I'll see who flies which flag, you finish your business!'

And so, there was a knot in Khoimon's birth canal, and it seemed that Chan Miya didn't want to be born; Abdul Goni and four other razakars arrived and made a round, Khoimon's belly continued to be swollen like an oil barrel, it didn't subside; and Mrs Zobeida Rahman told

Fakhrul Alam Ledu, 'After all, Chan Miya was a boy from a bundle,' and when Ledu wanted to argue with her, she said, '*Ki kawch tui, oytoh potlar bhitor thawn bairichhe, mayer pyate hoy naika!* What are you saying, he emerged from a bundle, he wasn't born from his Ma's womb!'

Perhaps this statement of Mrs Zobeida Rahman was correct, and a human baby could well be inside a bundle, but again, perhaps it wasn't correct, because a human baby couldn't be created inside a bundle, and perhaps Chan Miya wasn't either. But what was the reason for Chan Miya being called 'potlar pola', or 'bundle boy'? The reason was Khoimon, her stubborn nature, and her silence – Khoimon embroiled Chan Miya's birth with a bundle! After Abdul Jalil and Moyna Miya were taken away from the house with the tiger gate, when Abdul Goni said, 'You finish your business,' Khoimon actually got scared: what would Abdul Goni do once the business was over? And so, after Chan Miya's actual birth, Khoimon organized a false pregnancy, she stuffed a bundle of rags under her clothes, at her waist, and swelled herself up, Abdul Goni kept coming and going back, but there was no sign of Khoimon being done with her business, and if Abdul Goni asked, 'How many months has it been?', Khoimon stayed silent and let her anchal billow dangerously in the wind, but her Ma, Jorimon, did not want to have any further dealings with the razakars, she said, 'It must be six or seven months, why do you ask?' And so Chan Miya didn't get born – August went by, September went by, but Khoimon's belly stayed swollen, and Abdul Goni visited again and Jorimon said, 'It's about time,' but that didn't happen, there was no reason for it to happen, they fooled Abdul Goni by stuffing cloth at the waist. Perhaps Abdul Goni was bewildered, perhaps he lost track of the time, but he didn't give up – but why was Abdul Goni doing all this? Then October went by, and towards the end of November, Indian bomber planes dropped bombs on Dhaka airport, and the Pakistani F-86 Sabre fighter planes that raced after the Indian MiG or Mirage planes were unable to destroy them, but the Indian planes did lay and leave behind two eggs right on the runway, and after that in the beginning of December, one or two freedom fighters could be seen in the moholla, they would arrive all of a sudden and then leave just as suddenly, and fearing them, the razakars fled, or perhaps they hadn't yet fled, they were lying in wait, and perhaps their leader, Moulana Abu Bakr, said to them, 'Just wait, the Seventh Fleet has almost arrived; just wait, isn't the Chinese army arriving? They'll come down through India's NEFA region, and where will the fucking Indian non-believers go then! Just you see!'

And so Abdul Goni and his decrepit razakar squad remained in the moholla, and the bundle at Khoimon's waist wasn't taken down. The Pakistani army then surrendered on the 16th of December, and Niazi signed the Instrument of Surrender: 'The Pakistan Eastern Command agrees to surrender all PAKISTAN Armed Forces in BANGLA DESH to Lieutenant-General JAGJIT SINGH AURORA, General Officer Commanding in Chief of the Indian and BANGLA DESH forces in the Eastern Theatre ... The PAKISTAN Eastern Command shall come under orders of Lieutenant-General JAGJIT SINGH AURORA...'

In the evening of the 16th of December, a Thursday, amidst a mild chill, Group Captain A.K. Khondokar came and stood in front of a table set up on the Race Course field, he was accompanied by General Aurora; A.K. Khondokar said to Niazi, '*Surrender koro, astro namao, futo ei desh theika!* Surrender now, drop your weapons, and get out of this country!' Niazi stood with a grim face under the tall teak trees, with loose motions seeking to exit his arse, he removed his service revolver from the holster on his waist and laid it on the table, and then the bearded Kader Siddiqui stepped forward, he had been standing behind all this while and observing everything, but as soon as Niazi came near the table and placed his weapon on it, Kader Siddiqui advanced two steps and landed a terrific punch on Niazi's face, 'Son of a swine, whoreson, I fuck your mom,' he said, and Lt General Amir Abdullah Khan Niazi, alias Tiger Niazi, fell to the ground with his mouth gaping grotesquely, he began to weep and plead, 'I am a prisoner of war, I deserve protection and respect.' Lt General Aurora then raised his right hand to check if his turban was in place, and when he glared at Abdul Kader Siddiqui, the chief of the Kaderiya Force, and asked, 'Who are you?', Abdul Kader then replied in English, 'I am a *Bangali* youth, *shokto haddi* (strong bones) and *lomba* (long) beard, my name is Abdul Kader, I come from Tangail, doing *gulli* (shooting) and fighting for my country – who are you?'

Perhaps all this transpired on the Race Course field, it was what was supposed to happen, and when the people in Ghost Lane heard about it, they wondered, 'Hasn't the country just become independent?', and perhaps Jorimon then stopped her cooking in the kitchen and rushed to her daughter, and Khoimon said, 'Yes, now,' and they pulled out Moyna Miya's vegetable basket from inside the dark shack built in a corner of their inner veranda; a cloth bundle was visible inside the basket. Khoimon busied herself removing the cloth bundle at her waist, and as she undid each knot, Jorimon wept, and after that she undid the final knot and threw down all the old rags to the floor; when Jorimon picked up the bundle from the basket and clutched it to her bosom, it moved, and when Khoimon took the bundle from her Ma and loosened the cloths around it, a baby emerged from inside, and when it was held to her breast, it screamed; Khoimon then pressed it closer to her bosom but the baby screamed even louder – as if to bring the whole moholla down! On the 16th of December 1971, the sound of Khoimon's baby's screams echoed through Ghost Lane, but there was no trace of Abdul Goni – the son of a swine who had asked when the business would be finished – and thus, Chan Miya and independence entered Khoimon's life, but they had lost Abdul Jalil, Rashidul and Moyna Miya.

When the people of Ghost Lane heard the sound of Chan Miya screaming after he was brought out from the bundle, they exclaimed, 'What did Khoimon have, was it a boy or a girl?' Perhaps the womenfolk of the mohalla then arrived at Abdul Jalil's residence and saw Khoimon holding a big baby at her breast and feeding him, and when they asked, 'When was he born? How did you get such a big baby?', Khoimon replied, '*Eito ei changarir moidhye kapoder potlar bhitore achhilo.* Oh, he was in a cloth bundle inside this basket.' But in doing all this, it became difficult to establish exactly when Chan Miya was born, and when Khoimon took him to admit him to school, she complicated matters by saying that her son was born on Victory Day, the 16th of December, and the matter of Chan Miya emerging from a bundle too came to be recognized as the truth. After taking the baby out from Moyna Miya's basket, his Ma and grandmother promptly set to naming him, but though Khoimon liked the name Zafar Iqbal, it was rejected, because the name was too shiny, and then to match with the mother's name, they thought about a nice name beginning with 'K', but they could only think of Khabir, Khalil or Khyber, all of which were too ordinary, and when they brought the imam of the mosque, he told them, 'Name him Abdul Karim,' but before her Ma could say anything, Khoimon butted in and said to her Ma, 'Let it be, let his name be Chan Miya'; thus, with the offering of two goats to Allah, Chan Miya's name was decided upon.

Perhaps Mrs Zobeida Rahman's first son, Mamun, was born before Chan Miya, perhaps Zobeida Begum had observed Khoimon walking around with her bulging belly, perhaps she had spoken to her, perhaps she had run into Khoimon when she was on the way to her father's house with her baby boy, and when Khoimon asked her, 'What have you named your son?', perhaps Zobeida Begum replied, 'I haven't named him yet, I will. Tell me a nice name'; but Khoimon was unable to, she kept the name Zafar Iqbal for her own son. Perhaps they met again after that, and Zobeida Begum said to her, 'Your belly seems ready to burst!' Khoimon tried to remain calm, and when Khoimon once again asked her, 'What have you named your son?', Zobeida Begum turned dreamy, 'Oh I couldn't think of one, why don't you tell me a nice name?' But where would Khoimon get a nice name to suggest, and why on earth would she offer a nice name for Zobeida Rahman's son, because she would perhaps soon have to think of a name for her own son, so she said, 'Just pick some name or the other.' After that, they met again – that was the problem with living in the same moholla, there was no way you wouldn't encounter one another – they could well have met, and if they did, what else was there to do but to ask about her son's name? And so, Khoimon asked, 'Have you named your son?' But a name could not be given so easily, it took ten months and ten days to deliver a son, you couldn't name him just like that, in a day, or two, or five, and thereby sully the majesty of the womb, because once some peculiar name came to be attached to him, like Hablu or Dablu, his whole life was ruined. It was now Mrs Zobeida Rahman's turn to be piqued with Khoimon, and she retorted, 'Why do you need to know the name? You just go on asking … I haven't named him yet,' and then Khoimon said, most casually, 'Name him Dilip Kumar,' and the look on Zobeida Rahman's face changed, she replied, 'Name *your* son Dilip Kumar! Let's see what you name your own son!' But even after that, Khoimon retorted, 'Then name him Anda (egg) Miya!'

As a result of all these exchanges, Khoimon had good reason to not name her son Chan Miya, since that was a peculiar kind of name – what would the neighbours say, and especially Mrs Zobeida Rahman? But the boy's father had created the knotty problem, and when Zobeida Rahman heard the name, she remarked, 'It's a really lovely name, we can call him "Chandu"'; and so perhaps the teacher in Silverdale KG School, Mary Joyce, too called Chan Miya 'Chandu', perhaps she had heard Mamun or Ledu or Abhijit call him 'Chandu' and perhaps she thought, 'Let me show him how fond of him I am by addressing him by his pet name!' But this had just the opposite result;

Mrs Mary Joyce Clark was yet to learn a lot of things about this country – for instance, she didn't know that 'Chandu' was uncomplimentary, that it meant something like 'chump', or that it was 'Chan' Miya and not 'Chhan' Miya – although she was born in this very country, in Dhaka's Tejkunipara. Mary's grandfather, Albert Charles D'Souza had come from Goa eighty or ninety years ago and begun working with Fr Antonio Marietti's Catholic missionaries in the village of Shimuliya in Jessore district; perhaps Mary had told her daughter, Julie, all this while sitting at home in the lane housing the Women's Education Institute, and as she altered the long skirt, tucking in a hem and sewing it with a gold-tipped needle, she narrated all this to Julie, who was then reading *The Mousetrap* which Steven Arnold had brought, so whatever Mary was saying went in through one ear and out the other, Mary knew that, but still, gazing out of the window at a faraway building that was swathed in the soft light of evening, she talked to her daughter. Her grandfather, Albert, was of pure Portuguese stock, he had arrived by ship from Lisbon at the Portuguese colony of Goa on the west coast of India, and after staying there for a month or two, he was sent to Bengal; he stayed at the mission at Krishnanagar for a few days, where he familiarized himself with the people and the climate of Bengal, and after that he arrived in Jessore, to join Fr Antonio Marietti in the work of Catholic religious preaching and proselytization in the villages of Baxalpur, Shimuliya, Jagadanandakati and Jhikargachha; but he was very young, and having left his country he was melancholy and glum, he hadn't stayed very long in Goa either, but when he went to Jhikargachha for religious proselytization, he met the young local Christian ladies Kumari Labanyaprabha Das and her sister Kumari Bidyunmala Das, they conversed, and he liked them; perhaps at first Fr Antonio didn't deduce anything, perhaps he asked him, '*Albert, eto somoy ebong shrom keno Jhikorgachhay byay kortachho? Protestantder shoraya tumi okhane kichhui korte parba na.* Albert, why do you spend so much time and effort in Jhikargachha? You won't be able to do anything there after replacing the Protestants.' But Albert didn't heed Fr Antonio's counsel because he had already met the two sisters by then! Labanyaprabha's father, Bidhubhushan Das, was a Protestant Christian, he was in the jute business, he sent raw jute by goods train from the Jhikargachha station, which went to the jute mills in Calcutta via Bongaon. Bidhubhushan lived then with his family in a two-storeyed house on Station Road, near the Kapataksha rivulet, and he had no interest in matters related to Catholics, although he knew that one or two European saheb Catholic missionaries came to Jhikargachha from Jessore from time to time, and then one day he met Albert D'Souza at the Jhikargachha railway station; seeing his long cassock, Bidhubhushan advanced towards him – it hadn't occurred to him that this white reverend was Catholic. Bidhubhushan was more or less fluent in English, and so he tucked the pleats of his dhuti into the pocket of his punjabi and extended his right hand, 'Hello, I am a Christian, my name is Bidhu Das!'

While in Krishnanagar, in order to acquire a working knowledge of the Bengali language, Fr Albert Charles D'Souza obtained two books, one of them was the book written by the Portuguese missionary Manuel Da Assumsao, titled *Crepar Xaxtrer Orth, bhed* (The Meaning of the Bible, how it's different), in whose preface it was stated – *Doxto Bengali, xono: puthi xocoler utom puthi, xaxstro xocoler utom xaxtro* (Bengali friends, hear: here's the best book for everyone, the best scripture for everyone); the other one was a Portuguese-to-Bengali dictionary, *Vocabulario Portuguez E Bangalla.* Albert D'Souza began by saying 'namaste', and carried on the conversation in very deficient Bengali, and when he was at a loss for words, he began speaking in English, and it became apparent that he hardly knew English, but Albert D'Souza realized that Bidhubhushan was an amiable person who liked conversation and wanted to get acquainted, and he didn't want to lose Bidhubhushan in this Protestant bastion; he had two champa bananas in the pocket of his white cassock, and when he took out one banana and asked, '*Amar lawge duita kela roichhe, ekta apni khaun?* I have two bananas, would you like to have one?', Bidhubhushan understood the sad plight of this new white padre, and rather than saying anything, Bidhu Das accepted the banana offered by the padre and ate it, and he said, 'Sire, my house is just nearby, come to my place, let me offer you some refreshments.' When he set off with Bidhubhushan towards the house, Albert D'Souza felt that he ought to make his identity clear, so he told Bidhubhushan that he was a colleague of Fr Antonio Marietti in Jessore, and that Fr Marietti had sent him to Jhikargachha to preach the rules of the Catholic Christian prescripts; but Bidhubhushan's house and warehouse were very close to the railway station, by the time they exchanged just a few words they were at the doorstep, and there was no way for him to turn back now, and so when his daughter Labanyaprabha or wife, Jagattarini, opened the door, Bidhubhushan took Albert D'Souza inside and asked him with utmost courtesy to take a seat. While Jagattarini busied herself arranging refreshments for the guest, and achieved that by bringing a large, bell-metal plate bearing soaked chira together with curds-sandesh-banana, and four narkel nadus beside that, Bidhubhushan informed those in the inner quarters about Albert D'Souza's identity – he was a saheb, but a Catholic; but by then Jagattarini had reached the living room in the outer quarters with a bell-metal glass of water in one hand and the plate of food in the other, and her ghomta drawn over her face; their sixteen-year-old daughter, Labanyaprabha, had accompanied her out of curiosity to see a saheb, and observing D'Souza, Jagattarini thought that he was very young, perhaps he wasn't much older than her son Mihir. And so, after the refreshments, they engaged in casual conversation and it was almost noon, Jagattarini urged D'Souza to join them for their humble lunch; Labanyaprabha entered the room but didn't advance any further, she stood near the door and watched the saheb padre eat, she observed how he soiled his clothes by trying to eat with his hands. Labanyaprabha was used to seeing saheb padres all the time, Jhikargachha was a very small place, she joined the worship at the Baptist Church here every Sunday, perhaps she was a member of the church choir and sang 'Jesus's sweet name rings forever in my heart…' But she had never seen a real-life saheb in their house before, she thought the man ought to agree to her Ma's proposal, in which case she could teach him how to pick up the food with his hands and put it into his mouth. Although Albert D'Souza didn't agree to stay for lunch, he observed Labanyaprabha well and asked her name too, 'What is your daughter's name?' After Labanya said her name, he said, 'Wonderful!', drank another glass of water, wiped his mouth with the back of his hand and stood up, and then he joined his hands near his chest, bowed his head towards Bidhubhushan, Jagattarini and Labanyaprabha and said, 'Namaste, allow me to take your leave.' But although the master and mistress of the household gave him their leave, he seemed to have developed an attachment to the house, and while trying to go out through the small door from the olden times, he banged his forehead on the low lintel, and as he exited the door he spotted Bidyunmala; the fourteen- or fourteen-and-a-half-year-old younger daughter of the household, Bidyunmala, had returned from somewhere and was about to enter when she encountered the white padre, and when she looked at him and observed his plight, she began laughing, '*Aha, duyartar songe ki dushmoni go.* Oh dear, what enmity with the door,' she exclaimed, and Albert then remembered the second banana in his pocket, he took out the small champa banana from the cavernous pocket of his cassock and offered it to the girl, '*Amar lawge ekta kola achhe* ... I have a banana...' Mala Das was a bit bewildered at first, and then she accepted the banana; the tip of the yellow, thumb-sized banana had become soft, nonetheless, after Albert D'Souza left, she peeled it, and like a mouse, lovingly nibbled, bit by bit, at the low-grade banana – it could at least have been a sabari banana – and this did not escape Labanya's attention.

Perhaps as Julie Florence heard the tale of D'Souza, she wondered about these two unseen young women who were long dead and gone, and it occurred to her that Labanyaprabha could have become her mother's grandmother, but upon arriving at this point, Mary Joyce's tale took another turn; ultimately Labanyaprabha went to Jessore or Khulna and became a nun in a Christian monastery, and thereafter there was no news of her, perhaps she fell victim to destiny and coincidence, for had Albert D'Souza remembered the champa banana in his pocket when he was sitting in the living room of the house that first day, having eaten the refreshments prepared by Jagattarini, then perhaps events would have transpired differently, perhaps he would have offered it to Labanyaprabha, but D'Souza didn't remember; Labanyaprabha ruminated that D'Souza would surely accept their invitation and come to their house for a proper lunch or dinner very soon some day, that perhaps Bidhubhushan would first go and invite Albert D'Souza, and then there would be all the bustle of preparations in the household, and everyone at home would be feverish with excitement, they would be tired, and Albert D'Souza would sit to eat but wouldn't be able to eat properly, and then Labanyaprabha would teach this foreigner how to eat with his hands, she would say, '*Bura angul byabohar koren, bura angul diya thele daen.* Use your thumb, push it into your mouth with your thumb.' In short, D'Souza had no rescue from Bidhubhushan, no matter if he was Roman Catholic, but unfortunately for Labanyaprabha he didn't visit by invitation, it just happened unexpectedly; perhaps D'Souza encountered Bidhubhushan again one day, either at the railway station or at Jhikargachha Bazar, and Bidhubhushan pulled him home; perhaps Labanyaprabha wasn't at home then but Bidyunmala was, and so when Labanya returned, she found Albert D'Souza sitting in the lotus position on the large wooden aasan or floor seat and partaking of whatever there was in the house with rice. There was no limit to Mala's excitement in that regard as she reported to Labanya, '*Deki ki, Didi, bhaat tulte paare na go, ami boli ki buro angul byabohar koro, saheb, kintu amar kotha bujtei paare na, tokon ami haate dhore na shikiye dilam* ... You know what happened, Didi, he couldn't pick up the rice, oh dear, so I said, "Use your thumb, saheb," but he couldn't understand me, so then, you know, I held his hand and showed him...' Labanyaprabha felt the blow of destiny then, if one was not fortunate then that is what one was, and if one was, fortune would hold your hand and take you on the path of success. D'Souza's missionary work dwindled, he came to Bidhu Das's house in the morning or in the evening and chatted with Bidyunmala, he was more interested in whiling away his time with a young woman than in the well-being of Catholic folk, he brought along the book *Crepar Xaxtrer Orth, bhed*, he read out to Mala – '*xaxtri xocoler utom xaxtri Christor xaxtri, Crepar xaxtro ebong Crepar Xaxtrer puthi* (the greatest scripture of all is Christ's scripture, the Bible and the booklets from the Bible...' Bidyunmala was almost rolling with laughter, '*Tumi eigula ki poro, saheb, asho tomake Bangla shikai.* What's all this you're reading, saheb, come, let me teach you Bangla.' They went for a jaunt on the Kapataksha rivulet on a small boat, the people of Jhikargachha observed that; Fr Antonio Marietti in Jessore was worried, his other assistant, Fr Luigi Brioski was doing good work in the Bhabarpara area, but what had happened to Albert? He asked Albert again one day, 'I can't understand what progress you've made, D'Souza, you are just whiling away your time'; and so problems arose for Albert D'Souza, his heart was not in working among the local folk or the Protestants, it had been so long but he was unable to bring even one person into the fold by explaining the Catholic prescripts to him, and so after he returned from Jessore this time, he was in a worried and dejected state of mind, he told Bidyunmala that he was ill-fated, and then at night, when Bidyunmala lay in bed with her Didi on the first floor, she chatted about D'Souza: 'The poor man, see Didi, he doesn't bring bananas in his pocket any more, how rude, he says, "Where will I get the money to buy bananas?" I hardly know him and he says, "Where will I get the money?" *Ki fajil baba!* Gosh, what a wag!'

Labanyaprabha then fell asleep, but Mala couldn't sleep a wink, she said, 'D'Souza's Father scolded him, and so he's sad,' she said, 'The fatty's name is Father Anthony or something, he told him, "You couldn't make even one person a Catholic, why do you go to Jhikargachha so often?" It's good, let him face the music now, ask him to bring a banana and he says where'll I get the money!'

Probably Labanyaprabha didn't hear her younger sister saying all this, she fell asleep to the faraway sounds of an owl flying over the station and coming towards them, and of jackals howling. D'Souza wasn't seen for a few days, he wandered far and wide looking for a weak Hindu, or Muslim, or a Protestant yes-man; the padres of the

Baptist Mission had already taken the band of yes-men into their fold, but if there was a famine here now, if the Kapataksha or Betna rivers overran their banks and there was a flood, and the waters of the Budhkhan, Khormada or Somundar marshlands overflowed into crop fields and homesteads, there would be widespread lamentation and perhaps some service could then be rendered to the people. D'Souza roamed around, and at night, lying in the room on the first floor, Bidyunmala was immersed in worry, and perhaps then, from the direction of the Kapataksha, a solitary gull flew by in the darkness, calling, *'Kya-kya'*, perhaps Labanyaprabha drifted in and out of sleep, but her ears pricked up at the shriek of the nocturnal bird and she suddenly became aware of her younger sister's melancholy; she said to her, *'Sayeber bawl, Didi Kyatolik hobe – amare baaptaij korti bawl!* Tell the saheb your Didi will become a Catholic – ask him to baptize me!'

Albert D'Souza took Labanya by train to Jessore and presented her before Fr Antonio, and as she was departing, who knows what Bidyunmala surmised, she wept inconsolably, her grief seemed to know no bounds, 'I don't want anything, Didi, stay with me'; but Labanyaprabha didn't have any more time to stay, she left with Albert D'Souza and boarded the train. It took very little time to go from Jhikargachha to Jessore, so it wasn't a long journey at all, and after that Labanyaprabha followed D'Souza and got off at Jessore station, her tin trunk with a flowery design contained her clothes and suchlike, D'Souza walked with it resting on his shoulder, and then when he inserted his hand in his pocket he found that a champa banana lay in one corner, he took it out and offered it to Labanyaprabha, '*Amar lawge ekta* ... I have a...' Labanya ate the banana, in the way she had seen Bidyunmala eat one a long time ago, exactly like that, like fish underwater eating algae, with tiny nibbles, lovingly; after that she went away somewhere, who knows where Fr Antonio Marietti sent her, perhaps to Khulna, perhaps to Krishnanagar, or perhaps to the convent in the parish in Bhabarpara, in Nadia district, perhaps she found Sr Lalita, Sr Apolin, Sr Kumari Arnestina (Hashi) Gomez, they wore full-sleeved white blouses and grey-coloured saris with white borders, had a rosary in their hand and a cross hanging at their neck, and were busy with their routine, perhaps Labanyaprabha sang at the devotional singing on Sundays, '*Ami shokoli tyajiya jaibo choliya Srijishur chawron tawle* ... I'll give up everything and go, and sit at the feet of Lord Jesus...', or sang with the mourning procession on Good Friday, '*Jishu tumi momo tawre koto dukkho shohile* ... Jesus how much you suffered for me...'

Perhaps Julie Florence felt sad thinking about Labanyaprabha. And when Mrs Clark looked at her young daughter, smiled and asked, 'What happened?', Julie frowned, and then Mrs Mary Joyce Clark pushed up the spectacles on her nose and said, 'Beware of man and banana!' Nonetheless, Julie liked this tale – it was romantic and sad; the course of Albert D'Souza's life took a turn after he arrived in Bengal: by marrying Bidyunmala he turned from a renunciant to a householder, he discarded the cassock and trousers and donned dhuti-photua, he vigorously applied virgin mustard oil on his body and went with his wife's elder brother, Mihir Kanti Das, to the Kapataksha rivulet to bathe. Living in his father-in-law's house, he tried his hand at the jute business and failed, perhaps he didn't like his father-in-law's bossiness in this regard; he then worked for some time with the Raleigh Brothers company in Kushtia, and after that he took up a job as assistant manager in a zamindar's estate in Medinipur, but he didn't like this job either, and so he finally came away to Tejkunipara in Dhaka and remained there. He opened a bakery in Begunbari; Bidhu Das provided him the capital, because Bidyunmala went to her father and wept, '*O taka kotay paabe, padri manusher ki kichu thake?* Where will he get the money, does a padre possess anything?' Bidhu Das then had no option but to provide the money. Mrs Mary Joyce Clark told her daughter, Julie Frances, about how a D'Souza from faraway Lisbon spent his life baking crisp biscuits near Dhaka's Hathirjhil; after the formation of Pakistan, Mary Joyce's grandmother's family in Jessore left for Krishnanagar in West Bengal, in India. Before Jessore came under East Pakistan following the partition of British India, it came under the Christian diocese of Krishnanagar, and the padre, Fr Maro, was then the bishop of Krishnanagar, so with the assistance of his vicar general, Fr Louis Gobetti, many Roman Catholics of East Pakistan bought land in the villages near Krishnanagar and settled down there, and from Tejkunipara, four of the five sons of old D'Souza left, but Mary's father, old man D'Souza's fifth son, John D'Souza, didn't go, he said, '*Na, oikhane jaya ki korbo?* No, what will I do there?' Thus Mary's folks came to be in Bangladesh, but on account of the unprofitable business, old man D'Souza had few possessions other than the house built on a bigha of land. He was addicted to gambling on horses, he used to hang out at the racecourse in Ramna come Saturday; a few papers published details about the pedigree of the horses, as well as various tips, and a vendor used to come every week to the residence in Tejkunipara and deliver two such papers, one had race tips from the Gymkhana, and the other one was Chan Miya saheb's race tips; the racehorses had such a variety of names – Black Diamond, Queen of Calcutta, Phoenix ... Before Mary Joyce's uncles left for Krishnanagar, the house at Tejkunipara was sold and the brothers divided the money amongst themselves, Mary was then perhaps eight or ten years old. John D'Souza lived in rented premises after that, and thus began their life of floating around; in the midst of all that she passed the Senior Cambridge exam from St Francis School, became acquainted with Robert, a laboratory demonstrator at

Notre Dame College, and then married him; Robert was a very ebullient and handsome youth, he lived with his parents in a rented house in Lakshmi Bazar or Gendariya, and perhaps he first met Mary on some Sunday, during the Sunday prayer service at the Holy Rosary Church in Tejgaon, perhaps there was a tall shimul tree in the courtyard of this church, and perhaps it was spring then, and so a red-coloured flower had fallen beneath the tree; when Mary bent down and picked up the flower, Robert, wearing black trousers, black shoes and a white shirt, spotted Mary as he was about to enter the church, and said, 'A lovely flower!'

Mary could not recall whether she had seen Robert before at the Holy Rosary Church in Tejgaon, but hearing him, it seemed she was somewhat embarrassed, perhaps she didn't want anyone to see her picking up this wild flower because she was given to sudden likes and did things under that spell, and so when she heard Robert's remark, she smirked and said, 'Yes!'

'The tree as well!'

Mary suddenly wondered why this man was trying to talk to her. Nevertheless, she then looked upwards towards the tree, she liked this thorny tree too, she said, 'Yes.'

'Do you know the name of the tree?'

'Shimul, it's a silk cotton tree, I think.'

Robert found an opening to steer the conversation towards, he got down to showing beautiful Mary how heroically knowledgeable he was he said, 'The tree has a botanical name as well.' Mary smiled, she said, 'Every tree has a botanical name, isn't it? This one, too, must surely have one.'

'And don't you want to know what the name is?'

Mary had to give up then, the man was trying to build up credibility; she said, 'I don't mind, say it quickly if you can!'

Robert Francis thought that he was getting a response, that Mary was responding, or perhaps it hadn't gone that far; and he said, 'It's called *Bombax ceiba*.'

Despite her reluctance, Mary was immediately impressed, Mary's parents and D'Souza too didn't object; after they were married, they lived in rented premises, first in Lakshmi Bazar, and then in the lane housing the Women's Education Institute, which was close to Mary's school. Robert changed his job and joined the arboriculture department of the PWD, and then after the country became independent in 1971, he became the garden supervisor at the British Council, and one day, when he said to his boss, Steven H. Arnold, 'If only the winter in this country was a bit colder...' Steve came up to him, put his hand on his shoulder and said, 'You're a very fine man, Bob,' and then Bob told him that his daughter's birthday was on such-and-such date in such-and-such month, and asked him whether he would grace his humble abode with his presence on the occasion. Steven Arnold assented, and he arrived at the lane housing the Women's Education Institute on Julie's birthday; he had agreed to come especially when he learnt that Robert's wife was a teacher, and he brought an entire bundle of books for Robert's wife and daughter. Julie then read *The Mousetrap*, and her mother read *Madame Bovary*, or perhaps Mrs Mary Clark wasn't so keen, perhaps she didn't have the time either to read all these books, she was already struggling with the exam papers of the children at school, and so after the country became independent, Khoimon's battle continued, Mrs Zobeida Rahman's husband, Golam Rahman, returned to the moholla with the victorious freedom fighters, but none of Khoimon's folks did, and in fact, within a month of independence, she lost possession of half of her father's house; two long-haired fellows from South Moishundi arrived and said that half the house was theirs, they had bought it from Moyna Miya; Khoimon surmised that perhaps Moyna Miya had spoken to someone about half the property being made over to him, but he certainly wouldn't have sold the property to these people, however there was nothing she could do in free Bangladesh, these youths were kind enough to occupy only half the house, they left the other half for Khoimon and Jorimon; the usurpers plastered their premises afresh, whitewashed it and then rented it out, this part became No. 35/1 Ghost Lane. Khoimon's part continued to be No. 36, but then Jorimon too died for some reason, perhaps out of grief for her son, or because of the agony of outsiders occupying their house and breathing down their necks, and during such troubled times, the troop of monkeys arrived and began their high-handedness with Khoimon. When Khoimon took Chan Miya along and enrolled him in Rokeya Anwar's Silverdale KG School, a lot of people were astonished – Khoimon, who sold paper packets for a living, a bloody labourer, what standing did she have in the moholla? Nothing at all, and yet her son walked down Ghost Lane with a tie around his neck; they enquired, '*Porabi kemne, oyki ingraji parbo?* How will you educate him, will he be able to deal with English?' Khoimon then replied, 'There's no reason for him not to be able to, why wouldn't he?' Hadn't she employed a tutor for Chan Miya? But the moholla folk, and perhaps Mrs Zobeida Rahman herself, suspected that the monkeys were behind all this, perhaps she said, 'Plays with monkeys, was suckled by a monkey, just wait and see how much more the monkeys do!' That could well be, after all, weren't the monkeys of Bangladesh truly astounding creatures? Because it was Khoimon herself who chattered about all this when she went to Nurani Bilkis Upoma's house on No. 37, Khoimon observed that when she spoke about the monkeys and Chan Miya, Nurani Bilkis gazed at her enthusiastically, a faint smile spread over her face, her eyes lit up, she swallowed and absorbed whatever Khoimon said, perhaps she sometimes asked, 'Are you telling tall tales?' Khoimon seemed to fall from the sky then, and with an indifferent look on her face, she said, 'Why would I tell false tales, I'm telling the truth'; and she thought that that was an appropriate time to obtain something, and when she enquired, 'Aapa, don't you have paan in your house?', Nurani Bilkis got up and went and brought paan, she brought lime on a paan stem – Nurani Bilkis liked this tale, she was keen to hear about the amazing love between a human and monkeys! However, perhaps Khoimon really didn't make up tales about the monkeys, and the monkeys really did become roguish, but Khoimon was a poor woman who eked out her livelihood making and selling paper packets, she needed to earn in order to survive, and so she couldn't deal with the monkeys. The monkeys of Ghost Lane persisted in keeping watch over Chan Miya, perhaps the sensitivity of these monkeys of Dhaka city came to equal that of humans, perhaps not entirely equal to that of humans – because perhaps the idea of human sensitivity itself is a myth – however, perhaps these monkeys figured out that the boy had nobody, didn't have a father or brother, nor an uncle, nor grandparents, he had nothing, and so he grew up playing with the grey-coloured female monkey's baby – a human child could well grow up playing with a baby monkey. But the baby monkey was after all only a baby monkey, he grew up very quickly, his testicles grew large and dangled between his hind legs, his backside turned red like sindoor, he strutted just like Bangladeshi male ramp models along the walls or on the parapets of buildings, with his radiant posterior and tail held aloft; many young female monkeys from Ghost Lane, South Moishundi and Padmanidhi Lane were besotted with him, these female monkeys abandoned their own troops, and he could not be indifferent to these love matches, and then four or five female monkeys, with four or five babies fathered by him visible between their legs, hanging at their bosoms, came and presented themselves at some building or wall in the moholla; but this newly adult male monkey – Chan Miya's first playmate – didn't forget about Chan Miya, after all Chan Miya was a human child, at the age of three, four or five, he was hardly big, and so this monkey, accompanied by his five female monkeys and their babies, came to visit him, perhaps he said to his kids, '*Eita tawgo chacha lage, salaam de, bawl assalam aleikum.* This is your uncle, salaam him, say, "Assalam aleikum,"' and then the baby monkeys somersaulted near his feet and expressed their delight. Perhaps Khoimon narrated this new tale to Nurani Bilkis, 'You know what I saw one day, four or five female monkeys were sitting on the wall and plucking lice off each other and blinking, and when I went inside the room, five or ten baby monkeys were wrestling with Chan Miya, and seeing me, they bared their teeth.' The young male monkey perhaps turned into a rogue too, he became the terror of the moholla, perhaps he came one day with a grapefruit, and the five baby monkeys and Chan Miya played football with the fruit inside the room, one day he brought a bottle of Horlicks, they ate that with great gusto, and after that one day, this new father monkey brought a book for Chan Miya, although he was only a monkey, he realized that human babies needed to read and write, it wouldn't do to be a monkey, and so Khoimon told Nurani Bilkis Upoma that one day when she returned home, there was no trace of any monkeys outside, everything was quiet – 'I was in panic and terror, what's this, there's no sound from the boy, where's he gone, didn't he sleep? I entered the room and saw my son lying prone on top of a book.' But after all Khoimon couldn't read, she was an illiterate woman, so she took the book and went to Purnolakshmi; perhaps after having failed her matric exam, Purnolakshmi was then still waiting hopefully for her father, Chandrakanta, to find a boy from their Basak community to marry her off to, and Khoimon then appeared there with the book brought by the monkey, and said a load of nonsense to Purnolakshmi by way of explanation, because after all, she couldn't tell her that the monkeys in the moholla pilfered the book and brought it for her son; Purnolakshmi took the book with some of its pages torn, *My First English Book*, and began reading it, she asked Khoimon, 'Who'll teach your son?' When Mrs Rahman remarked that Khoimon had always been a woman with a cunning nature, did she exaggerate? After all, it was through irrelevant talk and excuses that Khoimon went through life, perhaps

Purnolakshmi had asked her just like that, as a way of making conversation, but when, almost as soon as the words left her mouth, Khoimon told her, 'Then you teach him,' Purnolakshmi was dumbfounded, she asked, 'How can I teach your son?'

'Why, have you forgotten to read and write? Teach Chan Miya instead of sitting idle, and if you want to be paid, ask me for money.'

Purnolakshmi began teaching Chan Miya, perhaps not for money, perhaps because she couldn't continue in her helpless state, or perhaps for the money too, but Chan Miya's monkey friends followed him around, his first monkey playmate came at any odd time with his children and wives, and when Khoimon wasn't at home, these male and female monkeys and their offspring crowded into the room, Chan Miya spent the time tumultuously with his guests; perhaps Khoimon scolded her son, '*Bandorer lawge thaika bandor hoya getachhoch.* You're becoming a monkey after being with monkeys,' and she once again narrated to Nurani Bilkis, '*Kemun pola hoilo, Allah, raitdin bandorgulir loya achhe.* What a son I have, Allah, he's with the monkeys night and day. Perhaps Khoimon threatened to hit Chan Miya too, she said, 'If you play with the monkeys inside the house I'll thrash you to bits,' but it was the monkeys who had made him their best friend, so at the mention of thrashing to bits, the oldest male monkey came and snarled at her to frighten her; some fifty monkeys, spanning three-four-five or ten generations became his playmates, and this number grew in geometric progression. Chan Miya went to Purnolakshmi's place for lessons, or Purnolakshmi came to their residence, and she said to Chan Miya, 'Read, C for cat, cat means *bilai*,' Chan Miya then read out, 'Cat means *bilai*,' nodding, and while he was reading, the monkeys waited atop the wall and Purnolakshmi thought that this boy would never learn anything, and yet one day Khoimon presented herself at Silverdale KG School on Rankin Street, but the watchman seated on a stool at the gate didn't went to let her in, he kept looking at Khoimon, she was wearing a shabbily draped, crumpled sari of faded print, with a pair of sponge sandals at her feet whose heels were worn out; perhaps the watchman thought, what business does this girl have here? Khoimon then revealed her intention, 'I want to admit my son, let me in, durwan bhai.'

The watchman, Ramdas, perhaps objected at first, because he thought that this low-class woman had no business inside the school, and if he let her in, the principal would chew him alive, she would say, '*Ramdas tumi gate-ey khadaya khadaya ki ghumao, ei shob lokjon bhitore dhuika jaay?* Ramdas, do you stand at the gate and sleep that all these people are able to enter?' But Khoimon had addressed him as 'bhai', he thought she was a good woman, so he let them in, and he acted as if he hadn't seen them, as if he had no idea where the two people had entered from, 'I can't tell you, madam, I didn't even see them entering!' Khoimon from Ghost Lane then moved the curtain at the door of Rokeya Anwar's room and barged in with her fatherless son, Chan Miya; and she reported to Nurani Bilkis Upoma that, seeing her, Rokeya Anwar suddenly fell off her chair, perhaps Khoimon made this up, because she had learnt to make up stories in the course of telling Upoma Begum about the monkeys, perhaps while chatting with her in the evening in the kitchen or by the well, when she had nothing more to say, Khoimon narrated these tall tales, and Upoma Begum didn't believe her, 'You're making it all up,' and then Khoimon said, 'Please give me some vegetable preparation so I can feed my son!' And so what could Nurani Bilkis do? She was silent for a while, she felt annoyed, yet she thought, the poor fatherless boy, and she said, 'Take it' – Khoimon took an eggplant or ridge gourd or potato curry in an enamel bowl belonging to Nurani Bilkis and returned home. Chan Miya ate that, and perhaps he scolded her, 'Amma, why do you bring eggplant curry every day?' During this time, Khoimon told Nurani Bilkis that when the plump Rokeya Anwar saw her and sought to sit erect and look down at her, she somehow fell off the chair, and Khoimon said, 'Perhaps she was sitting on the chair and dozing, sleeping in her own school'; and then, once she got up from the floor, she was embarrassed, and when Khoimon then said, 'Aapa, you fell off? Please admit my son,' perhaps Rokeya Anwar hadn't fully recovered her senses after her fall, but she then overcame her feeling of being at a loss and promptly got down to dealing with this problem; she realized that this woman was witness to her weakness and fall, and so she did not want to annoy Khoimon, she sent the ayah to call Mrs Clark from her classroom, and when Mary Joyce arrived, she said to her, 'Take him to your class.' Mary Joyce was a bit perplexed, because in the light of the principal's room – perhaps the light was inadequate – at first she only saw Khoimon standing in the room, and she wondered whom she should take to the class. Then, after a moment's hesitation she noticed Chan Miya standing by Khoimon's knee, clutching her anchal, and when the matter was still not clear to Mary Joyce, she said, 'Excuse me, ma'am?' Rokeya Anwar then lost her patience, 'Can't you see, Mary? Take the boy to your class,' and after Mary Joyce left taking Chan Miya along, she said to Khoimon, 'I didn't fall off!' Rokeya Anwar had perhaps started recovering her self-confidence, and so her annoyance increased, she put on an air of indifference towards Khoimon, she made a grim face and, looking at Khoimon, said, 'The fees in this school are high,' and Khoimon then showed her the bundle knotted at the end of her anchal and said, 'I have the money'; and then, amidst the grim creases on the face of Mrs Rokeya Anwar – whose family consisted of her lame husband and two adolescent children, Riya and Farubar – a faint smile could be discerned, this woman, or girl, or labouring woman wanted to educate her son in Silverdale with the money knotted in her anchal, how amazing, but she was certain that no sympathy would be awakened in some corner of her bosom for such women – after all, she had to send Riya to boarding school in Shillong! But when Mrs Mary Clark took Chan Miya's thin, almost non-existent hand in her own, left the principal's room and walked towards KG-1, she thought to herself, Rokeya Anwar is admitting kids like this to the school – what is she doing! But it seemed that through Mary Joyce's grasp, Chan Miya returned from the margins of non-existence, he learnt 'Jack and Jill' quickly, and Mary Joyce turned towards the tiny Chan Miya, she said, 'Very good, well done, Chan Miya!'

Silverdale KG School had a style of its own, the boys and girls wore uniforms, white shirts or tops with maroon-coloured shorts or skirts and a maroon-coloured tie, and there were two wooden see-saws and a slide near the school building – these were Rokeya Anwar's methods, her point being that if one ran a KG school, one had to do such things. At the beginning of every school year, once children were admitted, arrangements were made for their medical examination at Dr Nandy's residence, Mrs Rokeya Anwar gave this procedure the name, 'medical check-up upon entry'; at the time, Dr M.N. Nandy resided in the two-storeyed building next to the school, on Rankin Street, and his chamber was on one side of the ground floor, and so one morning, Mary Joyce, the teacher of KG-1, made the fifteen or twenty children from her class stand in line and cross the road, and arrived at Dr Nandy's chamber. Mary Joyce and the children sat on the sofas in the corridor and waited, the compounder called out names from a list and led the children to the doctor's room, and Dr Nandy examined them; he lifted up their shirts, applied his stethoscope to their chests and listened, he pressed their abdomens and felt whether the size of their spleens was all right, he looked at their tongues, he made them open their mouths wide and looked into the throats, he pulled down the lower eyelids to see how red it was underneath. After that he pulled down the boys' shorts and made them do sit-ups. Sitting outside Dr Nandy's room with the teacher, through the gap in the curtain at the door, Chan Miya observed naked boys inside doing exercises, and when two or three children were left, Mary Joyce discovered that one child was missing, Chan Miya wasn't there, and there was no trace of him; and so Mary had to face severe embarrassment, Rokeya Anwar scolded her, '*Tumi kemon meye, Mary, ei ponerota polapan dekhe rakhte paro na!* What kind of girl are you, Mary, can't you mind even these fifteen children!'

Mary was very angry with Chan Miya after that, and when he came to school the next day, Mary caught hold of him, 'What kind of boy are you, tell me?'

Chan Miya kept his eyes trained on the ground.

'What's your problem? Why did you go away like that without telling me?'

Chan Miya didn't speak, but he began crying, he sobbed.

'Why are you crying?'

Chan Miya then stopped crying and said, 'I felt scared!'

Mary Joyce went once again to Dr Nandy's chamber, taking Chan Miya along, she had to, or else Rokeya Anwar would scold her again – 'Why are you like this? Take him, get him examined.' At the chamber, Dr Nandy, fair-skinned and paunchy, and wearing suspenders, came up to them in the corridor, raised Chan Miya's arms up – and he then made a long-drawn-out sound, like 'Aah', and said to Mary, 'I see this is an amazing boy, madam, he says he's scared, what's there to be scared of!' The doctor then took him into the chamber and examined him, looked at his tongue, looked under his lower eyelids, and when Dr Nandy asked him, 'Why are you sacred?', Chan Miya replied, 'You took off the boy's pants, I was scared.'

Dr Nandy said, 'I see that this is an amazing well-mannered boy too,' and when Mary heard that, she smiled a bit, she ruffled Chan Miya's hair a little, and said, 'He is shy and brilliant,' and then Dr Nandy told Mary, who was seated across the table, 'Please go and sit outside,' and when Chan Miya was alone with him in the room, he lowered his shorts and made him do sit-ups in order to see whether there were any signs of a hernia, and putting on a thin, rubber glove on his right hand, he then felt and moved Chan Miya's testicles, which were like large-sized seeds of kidney bean, to see if there was one or two, after that he examined his eyes; with one eye shut, Chan Miya read out from the Snellen chart:

T
E P
L H V
O S T A
L C V E
F Z T H P
N L O S V H
O Z U F K L
T E P C L V O

The doctor then checked his colour perception, and he observed that Chan Miya got it jumbled up when he tried to read out from the Ishihara colour scheme, he read the number 74 as 21, and the doctor said, 'Read it again.'

Chan Miya said, 'Twenty-one.'

Dr Nandy realized that the boy was red–green colour-blind, and his pen made a rustling sound as he wrote on a piece of paper: protanopia/deuteranopia; but then Dr Nandy got a phone call, the black-coloured telephone whose top looked like a cow's horns rang in another room, and he got up, went 'Hello, hello, hello,' and returned to find the piece of paper missing, perhaps he was an absent-minded, philosopher type of doctor, and so it was concluded that he had forgotten the paper somewhere, and Chan Miya and his teacher then left. When Dr Nandy prepared the medical sheet for Chan Miya and all the others, he wrote: colour of hair, black; eyes, brown; eyesight 6/6 (without spectacles); no special medical problems; and thus the colour-blind boy remained unaware of his medical problem. And so Mary returned to her residence in the lane housing the Women's Education Institute and narrated all these stories to Bob, perhaps Julie was very small then, but perhaps she had got used to hearing her mother's school tales from the very beginning of her life, and new names were added to the list each year, Luthful, Masud, Dilwar, and then came Chan Miya; Julie then encountered Chan Miya on the prize-giving day, and when she asked her mother, 'Who is he?', Mary's mother said, 'He's Monkey Boy!' Perhaps Julie Florence had already heard about Chan Miya from her mother – 'There's a boy in class, a little one, everyone calls him Monkey Boy…', and so for that reason, when Mary told Julie, 'He's Monkey Boy,' Julie could place him, so that's him, she thought, and the girl, Julie, said to her mother, 'Why don't you ask him to come to our house, I'll play with him'; but that wasn't really possible, Mary couldn't ask Chan Miya to her house for no other reason than to play with Julie, but Chan Miya, together with Mamun and Ledu, attended her next birthday party. And as soon as she heard that her son had been invited to a memsaheb's house to eat, Khoimon couldn't control her excitement, she went to the Rathkhola crossing and got Chan Miya's black, 'naughty boy' shoes – now turned red with earth – polished, she applied mustard oil on Chan Miya's arms and legs, and Tibet snow on his face, and said, 'Go now,' and the boy left to feast at the memsaheb's house! Mary took the boys from school, and thus Julie met Chan Miya; Mary called her daughter, 'Julie, this is Chhan Miya, say "Hello", say "Hello, Chan Miya"!' Perhaps Julie then remembered that Chan Miya was Monkey Boy! Because all these little children never forgot anything; she said 'Hello' to him, and asked him, 'Are you Monkey Boy?' And Mary was unable to silence her and remedy the situation by saying, 'Hush, Julie, you shouldn't say such things'; and so Julie then sat and chatted one evening with Mamun and Fakhrul Alam Ledu at their residence in the lane housing the Women's Education Institute, and when she remembered Chan Miya, she asked, 'Where's he now?' Although Mamun pretended not to have heard the question, Ledu wondered why Julie was so eager to know about Chan Miya! And then one day, he managed to find Chan Miya; it occurred to him that he too hadn't met Chan Miya in a long time, what was he up to now, he wondered. What was that boy doing? Chan Miya? Perhaps his Ma, Khoimon, knew that best, after all, she had squandered her youth for the sake of the boy, hoping her son would become someone, like Zobeida Rahman had done for her son, Mamun; she went to Silverdale KG School and got him admitted there, she scorched her arse paying the school fees with her earnings from making and selling paper packets, but towards the beginning, Chan Miya too paid the price for this scorching, he was promoted from KG-1 to KG-2, he came second or third or something like that – Abhijit came first – and Khoimon went to the school and got the list of new books to be purchased; then she went to Nurani Bilkis Upoma and pleaded, '*Aafa amare koyta tyaka daen, noile amar polatar poralikhi ami kemne chalai!* Aapa, give me some money, or else how will I get my son educated?'

Nurani Bilkis was surprised to hear that. 'What the hell is the girl saying? Amazing,' she thought to herself, 'Did we ask you to send your son to the English-medium school that you now come and say, "Give me money for my son's education"? Hey, this wretch is a clever one indeed!' Nurani Bilkis pretended she had no idea what Khoimon was talking about, and after that she asked, 'How many ration cards do you have?', and Khoimon said that she had three ration cards, two were the white-coloured adult cards – the owner of one of them, Jorimon, was long dead and gone – and the third one was the blue-coloured child card, Chan Miya's; Upoma Begum pondered for a while and said, 'Get two sets of ration cards made,' and Khoimon did just that, she became the owner of twenty sets, i.e. forty extra white-coloured ration cards in all, and since Nurani Bilkis's husband, Fazlur Rahman, helped her in this regard, Khoimon didn't face any problems; every week she drew one and a half seers of rice per white card using two sets of cards in two ration shops, she drew sugar and wheat, and then she went to Thatari Bazar and sold it to provisions shops or rice vendors. With the money from making paper packets and selling the rations to the shops, she managed to keep Chan Miya in Silverdale till class four, and when he returned from school with the report card, she went with it to Purnolakshmi, who was still sitting and sleeping at home and getting fat, and she read Chan Miya's progress report four times in the year – it was a pleasant task that Khoimon gave her – and after reading the progress report, she said, 'Your son is a good student, he's come third, he scored hundred upon hundred in two subjects,' and after that, Purnolakshmi signed in the space provided for the guardian's signature, 'Khoimon Begum'. Khoimon was still hopeful about her son's future, she had got nothing out of marrying Moyna Miya, except for this boy; perhaps Mary Joyce Clark had thought that Chan Miya would go very far in life, but it wasn't at all impossible for Khoimon's son to lose his way in his life journey. Perhaps Mary Joyce Clark had thought that she would help steer the poor boy through Silverdale; but perhaps she didn't realize that love alone would not be enough to save Chan Miya, the peculiar kinds of difficulties besetting his life could not be erased by wiping away his tears with her thumb, so Mary succumbed to error, and one day, like Mamun, or Abhijit, or Ledu, she lovingly called Chan Miya 'Chandu', and unwittingly created a problem; Chan Miya didn't like that at all, he didn't go to school for three days after that, and Mary then became worried, what's happened to the boy, she wondered. Then Khoimon brought him to school, and holding the edge of the anchal of her sari in her mouth, she smiled, exposing her black, paan-stained teeth, and looking at Mary Joyce she said, 'Aapa, you called him "Chandu" and that's why he felt ashamed, he told me, "Teacher called me Chandu!"'

Mary was very sad, because Mary Joyce was born to be sad, she thought about how much she loved the boy, how much she did for him, and so she was grave for a couple of days, Chan Miya did this and that, he did a sum in his notebook and brought it to show her, but Mary didn't look in his direction and Chan Miya then burst into tears, so Mary went up to him and asked him, 'Why are you crying? Strange!'

What could Chan Miya say, then? He covered his face with his hands and cried some more, cried his heart out, and then Mary ran her hand over his head, 'Okay, okay, don't cry, okay!'

For the second time in his life, Chan Miya calmed down after wetting Mary Joyce's hand with his tears, perhaps Mamun told his Ma, Mrs Zobeida, everything, and after hearing that, she said, 'Allah, it seems there's no end to the drama'; but Chan Miya was a crooked kind of boy, he just could not be straight, and so when Julie Florence asked him at her birthday party whether he was Monkey Boy, he got so angry that when the photographer from Bari Studio at the Ramakrishna Mission Road crossing removed the cap from the lens of the camera dangling from his neck and held the flash gun high up with his right hand, Chan Miya moved away from there and went and stood in the balcony. Later, when Julie looked at their family album with Mamun and Fakhrul Alam Ledu, this picture formed part of their collective childhood memory, Robert was standing in the middle of the photograph wearing a bow tie, there were so many people in the picture, only Chan Miya was missing – '*Keno nai? Nai kyala?* Why is he missing? Why isn't he there?'

'Where was he?'

Mamun ul Hye replied, 'Perhaps he didn't come at all for the party that day'; but Julie Florence knew – it's difficult to say how she knew – that Chan Miya had definitely come, and she could remember that she had eaten a lozenge that Chan Miya had given her; sitting in their drawing room, Julie told Mamun and Ledu, 'But he was there, he gave me a toffee or something like that!'

The fatty Ledu too remembered that Chan Miya was there, and he told Julie that Chan Miya had given her a banana as well; that made Julie remember her mother's cautionary message about eating bananas, and she at once retorted, '*Kola khabo kaen, kola khaowar proshnoi ashe na!* Why would I eat a banana, there's no question of eating a banana!'

'You had it, I remember, I'm not making it up, what's wrong with eating a banana?'

Julie then became dejected, she thought that perhaps her mother had warned her too late about bananas and men – of course, Chan Miya was not a man then, nonetheless – and she asked once again, 'Ledu Bhai, where's your Monkey Boy now?'

Ledu wondered why Julie Florence hadn't forgotten about Chan Miya, she even remembered that she had eaten a toffee so many years ago, why? Why did this girl remember all that? Perhaps there was nothing unusual about it, Mamun had given him the best explanation in this regard, he had said that if someone was a Monkey Boy, people remembered him, that was normal, no one would remember people like Mamun ul Hye and Fakhrul Alam, that was normal too – and so Chan Miya had an advantage by virtue of being a Monkey Boy – and perhaps Julie asked, 'Why do you call Chan Miya "Monkey Boy"?'

'Because he was brought up by a female monkey.'

'It's quite possible, the two brothers Romulus and Remus were suckled and raised by a wolf, and later they established the city of Rome.'

'Is that true?'

'Of course it is! Why do you ask?'

Perhaps Mamun then said, 'Okay, let's forget it,' and Fakhrul Alam Ledu wondered where Chan Miya was now. Perhaps Khoimon knew, because after giving birth to him, Khoimon had kept him wrapped up in a bundle out of fear of the razakars, and said that her son was born on the 16th of December; perhaps Mary Joyce noticed the date when she was writing the progress reports for the first quarter of KG-1, when she wrote, 'Father's name: Late Moyna Miya'; 'Date of birth: ...'; Mary Joyce was then astonished, what a wonderful boy you are, Chan Miya, you were born on Victory Day, what an astonishing victory, and in the space provided for the teacher's comments, Mary wrote, 'He is exceptionally good, he is our hope!' But perhaps Mamun, or Ledu or someone else swore at him, calling him 'potlar pola', or 'bundle boy', perhaps one day in school someone was playing 'string cutting' with Chan Miya, using kite string daubed with glue and ground glass, perhaps Mamun's, or Ledu's, or Abhijit's string got severed because of Chan Miya's tug, and so he called Chan Miya 'potlar pola'! Returning home that day, he found that Khoimon wasn't at home, the monkeys were sitting in a row atop the wall, brother monkey, father monkey, baby monkey, grandson monkey, and a lot of female monkeys too, these monkeys began jumping up and down when they saw him, they came and sat on his shoulder, but Chan Miya was miserable, 'Monkey Boy' was one thing, but 'Bundle Boy' was something else, what did it even mean? Would such things never cease in his life? Oh Allah! And perhaps as evening was falling, Khoimon returned from Thatari Bazar after she had finished selling paper packets there, and she found the house lying in darkness, the brigade of monkeys was sitting silently on the wall with their hands on their faces, and she wondered, how did these monkey offspring become so well-behaved, amazing! She then pushed the door and went into the room and saw that Chan Miya was lying on the cot, something he never did at this time, she got scared, as if her very lifeblood had run dry, 'Oh dear, what's happened to you?' She went near and woke up her son, she planted a slurpy kiss on his forehead and asked him, 'What happened to you, my love, oh dear, are you feeling unwell?' And when Khoimon heard what Chan Miya then said, she blazed with rage, she felt like slapping someone and hitting them with a lathi; Chan Miya asked her, 'Why do the children call me "Bundle Boy"?' But what could Mst. Khoimon do when she heard that, perhaps she slapped her own face, she just sat helplessly, what could she say? He was hardly more than a baby and already he had started interrogating his Ma about his birth, he wanted explanations, oh Lord! Tears of rage, grief and humiliation ran down her cheeks, and she told him, '*Jara tawre potlar pola koy hyago thota fataya dech na kyala? Aya ghorer bhitore shuyya thakchaw!* Why don't you smash the faces of those who call you "Bundle Boy", instead of lying at home!'

Chan Miya's Ma, Mst. Khoimon, had thrown him a challenge; perhaps he had a fight one day in school with his classmate Liaquat Hossain – after all, the monkeys were not as big as children – perhaps when they were playing some game, or after a quarrel over whose turn it was on the slide, Liaquat called him, 'Bund—', and Chan Miya thought that perhaps Liaquat hadn't said 'bundle', so he continued to scuffle with his classmate regarding the slide, and perhaps Liaquat who was standing nearby looked at him and said, 'Bundle,' and even after that perhaps Chan Miya thought that it was all right, it didn't matter; but the boy Liaquat was a rascal, he then said, 'Bundle Boy,' and so Chan Miya had to do something, after all his Ma had told him to smash the face, and so when he came down the slide, he caught hold of Liaquat, dragged him to one end of the playfield and threw him to the ground, where he lay in the dust. That day, Chan Miya tasted disciplining in school; the watchman Ramdas held him by the hand and took him to the principal, and sitting behind her high desk, Rokeya Anwar asked him, 'Why did you hit Liaquat?'

What could Chan Miya say? His eyes were downcast, and Rokeya Anwar punished him for this act of violence, Chan Miya was made to stand in one corner of the office until the school got over. Perhaps word of this reached Mary Joyce, perhaps she inwardly wanted to do something for the poor boy, so she went to the office and brought him out holding his hand, but she was scared that Rokeya Anwar, being the imperious woman that she was, would scold her, 'Mary, why are you like this, you are spoiling the children'; and so she asked around until finally Chan Miya's class-two teacher, Rosalyn D'Costa, explained the matter to her, and naturally Mrs Clark was confused, 'What does "potlar pola" mean?'

'Son of a bundle, that's what it means!'

'Oh my God! But why should he be called son of a bundle?'

Then, the next day, or the day after that, or the day following that, Mary perhaps looked for Chan Miya and told him, 'Why did you fight with Liaquat, aren't you a big boy now?' He was big now, or else he would surely have burst into tears when Mary asked him that, he was truly a big boy now, he hardly cried any more, and so when Mary Joyce placed her right hand on Chan Miya's shoulder, he felt as if a pillar of light had settled on his scrawny shoulder like the oblique ray of light that came in through the gap in the door, and he turned his face towards this light, he looked at the face of Mary who was standing before him; Mary Joyce asked him, 'Why are you like this, eh? Why?'

'He called me "Bundle Boy"!'

'Does that mean you'll hit him?'

Perhaps Khoimon believed it wasn't good to be so tolerant, if someone threw a stone at you, sometimes it was best to throw a bigger stone back, but all the calculations went awry, and some time after being punished in school for hitting Liaquat, Chan Miya began skipping school, and back in Ghost Lane, he hit Mamun's younger brother,

Mahmud, too for some reason, since he was weaker than him; he slapped and punched him a few times, but Mahmud raised such a racket that Mrs Zobeida Rahman's entire household rushed out, caught hold of Chan Miya and thrashed him badly – until Khoimon arrived with a lathi and rescued her son. Chan Miya didn't want to go to school after that; Khoimon got angry, she scolded him, and wept, but after all, the blood of Moyna Miya flowed in Chan Miya's veins, there was lethargy in it, and so Chan Miya began to tire of schoolwork; the kids at school too were after him, like crows, they made life unbearable for him, and so he told Khoimon that he wanted to join her in making paper packets, 'I'll make paper packets with you and sell them, the children call me "Monkey Boy", they call me "Bundle Boy", I'm not going back to school'; and Khoimon then realized that the whole matter of the boy being born from a bundle had been wrong, and that her dreams were now consigned to dust. Perhaps the monkeys then heard about the misdeeds of Zobeida Rahman and her family, perhaps they thought, 'What! The gall! All of them got together and thrashed a fatherless boy!' And one day, a monkey – the monkey who had been Chan Miya's first playmate, perhaps it was that one – bared its teeth and snarled at Mrs Zobeida Rahman so fiercely at the well-side that Zobeida Begum slipped on the moss-covered paving and fell down with her pile of pots and plates, she didn't break the bones of her fat hips, but she hurt herself badly,

'*Amar maja gelo, ami shyash hoya gelam, bandorera amare maira falailo.* I'm finished, I'm dying, the monkeys killed me,' she wept, and so she was laid up in bed for many days, with Iodex balm massages and hot compresses on her hip; there was nothing she could do then, because there is nothing one can do against monkeys in this country, there was no way of catching them – although they could perhaps be shot with a gun, it would still be difficult to shoot so many monkeys. But couldn't one go to the police station and file a complaint against the monkeys? Couldn't the police do something in this regard? When Zobeida Rahman's husband, Golam Rahman, went to the Sutrapur police station, once the officer-in-change heard the nature of the complaint, he said, 'It's a very difficult case, these are wild monkeys, they have no owner, they are unclaimed, it's very difficult to bring the matter under the purview of public nuisance in accordance with the penal code, tell them to keep a lathi in hand instead,' and Chan Miya didn't go to school then, perhaps Mary Joyce imagined many things, so many things could befall a boy like him; later, when Julie asked Mamun and Ledu, 'Where's he?', Ledu thought Khoimon would certainly know where he was, because perhaps, observing Chan Miya's waywardness, Khoimon was dejected, but perhaps she also realized she had no other option. What was the point of beating and thrashing him, after all he was a fatherless child, it was all right, there were two sets of ration cards in his name, they would get by, and so perhaps she visited Nurani Bilkis Upoma's place one day and again made up preposterous stuff, '*Chan Miyato portei chay, kintu bhaiba dekhlam poraya labh ki, amra gorib manush, Aafa, amar lawge thonga banaile duijone milla ei kaam korte pari.* Chan Miya does want to study, but I thought about it and realized it is pointless to educate him, we are poor folk, Aapa, if he makes packets with me, the two of us can do it together.'

Nurani Bilkis said, 'Do that! Won't you take something today?'

'What can I take?'

'Oil, or vegetables.'

'*Na, Aafa, monta bhalo naika, polata lekhapora korlo na!* No, Aapa, I feel depressed, my son couldn't get educated!'

Khoimon should have been terribly sad, in effect Chan Miya's situation turned out to be just like that of his father, Moyna Miya, he grew up just sitting and lying around, and playing with the monkeys, and then when, perhaps in the face of pressure from the World Bank, the government discontinued the rationing system and closed all the ration shops in the city of Dhaka, Khoimon's two sets of ration cards became useless, and when Khoimon took out all of her forty-three ration cards from under the mattress on the cot and tore them up, the wind carried the bits away, and Khoimon observed how the pieces of what had been the last resort in her life were tossed about in the haphazard dusty wind, and then from the shack in the corner of the veranda she took out a very old bamboo basket and told Chan Miya, 'Here, since you won't go to school, go and sell vegetables in Thatari Bazar like your father, go and walk the streets crying, "Vegetables! Vegetables!"' Perhaps Chan Miya wondered at that, would he be a vegetable seller then? Impossible, never, so perhaps after falling into the clutches of a human trafficker he went to Nayapaltan and enrolled himself in Macadam Driving & Training Institute, the trafficker had perhaps told him, '*Deraibarita shikha falao, tumare Soudi Arobe Shapetko companite chakri diya pathaya dimune, Jedda-Modina route-e baas chalaiba.* Learn driving, I'll get you a job in SAPTCO in Saudi Arabia and send you there, and you'll drive buses on the Jeddah–Medina route'; and so Chan Miya told his Ma, 'Amma, arrange for some money for me, I'll learn driving and go to Saudi Arabia.'

Khoimon must then have said to Nurani Bilkis Upoma, 'Aapa, Chan Miya wants to learn driving and go to the Middle East,' and in response, Nurani Bilkis told her, 'That requires a lot of money, where will you get it?'

'I don't know where I'll get it!'

When Chan Miya joined the Macadam Driving & Training Institute, he got another chance to find out that he was colour-blind, but owing to inexpediency, corruption and irresponsibility, this too eluded him; the proprietor-cum-instructor of the driving institute, Rahman, or Dutta, or Gomez, arrived in a 1960s model Nissan Datsun car, affixed a 'Learner' plate, and taught Chan Miya to drive the car on the inner roads of Motijheel Colony and in the playground, and three more hopefuls for the flight to Saudi Arabia, or Dubai, or Kuwait, sat in the rear seat awaiting their turn, and Rahman, or Dutta, or Gomez – perhaps it was Rahman – lectured them: this is the bumper, this is the bonnet, this is the boot; see the three pedals in front of your feet, press on them with your feet, the one on the right is the accelerator, the one on the left is the clutch, the one in the middle is the brake; look into the distance when you drive, don't look at the bonnet of the car. He then sat in his office and taught theoretical things, and looking at the chart hanging from an iron nail on the wall, he said, 'Look, pay attention, there's a black arrow pointing to the right, and there's a red circle over it with a line running through it, what does that mean? It means you can't turn right'; after that, when he hung up a placard with an image of a traffic signal with the three lights, instructed Chan Miya to sit on a stool and asked him, 'How many lights do you see?', Chan Miya replied, 'Three.'

'What happens when the one at the top turns on? What colour is it?'

'It's grey, I'll stop the car.'

Rahman was confused, he asked, 'If the one in the middle turns on? What colour is it?'

'I'll slow down, this is yellow.'

'And the one at the bottom?'

'That's grey, when it comes on, I'll drive."

'What if the lights are horizontally placed?'

'I know that, when the one on the left comes on, I'll stop, when the one on the right comes on, I'll drive.'

Chan Miya completed his education by referring to top and bottom, and left and right, Rahman realized that the idiot was colour-blind, but he ignored it; because there was no remedy for that, and there was no way of getting a licence from the BRT if someone could not distinguish between colours. Khoimon then gave Chan Miya twenty-five hundred taka from the money she had saved with great difficulty, and Rahman paid a bribe and got him his licence; and so Chan Miya never found out that he could not see two fundamental colours. Perhaps Khoimon went to Nurani Bilkis Upoma's house and shed tears, '*Awkhone ki kori kawnto, Aafa, ami awkhone ponchaish shaait hajaar tyaka koi paai, kemne pathai Soudi Arob?* Tell me what I should do now, Aapa, where will I get fifty or sixty thousand taka, how can I send him to Saudi Arabia?'

Nurani Bilkis remained silent, she did not know any remedy for Khoimon's daily problems, she herself wouldn't be able to give her any money, so she looked blankly in Khoimon's direction pretending to be preoccupied, as if she had no clue about what was being said, but when Khoimon didn't say anything further, Nurani Bilkis said, 'The times we're living in, what can I say!'

'I just don't know what I'll do, the poor fatherless boy!'

'Put him to work, tell him you'll arrange the money later!'

'Where will I get it later?'

It had been Nurani Bilkis's intention to confuse Khoimon, to take the conversation elsewhere, so that she wouldn't say, 'Give me some money, Aapa,' but to her surprise, Khoimon didn't ask her for money, what had happened to her, had she changed? Upoma Begum said, 'If you put Chan Miya to work, perhaps he'll forget about going to Saudi Arabia, or earn himself and go with his own money, who can say'; and so, Chan Miya had to accept the reality, it wouldn't be possible on Khoimon's part to pay fifty or sixty thousand taka from her savings from selling the ration-shop rice, perhaps she didn't want to either – she had only one son, and if he went away, how would Khoimon survive? – so she took him to a motor garage behind the Food Department's silo in Kalta Bazar and got him a job there, the garage was called The Car-Home Motor Garage Ltd, and it was observed that although he had no interest in the work, he developed a penchant for cars, and he test-drove restored cars more often than he repaired broken-down ones, and one day someone pushed and brought a broken-down car to the garage – perhaps it was a Honda Civic – perhaps it wasn't anything serious, and his boss told him, 'Check if there's soot on the plug,' and Chan Miya then lifted up the bonnet and cleaned the plug by wiping off the carbon accumulated on it, and then he opened the door of the car, got in, started the car, reversed through the gate of the garage and went off. He wasn't seen after that, and the boss said, 'He's giving it a trial'; but for how long, how much does one need to test a car after cleaning the soot on a plug? The car owner's face turned grim, the garage owner's face was flushed red with rage – there was no sign of Chan Miya! He arrived with a princely air half an hour or an hour later, screeching to a halt, and the owner of the garage beat him with his shoe – 'You son of a swine, you disappeared with the car' – and after suffering the blows with the shoe, he said to his boss, '*Garita emon uira gelo bujhtei pare nai konkhan diya kohkan gelo shey!* The car just flew off and I simply couldn't figure out where it went!' When Khoimon heard from someone in Ghost Lane about all these goings-on in the garage, her face turned ashen, what would she do with this boy? She hadn't let him go to Saudi Arabia, and now the owner of the motor garage here had thrashed him with a shoe, someone had raised their hand against her beloved son, her fatherless child, so she said, 'You tell me what I am to do with you!' But Chan Miya's life didn't sit still, one day he said that he would get into the used-car business with a partner, and then it was as if the sky had collapsed on his Ma's head, 'What are you saying, son? Where will you get the money?', and so Nurani Bilkis Upoma gave Khoimon a bowl of eggplant or pumpkin curry and sent her off, but there was no trace of Chan Miya, and it was the monkeys who now ate the pumpkin curry provided by Nurani Bilkis; the monkeys waited for him at the house on No. 36 in Ghost Lane, they took down the pot from the shelf and ate the rice cooked by Khoimon, she had placed the vegetable curry given by Upoma Begum in the kitchen, and after the troop of monkeys entered the house, they threw the curry on the floor and wasted it. And while Khoimon lamented to Nurani Bilkis, 'Aapa, I can't keep any rice or vegetable curry at home because of the monkeys' torment,' the monkeys of Ghost Lane feasted on her rice and vegetable curry and thus turned fat, and when Mamun ul Hye's parents complained to the officer-in-charge of the Sutrapur police station about the formation of a monkey brigade, were they really exaggerating? Hadn't Khoimon herself told Nurani Bilkis Upoma all this, time and again, when she came to borrow some oil, or salt, or sugar – '*Chan Miya bawro hoya gele ki hobe, bandorto Chan Miyar pachh chhare na, haay Khoda ei jontugula ei polatar bhitore ki dekhlo!* What will happen when Chan Miya grows up, they don't stop following him, oh God, what did these creatures see in the boy!' After Chan Miya grew up, although Khoimon put two locks on the door of her house, and used a chain together with a local three-lever lock as well as a black-coloured Globe brand Chinese padlock with an iron hoop, was there really any way of obstructing the monkeys? It didn't seem possible, because Chan Miya removed a rod from the window for the monkeys, and they used that to get in and out, they went in and sat inside, so what could Khoimon do? After all, it was her fatherless boy! When all the monkeys – from ancient monkeys to old monkeys to middle-aged monkeys and so on, right down to tiny baby monkeys dangling from their mothers' bosoms – finished their daily business in the moholla, they landed up inside Khoimon's house in the evening for a veritable soiree, they sat waiting for Chan Miya to arrive, and Khoimon reported to Nurani Bilkis, 'I entered the room and found the troop of monkeys chattering away inside, and seeing me they bared their teeth and snarled, just imagine!'; and so, after Zobeida Begum was frightened by a monkey and fell down at the well-side, when the officer-in-charge of the Sutrapur police station asked, 'Tell me, what steps can I take against an animal from the jungle?', Zobeida Rahman's husband, Golam Rahman, was at a loss for words, he thought, what on earth is he saying! Astonishing! Because these monkeys were no longer ordinary monkeys, these were moholla monkeys that had been spoilt by indulgence, they weren't wild monkeys, and didn't everyone in the country know who indulged them? Then one day, Golam Rahman went up the stairs to the terrace and found it was full of shit, and when he told Zobeida Rahman, 'It seems all the monkeys in the moholla come and shit on our terrace,' she fell silent and pondered, Khoimon had been her enemy all her life, a pauper's daughter who was a pauper, and Golam Rahman went again to the Narinda or Sutrapur police station, and after hearing everything, the officer-in-charge said, '*Bandorerto paykhana kora lagbe, tai na?* After all monkeys need to shit, don't they?' What more could Golam Rahman say then? If the monkeys got the urge to shit, ought they to come only to their terrace to do their business and create a mountain of shit there! Wasn't there a solution to all this? If you can't say anything to the monkeys, then at least tell the godfather or the godmother of the monkeys, everyone knew that the godfather of the monkeys of Ghost Lane was Chan Miya, haul him up, thrash him, cut him up; but the officer-in-charge smiled, he said, 'Monkeys are part of the heritage of old Dhaka, and as for the godfather, if he's apprehended, perhaps they'll go and demonstrate outside the magistrate's court, and the honourable court will be embarrassed, pictures will be published in the newspapers, and I will be finished for no fault of mine!' And so a new nuisance began in Zobeida Rahman's life, and one morning or evening a man arrived and said that his name was Mamun, and that he had come from Chittagong; 'I've come from Chittagong,' he said, 'I'm a son of this house, my name's Mamun, I was lost for a long time,' and then Zobeida's old fears returned, she thought that this was all Khoimon's doing! But Khoimon was then entirely preoccupied with Chan Miya, she was full of remorse, why on earth did she allow him to learn driving when she didn't even have the money for him to go abroad; and so, after monkeys, it was with other people's cars that Chan Miya now became acquainted. Although the proprietor of The Car-Home Motor Garage Ltd had thrashed him with a shoe one day, he felt no shame at that, he stuck to his job at the garage so that he could satisfy his urge to drive, and he repaired cars, his body covered in grease, and then test drove them, and thus one day he observed a parked Honda Civic, perhaps in Lakshmi Bazar itself, perhaps right beside the roundabout at Bahadur Shah Park – perhaps this was the very car for which his boss had beaten him with a shoe – and Chan Miya inserted a metal cord, unlocked the door and disappeared with the car. He returned after thirty or forty minutes, or an hour, parked the car close to the roundabout, and vanished, and perhaps the owner of the car returned and saw that the car was not exactly where he had left it, but he didn't suspect anything, he thought, it's all right, do people always remember everything? After this, Chan Miya didn't feel like working in the garage any longer, because he no longer lacked cars to test-drive, and so he went up to the owner of the garage one day and said, '*Apne amare juta diya marchhen, amar baap nai, ami ekta etim pola, ami aar apner kaam korum na.* You beat me with a shoe, I don't have a father, I'm a fatherless boy, I won't work for you any more,' and perhaps a white-coloured Toyota Mark 2 vehicle, parked at Bahadur Shah Park, or Lakshmi Bazar, or in front of the Police Club on Nawabpur Road, caught his attention, he disappeared with the car; he went via Aminbazar, past Savar and then returned after a visit to the National Memorial, perhaps he laid flowers too at the memorial, he thought that it was really wonderful, but when he returned after three or four hours and tried to drop the car in the vicinity of Raysha Bazar, he was spotted by a policeman at the Dolaikhal crossing; as he pushed the lock of the car door into place, slammed it shut with a thud and turned around, he saw a policeman standing in front of him; the man said, 'My name is Sergeant Rafiq, whose car is this?'

There was nothing Chan Miya could say, but the sergeant was an expert, once he got chatting with Chan Miya he was astonished, where is this creature from, he wondered, and then he asked, 'When you do this business, why do you leave the car behind? If you're caught, you won't be spared – you've got caught, you'll go to jail now – Offence Against Property, Theft, Section 374 of the Penal Code, imprisonment for three years, or a fine, or both, and in your case it will definitely be both!'

Sergeant Rafiq then felt pity for this boy, he put his hand on his shoulder, and that day Chan Miya once again inserted a metal wire through the door of the Toyota Mark 2 vehicle, opened it and made a long trip to Tongi, and when he dropped the car behind the Gazipur intersection, at Basumati Motor Garage, which was owned by Arfan Ali, and gave him a note written by Sergeant Rafiq, Arfan Ali told him, 'You'll get fifty once it's sold.'

'Fifty what?'

'Thousand.'

Chan Miya turned into a car thief, and when he told his Ma that he would get into the used-car business, Khoimon was unable to sleep with worry, she said all kinds of nonsense to Nurani Bilkis Upoma, that her son Chan Miya was capable, if he wanted to he could have done well in life, after all, hadn't he been a good student? Wasn't Purnolakshmi witness to that? He was good at his work in the garage too, just go and ask in Rokanpur, go and find out what a fine mechanic he had become, and that's when the idea of the used-car business got into his head! Looking at Upoma Begum's face, Khoimon then said, 'Chan Miya wants to get into the used-car business.'

Nurani Bilkis had no clue about the matter; after the ration shop closed down, her husband, Fazlur Rahman, had now become a wholesaler of rice in Shyam Bazar, so she asked, 'What kind of business is that?'

Perhaps Khoimon too didn't really know, she said, 'Buying and selling cars.'

'Where will he get the money?'

'A garage owner will be his business partner.'

Perhaps Nurani Bilkis once again felt uneasy, and so Mamun ul Hye and Fakhrul Alam Ledu went to the lane housing the Women's Education Institute and found that Robert was very unwell, he had an ache in his chest and a cough; in order to go to the doctor, he came down the stairs with his arms around Mrs Clark's and Julie's shoulders, and the situation turned into an opportunity, and Mamun and Ledu lent a hand – although this didn't cut any ice with Julie, perhaps being of help to her father would do Mamun some good! Julie then glanced obliquely towards Mamun, and he wondered, why do you look at me for no reason? Perhaps they met again, perhaps Robert's condition was nothing serious, perhaps this problem was on account of the cold, perhaps it had the looks of pleurisy, and then Mamun asked Julie, 'Why don't you take care of your father?'

'How much longer will I take care of him? After all, once I'm married, I'll go away!'

'When are you getting married?'

Perhaps Julie's parents thought about Julie's wedding, after all, their daughter had grown up and it was the norm to get one's daughter wed when she grew up, perhaps Julie too thought about the subject, or perhaps she didn't think about it, but where were the boys in this country to whom Julie could be given in marriage? Then one day, Mamun ul Hye asked her, 'Do you read Bengali books? Or only *The Mousetrap*?'

'Why?'

'Have you read the poem "Kaaler Jatrar Dhwani"?'

'I think so.'

'May I give you a book on your birthday?'

'Give it, but don't write anything inside.'

Mamun realized how shrewd this girl was, and on the 21st of September, the two of them – Mamun and Ledu –

bought two books for Julie and arrived, Mamun was keen to write on the first page of the book, 'To My Love Julie', or 'To Julie of My Dreams', or 'To Dear Julie with Love', but his hopes remained unfulfilled; he said, 'Isn't there a party for your birthday?'

'Dad's not well, and I am already an old woman, how many more birthday parties can I have!'

'Do you know what Ledu is doing?'

Julie was curious, 'No, I don't know, what's he doing?'

'Ledu is wooing his love, Shefali Aapa!'

'Great! Aren't you doing the same?'

Mamun became melancholy, what kind of female was this, playing around with a helpless, drowning man! Why did she have to ask such a question? Be that as it may, Mamun said that he wanted to!

Julie then said, 'I really want to meet Monkey Boy!'

And so, when Fakhrul Alam Ledu finally met the adult Chan Miya, he had started coming to the moholla in a car, and the people of Ghost Lane were all agape seeing his business, they found it very strange, and Zobeida Begum wondered whether this was at all possible. Wasn't this the son of the vegetable seller, Moyna Miya? Wasn't he the son of Khoimon who made paper packets for a living? He should have been driving a bullock cart, and here he was, arriving in the moholla in a motor car! Then one day, Chan Miya was standing in front of the temple, beside a white- or blue- or black-coloured Proton Saga, or a Wira Sedan, its door was open, three monkeys were seated on its roof, and Chan Miya was eating bananas with them, and Ledu then came and asked him, 'What business are you in?'

'In the motor-car business.'

'What business with motor cars?'

'I buy cars and sell them.'

'What are you saying!'

'Yes, have a banana!'

Ledu stopped asking questions, ate a banana and was pleased, and when he told Chan Miya about Julie Florence, 'Mary Teacher's daughter, Julie, asks about you,' did Chan Miya's childhood appear in the window of his mind? His childhood life had been an unreal one, as ramshackle as a scarecrow made of straw, full of fear and the dread of being blown away by the wind – did he then remember Julie from within the mist of the past? He asked Ledu, 'What does she ask?' And so it was clear that he remembered Julie; but what would Ledu tell him? That Julie asked where Monkey Boy was? After all, Ledu couldn't say that to Chan Miya's face, although he was fat, he had a fine sense of discretion, and perhaps that was why their next-door neighbour, Shefali Aapa, called him one day and said, '*Dekhto Ledu, bandor amar bodice-ta chhader upore niya gechhe niki?* Ledu, can you please go and see whether the monkeys have thrown my bra on the roof?' There were no stairs to go up to the roof of the house on No. 18, the one-storeyed building where Shefali's family lived, so what choice did Ledu have, he scaled the wall of the building with his heavy body and climbed up to the roof where he did spot a white-coloured bra lying in one corner. Perhaps Ledu was tired after climbing up to the roof, he put Shefali's bra into his pocket and rested for a while, meanwhile Shefali was standing below and gazing up, a long time went by with no sign of Ledu, she rubbed her eyes in disbelief, what's the fat rascal doing, she wondered, and then she called him by his name, 'Ledu, hey Ledu, where are you?', Ledu climbed down the wall, whose bricks were sticking out, Shefali took her bra and snapped, 'What were you doing for so long?' Ledu said that he was doing nothing, but Shefali was a woman, why would she believe that, after all she had suspicions in her mind, so she said, '*Boya boya eita shungchhoch, bodmaish!* You were sitting and sniffing this, you rascal!' But Ledu hadn't done that, the thought had never entered his head, he said, 'I don't do such things,' and Shefali then became more enraged; she was a newly married, beautiful woman, separated from her husband, Abdur Rahman, who had gone abroad; he left for Qatar a month after he married her, and he now recorded all kinds of details and exaggerations on a cassette and sent it to his wife – 'How are you, I haven't received any letters from you in a long while' – and then after a monkey took away her bra, when she encountered Ledu, she thought, let me make this fatty toil; but hearing what Ledu had to say, she said, 'If you don't do such things, what do you do, my angel!' What could Ledu say to that? He didn't say anything, and after that, Shefali called Ledu one day, they had a guava tree in their compound, a branch of the tree was hanging down crookedly like an inverted umbrella, and one day a ripe fruit was visible on the branch; Shefali spotted Ledu across the wall and said to him, 'Hey Ledu, please pick the fruit!' Ledu was a tall and big boy, but nonetheless the branch was out of his grasp. He couldn't reach it even with a jump, so Shefali then said, 'Hold me up high, I'll get it'; and Ledu bent down, held her firmly near her knees and lifted her up, and Ledu's face was squashed against her fat, round buttocks. That day, Shefali pulled and dragged down the branch and plucked off the guava, and after that she needed to come down, but it seemed Ledu had forgotten about releasing her, so Shefali shouted, '*Ki re chharosh na kyala?* What's up, why don't you let go of me?' Ledu then lowered her to the ground. Another day, another fruit on another branch ripened, and Shefali slipped away from the attention of the menfolk of her house and called Ledu to get her the guava, 'Please pick the fruit for me'; perhaps this branch of the tree wasn't very high, it was within reach, but it wasn't really visible, even though Ledu thought he had caught hold of the branch, he hadn't, perhaps he would have been able to grab it if he jumped, but because his leg was aching, he couldn't jump either, and so it was necessary for Shefali to be lifted up, this time Ledu held her up by the knees from front, he kept his face pressed between her thighs; and then perhaps he waited every day for Shefali's call, and one day he observed that a ripe fruit was dangling on the tree, but Shefali Aapa didn't call him, bats ate up the ripe fruit at night, perhaps monkeys too ate it during the day, and then another fruit ripened, and another one, but there was no word from Shefali. Ledu then went to Shefali's house and said to her Ma, 'Khalamma, where's Shefali Aapa?' and then Shefali's Ma told him, 'Oh Shefali's gone to her in-laws' house, she's going away to Qatar'; perhaps Ledu narrated this story about the guava to Mamun, and Mamun asked him, '*Aar ki korochh?* What else did you do?' But Ledu hadn't done anything else; because he was a fat boy, he had a fine sense of discretion, and that's why Shefali did all that with him, thinking that there wasn't any possibility of trouble, and then, one day she went away joyfully to her in-laws' house. That's how the fatty Ledu's sense of discretion could grow, he was certainly a good boy, although his mind was restless for a few days after having nuzzled Shefali's thighs and buttocks, but he never saw Shefali again, and yet he told Chan Miya that perhaps Julie was asking about him just like that, 'Perhaps she remembers the childhood days, and that's why she asked.'

'Just like that!'

'Why?'

'She called me Monkey Boy!'

Fakhrul Alam Ledu then tried to reflect on the deep significance of human life, in effect, human life was not possible without memory, it was memory that saved and killed, he gazed at Chan Miya, and in the lane housing the Women's Education Institute, when the sun began going down, Julie Florence switched on the tube light and continued to read *Madame Bovary*, which Steve Arnold had brought for her mother – that man gave such a book to her mother! She asked her mother, 'Ma, did you read the book that dad's boss brought?'

Mrs Clark hadn't read it, the examination papers from school took up all her time, she said, 'I haven't read it. Why did you ask?'

'You should read *Madame Bovary*.'

'Why?'

'It's a sad tale of a married woman, in desperate, adulterous love.'

'Ah, you are becoming very possessive, Julie, I'm quite old now!'

Perhaps age troubled Mrs Clark, there were lots of zeros, errors and scratches in the old accounts ledger; there was no time to open a new accounts ledger, her hair had turned grey, her skin had become wrinkled. Mary was cheerless because Robert Clark's illness was not an ordinary one; suddenly one day, Robert forgot the scientific name for shimul, and Mary wept again after a very long time on account of Bob. Tears rolled down her fair-skinned, middle-aged cheeks, like rain descending after ages on scorched earth; she told Bob, 'Try to remember it.' But Bob could not, he had entirely forgotten the botanical name for shimul, and after he realized that, it seemed as if Bob's life lost its fulcrum; it was when he went for prayers with Mary and Julie one Sunday morning and entered through the gate of the Holy Rosary Church that it struck him that he could not remember the name of the tree, he told Mary, 'Mary, I forgot the name!'

'What name?'

'Of this tree.'

'Shimul!'

'No, the other name!'

When Mary understood, she could not believe that was possible, 'You forgot the botanical name for shimul! Didn't I marry you because of this scientific name, Bob, leaving the world behind and coming to you?' Oh Jesus, she was upset all through the church service, she wept to the Lord, have mercy on me, Lord Jesus, I never sinned knowingly, my Lord, have mercy on us; the pastor of the church led the prayers.

Pastor: 'In the name of the Father, the Son, and the Holy Spirit.'

Everyone: 'Amen.'

Mary folded her palms together, and bowed her head; perhaps Julie could not understand why her mother was anxious, so what if he could not remember the name of a horrid, ugly – and thorny – tree, her father was getting old, and his memory was failing, perhaps it was dementia, something like that could well happen; but it seemed her mother knew more, her mother, Mary Joyce, continued to be disheartened, her mind wailed inwardly, if Bob forgot even the name of a tree, then nothing would remain of his life, and she told her daughter, 'He will not live long!'

Steven Arnold was very worried, after all Bob wasn't supposed to be in this condition, he granted Bob leave, 'Take a break for a few days, rest at home, just see, everything will be all right'; but Bob didn't survive, he was admitted to BSMMU for lung cancer, and then one day, Mary left Julie at her father's bedside and went over to the Shahbagh market to buy pethidine injections, and when she glanced at the National Museum, she felt that the world was utterly indifferent to her personal crisis, the stream of people and vehicles on the streets flowed on, and the leafless shimul tree inside the compound of the National Museum was full of red flowers. So Mary went into the museum compound, and after a very long time she picked up another red shimul flower from the ground, and in the quest for the botanical name of the shimul flower, she went into the public library; but she wasn't able to find out even the correct English name for the shimul, was it the 'silk cotton tree'? But there was no entry against that name, there was nothing in the *Encyclopaedia Britannica*, nothing in the *Encyclopaedia of Botanical Names* either, and finally she found the botanical name for shimul in the *Banglapedia*, Bombax ... She noted down the name on a slip of paper, and returning to Bob's bedside, she said, 'Look Bob, a shimul flower,' and she took out the slip from her handbag and read out the scientific name for shimul, and Julie thought a smile had spread across her father's face then despite the terrible agony he was in, but he didn't live for more than fifteen days, he was buried in the Christian cemetery at the head of Tipu Sultan Road, and it seemed that trepidation rained down on Mary from the heavens; Steven Arnold then came one day to the lane housing the Women's Education Institute, and not knowing what to say, he asked Mary, 'Did you like *Madame Bovary?*'

Wearing a black scarf over her head, grief-stricken Mary remained silent, she hadn't read *Madame Bovary* at all, but she asked Steven Arnold, 'Can you help my son go abroad somewhere?' And as a result of this endeavour on Mary's part, a crisis was created for Joseph Eugene, because he said to Shakila Banu as he sat in the Job Section of the Government Press that he didn't like all this any more, and looking at him, Shakila Banu from Nakhalpara scratched the top of the wooden desk in her office with her nail and drew tiny hopscotch squares – so it was finally with a Christian boy, Joseph mistri, but how did it start? Shakila Banu's co-workers in the Job Section of the Government Press were of the view that this was nothing, it was pointless; when Shakila's father, Faruk Hossain retired from his job, thanks to the influence of the leaders of the trade union, his elder daughter, Shakila, a BA graduate, was hired in the Job Section; Shakila sat at her desk the whole day, and when work-related requisitions reached her, she wrote the relevant description in a ledger book, gave it a number and sent it to the concerned section. She did that all day, her co-workers observed her, she wasn't dark-skinned, or fair-skinned either, her figure wasn't bad, but her row of upper teeth hung down like a first-floor balcony, so she didn't smile, and in order to cover up her teeth, she pulled down her upper lip and kept her face grim; there was no enthusiasm regarding her on the part of the unmarried employees of the Government Press, and Shakila's boss, the section-in-charge, had made a suggestion to an Intermediate Arts–failed binder in the Binding Section, but it didn't work out. And then she somehow met Joseph, how that happened was a mystery, however, one afternoon, Joseph, all black with grease, came and sat at Shakila's table, and said, '*Tahoile khaowan.* So treat me then,' and hearing that, the folks in the Job Section were astounded, what's he saying, asking a woman for a treat was a tremendous feat in this country, because in this country, women too were consumed like foodstuff; what was Shakila going to treat him, what did this Christian son-of-a-Christian want to have – what was the matter? It was hard to figure out what the matter was, but perhaps the girl had never imagined that Joseph mistri would really come and sit at her table, in front of so many people, and Shakila was unable to drive him away, and so she took out the handmade rotis and scrambled egg that she had brought for tiffin and shared it in full view of everyone; Joseph ate one and a half rotis and half the scrambled egg, with a piece of onion and a green chilli to go with it, burped, and said, 'I ate to my fill,' and so the row of teeth defied the resistance of her upper lip and emerged, and she opened her handbag, took out a tissue paper and offered it to Joseph; as he took it, he touched Shakila's fingers. Perhaps Shakila sat at home, trembling, for two days, and her co-workers in the Job Section thought that womenfolk were always skiving, they were delighted if they could avoid coming to office, but the following day, or two or three days later, she returned, and brought along with her a small tiffin carrier with three containers, and in the afternoon the employees in the Job Section observed with wide eyes that Shakila sent the peon in their section to find Joseph mistri and fetch him, and after Joseph Eugene arrived, she opened her tiffin carrier, there was pulao in one container, chicken curry in another, and four pieces of something like tikka kebab in the third; perhaps Joseph was embarrassed, but after that, they divided the pulao between themselves, poured the chicken curry gravy over it, and began to eat, and in this way, Joseph mistri got more and more involved. Perhaps a couple of days went by and Shakila fed him again, perhaps it was rotis and scrambled egg once more, and then the people at the Government Press learnt what all Shakila Banu of the Job Section fed Joseph mistri, egg-roti-pulao-chicken and suchlike, and perhaps they then thought that there was nothing wrong with providing all that, so long as she did not serve herself on Joseph's plate, or was there really nothing wrong? Didn't such behaviour prod a man to go astray? It definitely did, it instigated him, and there was no doubt that Shakila and Joseph Eugene fell to such nudging, Joseph even presented himself at Shakila's residence in Nakhalpara, he fawningly addressed Shakila's Ma, Firoza Banu, as 'khalamma', and after having tea together with a hard, dry, pakon pitha, a kind of rice cake, as he took his leave, he said, '*Jaai,* I'm leaving, Khalamma, assalam aleikum'; and Shakila Banu was pleased with this behaviour on the part of Joseph mistri, a weight seemed to have been lifted off her chest, her breathing became normal, and when her Ma told her, '*Awre Musholman hoite kaw.* Tell him to become a Muslim,' she said, '*Kawmu!* I'll tell him!'

But did Shakila really ask Joseph to become Muslim? Perhaps she did; perhaps she said that her Ma wanted them to get married, but there were matters of society, family, religion, weren't there? And what did Joseph mistri then say? Perhaps he stammered and stuttered, perhaps he got angry, perhaps he didn't say anything and stayed silent, and gazing at his mute face, she said various things haphazardly, perhaps she did not want to shut this door of possibility for her. And so, perhaps another two, or four, or ten months went by, clouds rumbled in Dhaka's sky and there was rain, and after the rains came winter, and because Shakila was feeling very cold, she wore socks to office, and Joseph mistri laughed when he observed that, he said, 'You wear sandals with socks, what a yokel you are,' and Shakila's teeth were freed and her face turned crimson; but then Shakila's mother's anxiety turned critical, her brothers were about to explode, and one day the local goons of East Nakhalpara stopped Joseph Eugene near the MP Hostel while he was returning from Shakila's residence, they landed slaps, blows and punches on him till he was bloody, and he then ran, went through the hostel gate and into the compound – seeing the policemen at the gate, the goons turned back. After getting beaten up by the youths of Nakhalpara, with cuts on his jaw and chin, Joseph Eugene went to work the next day, he said he had fallen from a rickshaw and injured himself, and Shakila heard about the incident of Joseph being beaten up in the moholla, but all she could do was hide her face and weep inside her room at her residence! Joseph then met Nimchandra Banik, a member of the Government Press branch of the Bangladesh Hindu Buddhist Christian Welfare Association, Nimchandra was a typesetter in the linotype unit and lived in the Government Press colony at the seven-point crossing in Tejgaon, he knew Joseph well and so, no matter how much Joseph insisted, it was difficult for him to believe he had fallen from a rickshaw and cut his face; he asked, 'What happened, Joseph dada?' But Joseph didn't reply, or perhaps he told him, and after hearing everything, Nimchandra asked him, 'Do you love Shakila?'

'Who knows!'

'Will you marry her?'

'She asked me to become Muslim!'

Perhaps Joseph Eugene tried to reflect on how so much had come to pass, he had gone so far for a girl like Shakila, why was that? Was he in love? Nimchandra Banik then asked, '*Shakilare khaichhho?* Have you had Shakila?'

The matter of having a woman was uttered again, and Joseph mistri was silent.

'*Khaite chaile khaya deo, jayga lagle amare boilo!* If you want to have her, do it, let me know if you need a place!'

And so Mary was worried about Joseph, and after Robert's death, when she sat in their residence in the lane housing the Women's Education Institute, and looking at Steven Arnold, she asked him, 'Can you help my son? I want to send him away quickly,' Steven Arnold understood, children were everything in a woman's life, and he replied that he would try; and as a result of this, a new disaster descended upon Mary Joyce's life. Because Steven arranged a visa for Joseph to go to England, Joseph went and settled down in Birmingham, a mid-country city north of London, he got a salesman's job there at Marks & Spencer, he shopped at the Tesco Superstore, he stood with old white ladies at the tobacco-and-newspaper store and bet a pound at Lotto, and because he was too lazy to cook, he survived on chicken burgers from Burger King; perhaps a change was taking place in his life, but because of the colour of his skin, it became difficult for him to become Joseph Eugene, and one day, while he was walking homewards along the canal from his store in the downtown area, and neared Birmingham's Sea Aquarium, some middle-aged white men stared at him and contemptuously swore at him, calling him 'Paki'. There had been riots then in Manchester and Birmingham between the local white youths and youths residing in the South Asian and Caribbean localities; Joseph Eugene was scared, 'Where have I landed, Lord,' he wondered, and perhaps Lord Jesus wept for him, because that weekend it rained incessantly and he arrived at the terminal moment of his life. Because of it, although he knew that the wages for working during the weekend were higher, Joseph thought, 'I don't like it here.' Sir Andrew Lloyd Weber's musical, *The Phantom of the Opera* was running then at the theatre hall of the City Convention Centre – and Joseph Eugene thought he ought to go and see it, and that was when, in the drizzling rain, some miscreants stabbed him as he walked along one side of the immense open plaza in front of the City Convention Centre, and when his innards spilled out, he fell on the wet plaza paved with light brown ceramic bricks.

Joseph Eugene's mother brought her dead son back to Bangladesh, she refused to allow him to be buried in England under any circumstances, so she communicated with the police through the office of the Assistant High Commissioner, and under the supervision of the High Commissioner, the police took Joseph's coffin to London in a van and loaded it on a British Airways flight at Heathrow. In Dhaka, Mary opened the coffin and looked at her son, he was lying with his eyes shut, there was a dry bloodstain under his shirt on the bandage over his abdomen, Mary Joyce then ran her hand over the bandage on her son's wound; Joseph Eugene was buried beside Robert, and afterwards, Mamun ul Hye went to the lane housing the Women's Education Institute and waited for a long time, and when Julie arrived at the sitting room like a pale shadow, Mamun wept, perhaps Julie asked him, '*Apne kanden kaen, bhonda pola?* Why do you cry, silly boy?', and perhaps the emotions within her swelled, and although she was in a state of deep grief, for once in her life it occurred to her to gaze at the boy and run her fingers fondly through his hair; Mamun then wiped his tears and said that he didn't know why he wept, 'Nothing is going our way, my way, Julie, why?' But Julie Florence was steadily getting older and she was confronted with the inevitable: what would she do now? Her mother dragged herself to school every morning, she returned in the afternoon, and then she lay in bed; if Julie was at home, perhaps she went and sat beside her and asked, 'Mom, would you like to have a glass of lemonade, shall I make it for you?' She thought that her mother, Mary Joyce, was sinking, that she was drowning, one needed to reach out and hold on to her, and so she took a job at Green Herald School, and sitting in their living room, Mamun ul Hye and Fakhrul Alam Ledu asked, 'How is Teacher's health now?' Mamun ul Hye had recently got a job in Eastern Bank, as Assistant Vice President, and Julie asked him 'Won't you give us a treat?' Perhaps Mamun ul Hye felt thirsty then, Julie went inside and brought a jug of water, she poured it into a glass and gave it to Mamun, and she asked Ledu, 'Shall I give you some, Ledu Bhai?' Ledu then told her, 'Do you know Julie, I met Chan Miya, he's furious with you, apparently you called him "Monkey Boy" when you were young, he hasn't forgotten that'; and it was then observed that at the mention of 'Monkey Boy' some excitement entered her monotonous, melancholy life; she asked, 'Where did you find him? And why would I call him "Monkey Boy"? Astonishing!' But Chan Miya was in an altogether different situation now, he was 'The Car Thief of Dhaka', perhaps Ledu had encountered him, Chan Miya had been standing in the lane of the moholla beside a vehicle of some make with two, or four, or ten monkeys seated atop, an entire stem of bananas was kept on the rear seat, and the monkeys were plucking the bananas and eating them, perhaps they offered them to Chan Miya as well, and that was when Ledu appeared and said, 'Let's go to Teacher's house one day, Julie likes you very much'; but at the residence in the lane housing the Women's

Education Institute, Mamun ul Hye then said to Julie, '*Ami ki tomar Jishuke ekta chuma dite pari?* Can I kiss your Jesus?'

Julie replied, '*Oi je deowaler songe jhulan achhe, jaya diya ashen!* It's hanging on that wall there, go and kiss it!'

'The one on your neck.'

Julie took off the very old sterling silver chain around her neck and gave it to him, Mamun Miya cupped it in the palm of his right hand, 'Can I take this?'

'Why? No!'

'*Amake Christan banao, Julie!* Make me a Christian, Julie!'

'*Dorkar ki?* Where's the need for that?'

After all, nothing remained of childhood, it had vanished like the image in a mirror, hadn't it? Be that as it may, Mamun Miya therefore had to return Julie's chain and crucifix, Julie extended her hand and took the chain, and Mamun then clasped Julie's hand. Didn't Julie understand anything? Was it possible? Perhaps Julie played along, or was being courteous – but couldn't such courteousness be life-threatening? And as if he were a beggar, Mamun Miya said to her, '*Tumi jano ami tomake kotowta chaichhi.* You know how much I desire you, can I kiss you once?'

'I don't think so – I'll be available only to my husband.'

'Where's he, this husband-god of yours?'

'He's here, I'm going to marry him soon.'

'You're just making it up!'

'Why should I make it up – you know him!'

'Who is he? Who?'

'Your teacher Ms D'Costa's son.'

'Pius? Oh my God!'

Through the gap between the curtains, the evening light then fell once again on Julie Florence's face, and it occurred to Mamun that if a woman's heart didn't want someone, then she never ever wanted him; so would Julie become Ms Rosalyn D'Costa's son's wife? How was that possible – she was so proud and beautiful – it couldn't be, because Asmantara's Rabbit arrived then from Chittagong and presented himself in Ghost Lane, and after Mrs Zobeida heard what he said, she hurriedly took him inside and seated him, 'Sit down, my precious, don't say all this aloud on the street, listen, my son did not get lost,' and Rabbit Miya sat and listened to Mrs Zobeida and had refreshments.

'We already have a Mamun here, don't you have any other name?'

'You can call me Qutubuddin, you can call me Aibak too, or Rabbit.'

'Is your name Rabbit?'

'Yes.'

'I'll call you Aibak!'

Rabbit wondered, if he wasn't Mamun, then who was he? He had to find the answer to this question, he had travelled through so many pathways and unimagined trajectories and arrived here, after all, he had to attain the objective of his life, to seek and find – who he was, 'Who am I?' But after all, Asmantara Hoore Jannat was Abdul Wodood Chowdhury's whimsical and obstinate daughter, Dolly Akhtar too hadn't forgotten about her behaviour during her infancy, and so after they put a rope around the rabbit's neck, they had a cage made with iron rods and placed in a corner of Asmantara's bedroom, and Rabbit Mamun grew up living inside that, eating the rice and vegetable curry provided by the servants and receiving Asmantara's affectionate caresses; by the time Asmantara began going to school, it was observed that Rabbit Mamun had grown too tall for the cage, so Dolly Akhtar got a new one made of shil-kodai wood, and then when the rabbit outgrew that as well, and lay curled around inside, perhaps Abdul Wodood told his daughter that there was no need to keep the rabbit confined any longer, and Dolly Akhtar perhaps said, 'Can't you see, this is not a rabbit, it's a man, I'll get you a real rabbit, release this one!' But Asmantara refused, she wept, 'I don't need that, I don't want it, I'm not letting go of this one!'

The captive life of Rabbit was thus prolonged, he grew taller and curled up even more inside the enclosure, and the fear, anxiety and feelings of an imprisoned creature grew in him; perhaps Asmantara herself found his behaviour strange; returning home from the Satipara Primary School, she observed that Rabbit was sleeping curled up in a circle, and Asmantara prodded him with a wooden ruler, 'He's sleeping,' she said, and a single prod was sufficient, Rabbit woke up like an angry wildcat, he bared his teeth and a violent gleam flashed in his eyes; perhaps Dolly Akhtar too observed the changes in Rabbit's behaviour, but after seeing the look on her daughter's face, she and Abdul Wodood Chowdhury once again had to simply accept the matter of Rabbit's continued presence in her room. Asmantara then reached class four, and one night Rabbit had an ejaculation inside his lungi, perhaps this happened in the course of a dream, perhaps he imagined various poster images, of Shabnur and Poppy, perhaps he saw the Taj Mahal in Agra and the Qutub Minar in Delhi, perhaps in his dream he fell down the stairs of the Qutub Minar and kept rolling down, and he was overwhelmed by the swelling between his thighs, which was like the waters of a flood tide; when he ejaculated explosively in alarm, panic and excitement, even in his sleep he felt his lungi get wet. When he woke up, he touched the sticky substance – the sap from his own body; his nose got the first moist-earth smell of his semen, and in the semi-darkness of the dim light, he seemed to become crazy, what kind of smell was this, what mood was it evoking, he felt like breaking out of the cage, lifting up his arms and running down the bank of the Dolu river – he dashed through woods and forests, and over the blue mountains far away, he kept going – he smeared this sex-juice of his on his arms, face and neck, and he shook the grille of the cage and screamed, bringing the house down. That day, everybody in Abdul Ali Chowdhury's house witnessed Rabbit's shenanigans, and everyone in the neighbourhood of Boyaliya heard about this, perhaps everyone in the town of Satkania as well; because when the people at home came running upon hearing his frightening screams, they saw that Rabbit was naked, his lungi was wound around his neck, and he was sitting on his knees inside the cage, banging it, Dolly Akhtar was frightened then, would he bite? Abdul Wodood Chowdhury was dumbfounded, he could not for the life of him figure out what had happened to the boy, and then perhaps the servant of the house, Abuilya, or the imam of the Daroga Mosque, who had permanent quarters in Abdul Ali Chowdhury's house, brought a large pail of water, went up to the cage, and flung the water at Rabbit Mamun, who was squatting on his haunches like a gorilla in a zoo, his balls dangling; the excited Rabbit was knocked down by the force of the water, and perhaps someone asked him, '*Oda khorkosh, in kyan korodde oda!* Hey Rabbit, why are you doing this!'

'*Aain khanchar bhitore naw thaikkom, aantthe gom naw lar, aanre bair goron!* I don't want to be inside the cage, I don't like it here, take me out!'

Like the smell of the chhatim flowers that wafted into the room on a gentle breeze, the faint smell of Rabbit's semen pervaded the room, and then perhaps someone identified this smell, perhaps Abdul Wodood did, perhaps Dolly Akhtar did, perhaps it was the imam of the Daroga Mosque; and then the imam of the mosque said, 'The boy has turned adolescent, Alhamdulillah, free him now!' But where was Asmantara then? It was found that she wasn't in her room, her bed was empty; they searched the whole house for her, she wasn't there, and after that she was pulled out from under her own cot, and when her Ma asked her, 'Hey, what are you doing?', she replied, 'Amma, I got scared seeing Rabbit!'

Come morning, Rabbit was let out of the cage, Asmantara wept, but she hadn't forgotten what had happened the previous night, and so the fear didn't leave her, and then Rabbit Miya walked all by himself, along the bank of the Dolu river and sat at the base of the concrete bridge, there was no leash around his neck, and no Asmantara behind him holding the leash, he lay there like a helpless soul; perhaps Abuilya discovered him after he returned home in the evening, Rabbit was sitting all by himself at the edge of the pond and weeping, and then everyone in Abdul Wodood Miya's household learnt that Rabbit was in depression, and so Dolly Akhtar arrived there, took Rabbit by his hand, led him to the house, spread out a mat and served him food, and she said, 'Hey, why were you crying? Aren't you a man? Stop crying!'

Consequently, Rabbit Miya wept some more, he wept loudly, the atmosphere in the house turned gloomy with the sound of his bawling, and when a piece of rice got stuck in his windpipe, he began coughing, he was about to choke to death, and then Dolly Akhtar or Abuilya thumped him gently on his back two or four times, gave him a glass of water, laid him down flat on a mat, and perhaps when Asmantara then peeped from behind Dolly Akhtar, Rabbit noticed that, and when he asked, 'Aren't you afraid of me?', it seemed the girl had forgotten what had happened at night, she replied, 'No, I'm not afraid'; but Dolly Akhtar and Abdul Wodood didn't let Rabbit stay in Asmantara's room any longer, he had a place with Abuilya in the tin shed by the pond behind the house. As he lay in the tin shed, he began to weep once again, and when the old servant Abul asked him, 'Why are you doing this?', Rabbit Mamun said, '*Aantthe gom naw lar, aain faanlar naw baichchom, Abul Kaka!* I don't feel good, I won't survive, Abul Kaka!'

But eventually Rabbit didn't die, he lived comfortably with Abul in the tin shed, and then, or some time subsequently, he learnt about Qutubuddin Aibak, and perhaps he told someone about ejaculating while rolling down the steps of the Qutub Minar, perhaps it was Abul whom he told, although he was much older than him, perhaps Abul had prodded him and wanted to fuck his arse. Dolly Akhtar and Abdul Wodood had certainly not thought about this danger, if they had they would perhaps have warned him, 'Beware, we'll break your bones'; perhaps Rabbit then told Abuilya about rolling down from the Qutub Minar, and when he visualized himself slipping and falling, his organ turned erect inside his lungi, and when semen emerged from the tip of the organ and wet his lungi, there was nothing the swindler of a servant could do, on the contrary, Rabbit held him tight, lifted up his lungi, and fucked his arse! Abuilya then opened the door of the shed and was lost in the darkness outside; the next day, he spread the tale about Rabbit visiting the Qutub Minar, and he told Abdul Wodood and Dolly Akhtar that he wouldn't live with Rabbit, saying that Rabbit harassed him a lot at night and didn't let him sleep! Qutub Minar then became the name of the rabbit, and Wodood Miya decided that he would take him to his fishing trawler and put him to work there, and so Abuilya would have to wait for two or four days; but when Rabbit's male organ became erect at night, Abuilya's throat turned dry with fear, 'No, my nephew, don't do that!' But Rabbit had no time to waste, so Abul went into the house and fetched the household maidservant, Asiya Bua, she was a poor man's wife, but her body was youthful, squandered away in furtive or forced encounters among bushes and shrubs, but perhaps she didn't know what Abuilya's intention was because Abul had never harassed her, and that's why she didn't think twice and simply followed him, and although the *charchala*, or four-roofed tin shed lay in darkness, she went inside. Abuilya then said that Qutub Minar wasn't well, and so Asiya approached Rabbit lying on his side on the cot, what's happened to the boy, she wondered, and all the while, Rabbit, aka Qutub Minar, lay waiting; when Asiya stretched out her hand in the darkness, it found Rabbit's hot, erect pole. That night, after many years, Rabbit Miya slept once again with his body wrapped around a woman, and Abul then disappeared, but the next dawn, even before the azan for the Fajr prayer sounded at the Daroga Mosque, when it was still dark, he fetched Wodood Miya and Dolly Akhtar; and so Asiya lost her job, and Wodood Chowdhury took Qutub Minar to Gohira, which fell under the jurisdiction of the Anwara police station, and put him to work on his operations of smuggling urea-based fertilizers to Burma, and as a sailor's apprentice on the wooden trawler, MV *Mother's Blessing*, which was used for fishing. Rabbit fell into a dilemma on board the MV *Mother's Blessing*, there were three people in the trawler, Jaan-e-Alam, Shamsu and Zakir; it was difficult for Rabbit to protect the hole in his backside from these three people, they disturbed him the very first night, but he saved himself by squirming this way and that, and the three sailors thought, 'Hey, wait, let's get to the waters first!' The trawler departed the next day, the objective was to catch fish at sea, MV *Mother's Blessing* raised anchor, the engine started with a loud putter, and the vessel raced ahead on the deep, murky waters of the Bay of Bengal, the 12' x 30' wooden trawler seemed to be in a veritable state of intoxication over the waves of the sea; perhaps a long time went by, the captain, Jaan-e-Alam, was a seasoned sailor, he steered the trawler at top speed to where the shoals of laeta fish dwelt, and after travelling for two or two and a half hours, they were perhaps approaching a shoal of fish, Zakir and Shamsu began casting the net with large, round, football-sized plastic floats that was lying in a mound-like pile on the deck of the trawler, and a girl then climbed up the stairs from the ship's hold; making a retching sound, she vomited on the deck and messed it up, and then fell on her side. Seeing that, Jaan-e-Alam's eyes turned red with rage, Zakir and Shamsu grimaced, and Jaan-e-Alam asked, '*Jahajete raandi ainye kawn?* Who brought a whore on board?'

'I brought her, why?'

Since they were in the middle of the sea, there was nothing Jaan-e-Alam, Shamsu and Zakir could do, but they remembered the incident; it was learnt from the woman that her name was Arati Jaladas, she was the widow of Radhashyam Jaladas, her house was in the village of Gohira-Khardah, close to Gohira; she said she was twenty-six years old, and that the fourteen-year-old Rabbit had hired her for fifty taka, but she wasn't a whore, the three children of Radhashyam lived with her. Jaan-e-Alam was astonished, gosh, this boy was indeed a wily one, how did he get the time, and when did he do all this? Jaan-e-Alam then took out a couple of Stemetil tablets from a tin container and gave them to Arati, she swallowed the tablets and remained lying on her side on the deck; and so, because he was with a woman at night, Rabbit's dignity was saved; but Jaan-e-Alam, Zakir and Shamsu could not forget about this depravity, this boat provided them their livelihood, and the son of a whore Rabbit had brought along a prostitute on board, and so a conflict became inevitable. Perhaps Jaan-e-Alam told Abdul Wodood Chowdhury about the incident, Abdul Wodood was very sad to hear that Qutub Minar Rabbit was thus defiling the trawler he had built with great effort, perhaps he took Dolly Akhtar's advice as well, but they could not find any solution, the boy had no one, where would he go? And so, Abdul Wodood Chowdhury told Jaan-e-Alam that the boy was like his son, he had been with him since he was a child, so he would scold him; but nothing was gained by scolding Rabbit, whenever he boarded the trawler, he was accompanied by Arati, and Jaan-e-Alam and his two companions burned with outrage, they did not want a spurious girl to be present when they were busy grappling with the sea and fish. But this time they were on a trip to Burma, and five or six sampans from Chittagong followed the coastline and arrived at the estuary of the Sangu river in Gohira under the cover of darkness and loaded stuff into the trawler *Mother's Blessing*, they brought drums of octane and sacks of nitrogen-urea fertilizer; Abdul Wodood communicated with Jaan-e-Alam via Grameenphone to Grameenphone (GP-to-GP), 'Hey Jaan-e-Alam, you've got the goods, haven't you?'

Jaan-e-Alam thought he had received the goods, but it took the whole night to unload them from the sampans and then load them in the trawler, so he postponed their departure; the goods were to go near Akyab, perhaps to Mungdu, so Jaan-e-Alam did not want to set out during the day, all kinds of eyes wandered around then, but they could advance a great distance in a single stretch once they set off at night, so he told Wodood Chowdhury that everything was all right, he would depart as soon as night fell, and that Shamsu, Zakir and Rabbit were also with him. But he mentioned the matter relating to Rabbit again to Wodood Chowdhury, 'You should warn him now'; and so, on account of Wodood Chowdhury's stern instructions, Rabbit's first smuggling expedition commenced without Arati Jaladas; perhaps he had met Arati, and glancing at the thick moustache on his upper lip, she had asked, 'Aren't you taking me along?'

'I'll take you, but later!'

But during his time in Gohira, perhaps Rabbit Miya learnt some more about Qutubuddin Aibak, perhaps some sailor or fisherman on some other fishing boat knew about that, and perhaps he told Rabbit about Qutubuddin Aibak, or perhaps Rabbit met Arati's elder daughter, Pratima, when he went to Arati's house one day, perhaps Arati was doing something in some other house then, or she had gone to the field to collect something, and so, because Pratima had washed her only frock and pair of knickers, she came and stood before Rabbit wearing her Ma's petticoat, with a gamchha covering her bosom, she was a vulnerable, fatherless girl, and Rabbit became acquainted with her; perhaps Pratima went to the primary school in the village of Gohira-Khardah, she was very amused when she heard that Rabbit's name was Qutub Minar, and perhaps she said to Rabbit, 'But the Qutub Minar was built by Qutubuddin Aibak,' perhaps Pratima read about this in her social studies textbook: 'Upon the death of Sultan Mohammad Ghori, his commander-in-chief, Qutubuddin Aibak, declared himself emperor of Delhi in 1206 CE.' After he heard this, Rabbit gazed at Pratima's budding breasts beneath the thin gamchha and felt overwhelmed, he said, '*Aain tunyare loi bhagi jaiyum goi!* I'm going to run away with you!'

Arati returned then, and Rabbit explained to her that they were going very far for their fishing expedition and so he couldn't take her along, he would take her the next time; Arati was dejected at not being able to earn fifty taka, but on account of Rabbit having heard the name of Qutubuddin Aibak for the first time, and because the memory of Pratima was still fresh in his mind, he looked at Arati and held out a currency note. Jaan-e-Alam and his boatmen knew that Rabbit's other name was Qutub Minar, but they knew nothing about Qutubuddin Aibak, there was no reason for them to know, and so, unfortunately they hatched a conspiracy against Rabbit; that day, after Rabbit took leave of Arati and Pratima and returned, they raised anchor in the wee hours of the night; the trawler wobbled under the weight of the sacks of fertilizer in the hold and the three drums of octane fuel, and except for the trawler's bow, the whole vessel was covered with a grey-coloured tarpaulin sheet that was fastened over it to camouflage it; even if one looked through a pair of binoculars it would be difficult to make out that there was a vessel at sea, and because of the tarpaulin sheet, the trawler wouldn't be spotted on a radar either. Jaan-e-Alam feared the coastguard and the navy but Allah's sea was huge and immense while the navy carried out its patrol with merely two or four ships; it wasn't as if Jaan-e-Alam hadn't been chased two or four times, he had been, but he managed to make MV *Mother's Blessing* indistinguishable from the water, exit the maritime boundary of Bangladesh and enter Burmese waters, and so the naval ship had to halt, and Jaan-e-Alam, Shamsu and Zakir then stood atop, waved and said, 'Bye bye, ta-ta!' That's why Jaan-e-Alam was not afraid, but nonetheless they took all necessary precautions and set off, and Rabbit sat with Zakir and Shamsu inside the trawler, whose interior looked like a dark cave, covered as it was with tarpaulin on all sides. Perhaps after the trawler had sailed all night, they had reached close to Bangladesh's maritime boundary, and then Rabbit woke up on account of his bladder being full of piss, and he realized that Jaan-e-Alam and the two boatmen were awake; they were talking in whispers, and that was how, by dint of sheer good fortune, Rabbit found out about their conspiracy; these three men hadn't forgotten about the time a woman was brought along on the trawler, so they had decided to tie Rabbit's hands and feet and throw him into the water, and when they returned, to tell Abdul Wodood Chowdhury that Rabbit had slipped and fallen into the sea! But Rabbit had heard everything while pretending to be asleep, so he then quickly did two or three things even as he lay in the darkness; first, he stretched his leg towards the bundle of rope lying near his feet, he brought it to his hand, rolled close to Zakir and Shamsu who were lying nearby, and grabbed the two of them as if he was still fast asleep, but in the course of that exercise, he passed the rope through the belt loops of their trousers and tied it to a post nearby, and then he rolled away again and went to one end of the trawler; Shamsu and Zakir hadn't noticed anything, and Jaan-e-Alam had been busy at the helm; in the darkness, Rabbit picked up the zigzag iron crank handle used to start the trawler's Yanmar diesel engine, and with a single blow smashed Jaan-e-Alam's skull and split his head open; Shamsu and Zakir didn't survive either, when they sensed danger and tried to flee, they realized that they were tethered together like a pair of goats, and they died like tethered goats as well, Rabbit beat them to death. Dawn then came up over the sea, and when MV *Mother's Blessing* went past Teknaf, the southernmost point of the Bangladesh mainland, and Abdul Wodood was able to get mobile connectivity for the final time, the mobile phone inside the pocket of the dead and gaping Jaan-e-Alam rang, but Rabbit didn't take the call out of fear, and then it rang again but Rabbit knew that it was Abdul Wodood Chowdhury calling, so once again, he did not answer it out of fear, and then when it rang yet again, Rabbit took the phone out of Jaan-e-Alam's pocket and informed Abdul Wodood that the three men had perished in the attack by the navy, he was the sole survivor, but the trawler as well as the cargo were safe in his custody, 'I can take it there,' he said. Abdul Wodood Chowdhury had to do a lot of things then, he made an ISD call to Akyab and spoke to the people there, and then he called Jaan-e-Alam's mobile again and told Rabbit that he need not be afraid, he didn't need to know the exact location, all he had to do was hold the wheel steady and just head eastwards; Abdul Wodood also instructed him to hoist a flag on something atop the boat, so that the Burmese party could spot the trawler; Rabbit did as directed. And so, after Wodood Chowdhury's friends in Akyab received the goods, they sent the trawler back to Gohira with a seasoned helmsman and his boatmen, and Abdul Wodood Chowdhury himself was present to witness the arrival of MV *Mother's Blessing* from the Bay of Bengal, the trawler entered the Sangu river, reduced its speed, and came puttering to dock at the bank, and when Rabbit jumped to the ground out of a large window, Abdul Wodood went and hugged him, and he declared that Qutub Minar Rabbit would henceforth be the captain of MV *Mother's Blessing*, and to help him learn the craft of navigation quickly, he appointed the most experienced sailor in his fleet of three ships, Azizya, and so, at the age of fourteen-and-a-half, or fifteen, a kingdom came into Rabbit's possession, as well as two women – Asiya and Arati. However, perhaps Azizya didn't recognize Rabbit, or perhaps he did but pretended not to, so he asked, 'Who's he?' Qutubuddin Aibak then told him that he was Aibak, and that he wanted to learn the craft of navigation from Azizya, '*Awne aanr ustad.* You are my teacher,' and with Azizya's training, Mamun, aka Rabbit, aka Qutub Minar, aka Qutubuddin Aibak, became an expert sailor; he remained in Gohira for four years, he never mentioned returning to Satkania, and meanwhile Arati died of a stomach ailment, Pratima got married to a man from the village of Jaladi, in Banshkhali, and Rabbit then called a carpenter and got a wooden throne made, it had a high back and three stars carved on it – one on top, and two on the sides – and at the end of each of the two arms was a lion's head with its mouth wide open; the carpenter concluded the task of building the throne by plating the arms and the spot behind the head with golden foil. Rabbit liked it very much, he placed the throne on the small, open deck of MV *Mother's Blessing*, and he fastened its legs to the deck floor with ropes; when the ship raced towards the Swatch of No Ground that lay on the Bay of Bengal to the south of the Sundarbans, or went towards the Southern Fishery Zone a short distance away from Cox's Bazar, Rabbit sometimes handed over the wheel to his assistant, Muzaffar, and went and sat on the throne of golden foil on the deck, the wind whistled past his ears, ruffling his hair, and Rabbit gazed at the horizon on the lookout for some shoal of fish somewhere in the distance; after that, when he observed a lot of seagulls hovering over the sea and reckoned that there were fish there, the sailors on MV *Mother's Blessing* cast the long net into the sea, the plastic floats spread over the water like a huge, long pearl necklace beside the ship, and the ship sailed into the shoal of fish; then one day he returned to Satkania, and touched Dolly Akhtar's feet to pay her his respects; 'How are you, Amma?' He was asked to stay with Abuilya in the tin shed at the pondside, and when Asmantara returned in the evening from Satkania Girls School, he met her; seeing the moustachioed man, Asmantara couldn't recognize him at first, 'Who are you?'

'I am Qutubuddin Aibak.'

But Asmantara didn't know anyone by that name, there was no reason for her to do so, so she said, 'Who is Qutubuddin Aibak?'

'I'm Rabbit!'

Asmantara then recognized him; she had grown up, she wore a salwar-kameez now, she had a dupatta on her bosom, her earlier girlish demeanour was gone, and she never forgot that she was Abdul Wodood Chowdhury's daughter; and so encountering Rabbit now, she wrinkled her tiny nose a bit and said, 'Oh, so you're Rabbit, why didn't you say you're Rabbit, since when have you become Aibak!'

When Rabbit told her that Qutubuddin Aibak was the emperor of Delhi, and that he had established the Slave Dynasty, Asmantara said, '*Aain jani, tuin kawn bashsha hoiyachhaw?* I know, but how are you an emperor?'

Rabbit was no match for Asmantara, and then two new, steel-bodied ships were added to Abdul Wodood's fleet of trawlers, they were given the names, MV *God's Gift* and MV *God's Grace*, and following Dolly Akhtar's advice, Abdul Wodood Chowdhury made the eighteen- or nineteen-year-old Rabbit the head sareng, or captain, of his flagship, MV *God's Gift*; Rabbit, aka Qutubuddin Aibak, was happy, although he was also sad to be leaving his vessel, MV *Mother's Blessing*, but he brought along his gold foil–encased wooden throne, the wheelhouse of the new ship was on top, on the second deck, so he placed the throne on the open bridge beside this cabin, it was fastened to the deck with screws, and at the top of the mast, just below the navigation lights, two strips of cloth, yellow and red in colour, fluttered like flags. And then, perhaps *God's*

Gift was once chased by the navy, near Sonadiya; the depredations of the navy had increased of late, added to that was the torment of the coastguard, it was the coastguard that Rabbit was more scared of – naval ships were mostly large vessels, one could spot them from afar and take precautions, but the sons-of-swine coastguard moved around in small gunboats, they could hardly be seen until they came near, removed the cloth hood from the muzzle of the cannon, and *boom* – finished! Perhaps on that day too there were octane drums and sacks of fertilizer on the deck and in the hold of MV *God's Gift*, there was no end to the Burmese demand for fertilizer and octane fuel, it seemed as if they consumed fertilizer and drank octane, and a part of all these goods perhaps went via the Arakan and reached Tripura, in India, as well, and so business was good; standing on the bridge of MV *God's Gift*, Qutubuddin Aibak spotted the patrol vessel of the coastguard, and he was certain that the coastguard had noticed him too, so there was no way to hide, and the only option was to try to escape, and although the coastguard's vessel was faster, one's navigation skills in the deep, turbulent seas could also create opportunities of escape, and that's what Rabbit did. The coastguard vessel fired a warning shot to order a halt, *boom-boom*, but could one halt here? Rabbit didn't halt MV *God's Gift*, he decided to trust fate, and so the wheelhouse at the top was riddled with bullet holes from the coastguard's machine gun, the shell from the cannon broke the mast, the tarpaulin cover was torn to shreds, but after a long chase, MV *God's Gift* did escape, and before going out of range of the network, he made a GP-to-GP call to Abdul Wodood's mobile and told him that the coastguard had attacked and wrecked the wheelhouse and destroyed the mast, but there was no other damage to the ship, and everything was fine now. Perhaps Abdul Wodood Chowdhury was in the sitting room of his house then, he listened to the report and said, 'Alhamdulillah,' and Asmantara arrived then, after all she was an adored daughter, so she asked her father, 'What's happened, Abba?' But Abdul Wodood the merchant could not tell his daughter all that had occurred, if Asmantara found out that she was the daughter of a great smuggler, perhaps she would burst into tears, her flower-like life would come to an end, perhaps she would stop eating, her father would cajole her, as would her mother, but she wouldn't eat; and after that, when bells started ringing in her tummy, she would eat, and conclude: Fine, it's better to be a smuggler, after all, who has any worth in Bangladesh? No one. Such was the chatter the frisky-as-shrimp class-seven students of Satkania Girls High School engaged in: What salary do engineers and doctors earn, they're all paupers! They wouldn't marry such folk, and Asmantara had thought that she could marry an officer of the BCS administrative cadre, it would be good if her father could fetch one, officers of the administrative cadre had worth, but what bearing the

UNO wives had! – one of them had come to cut the inaugural ribbon of the new laboratory in the science department of Satkania Girls High School, and after she cut the ribbon, everyone was agog and going, 'Bhabi, bhabi'; a glass of sherbet was offered to her, a plate of grapes was offered, tea was poured into a cup, but she didn't touch a thing, '*Na bhai, amar ashubida achhe.* No dear, I have a problem,' she said, and after staying a little while, she got into the UNO jeep and left; Asmantara decided she would marry some UNO fellow, and if an unmarried UNO type couldn't be found, then some Assistant Commissioner, Land, who would subsequently join the UNO; wouldn't her father be able to look for and find one? If he was told that the girl's father had a house in Chittagong, or in Dhaka – after all, her father could certainly buy a house in Dhaka – could he refuse? And then if this husband was posted in Lohagara or Chandanaish, she too would cut ribbons, and not have anything if something was offered, she would say, '*Na bhai, amar ashubida achhe,*' and she would come for an outing to Satkania in her husband's government jeep, and what a grand fit her school friends would have on seeing that! But that fancy of hers came to an end when she observed the Assistant Commissioner, Land, of Satkania sub-district in her father's sitting room, her dad was rebuking the young fellow, 'Why are you unnecessarily bringing up all these things, go and get the big pond in the marketplace registered in my name, and don't bother me any more,' no, Asmantara would not marry such berated men; and so Asmantara was not so touchy about being a smuggler's daughter, but still, a father could certainly feel some restraint in front of his daughter, and so Abdul Wodood told Asmantara that Rabbit had called, he was taking the ship to Cox's Bazar; and at that moment, close to Teknaf, as Rabbit moved out of range of the mobile network, he remembered the slaying of Jaan-e-Alam; that day, after being struck by an iron rod, the brains inside Jaan-e-Alam's head had spilled out like mashed potatoes, and Shamsu's and Zakir's heads, ribs and the bones of their arms and legs were smashed to bits, and that day, as he sailed close to Teknaf, he had thrown three bodies into the water. Rabbit now raced MV *God's Gift* over the sea like a crazy horse, and when he finished talking to Wodood Chowdhury, he put the mobile phone into his pocket and gazed at the coastline of Burma in the distance, land seemed to be so close by, and yet so far away; he then remembered what Asmantara had remarked, 'How are you an emperor?' So when Wodood Chowdhury called him on the phone one day and asked him, 'Aibak, when are you coming to Satkania?', Rabbit felt pleased to be called Aibak, he replied, 'Why, is there some work?' Of course, Rabbit had gradually become Abdul Wodood's favourite, but he had never imagined that Rabbit would become Aibak, perhaps Dolly Akhtar had said to Abdul Wodood, '*Polata khubi kaajer.* The boy's really useful,' and at the time, perhaps Abdul Wodood wanted to discuss some complication that had come up in his Burma business, and he wanted to include Aibak in the conversations he had with his sons on the matter. Aibak arrived then, and at night, a mat was spread on the floor, close to the dining table, and he was served food while Dolly Akhtar supervised from her seat nearby, and Abdul Wodood then conversed with him; perhaps Rabbit heard him, or perhaps he didn't hear properly, because his eyes were fixed on Dolly Akhtar, he marvelled at how much affection this mother-like woman showered on him, but who was she to him really? After that, he said to Wodood Chowdhury, 'Why don't you come to Gohira one day, come with Amma and the brothers, I'll take you on a trip to the deep seas, you haven't even set foot on *God's Gift* yet!' Dolly Akhtar was very pleased with the proposal, once Asmantara's and Abdul Wahab's school examinations were over in November or December, they would go on a Bay of Bengal pleasure trip aboard MV *God's Gift*, the weather too would be pleasant in winter, but it seems that turned out to be a decree of fate; in the end of December, on the eleventh day of Poush, Abdul Wodood and his family went for a sea jaunt, and they drowned, only Asmantara, who couldn't join them, survived. On the morning of the trip to Gohira, after she had a cup of tea, she mysteriously developed a running tummy, it was so bad that she had to rush to the toilet again and again, she declared, 'I can't go'; so the trip was about to be cancelled, but then Asmantara said that she would be able to stay alone at home, so Dolly Akhtar agreed, and Rabbit too assured them that they would return the same evening, so there shouldn't be a problem. They left very early in the morning that day, and went by motor car through Dohajari to reach Gohira, and then around ten in the morning, MV *God's Gift* cast off, heading southwards, and when the trawler was along Maheshkhali, it turned westwards and advanced towards deep waters, and once Maheshkhali receded into the horizon behind them, they spotted the gunboat, it seemed as if it had been waiting for them; but since there was nothing suspicious on board the trawler, there was nothing to fear, but nonetheless, perhaps Aibak or Rabbit got scared and lost his senses, he turned the trawler and sought to flee; Abdul Wodood, who was sitting on top in the wheelhouse and observing all this, shouted out, 'Why are you doing this, boy?'

Aibak then replied, 'Just watch!'

But this time, MV *God's Gift* could not outmatch the speed of the gunboat; the coastguard kept catching up with them, they fired a warning shot, but Rabbit didn't stop, and Wodood Chowdhury and his family members went down to the ship's hold and took shelter there; Rabbit took out an automatic weapon from under the cushioned seat of the master sareng, aimed at the gunboat of the coastguard and opened fire, but the use of the weapon sealed their fate; the coastguard was certain that the rogue vessel was armed and engaged in some nefarious activity, so they immediately turned the muzzle of the cannon towards the target, and when the first shell wiped out the wheelhouse, Rabbit grabbed a buoy and hung down the side of the trawler, and fired again from that position, and so the coastguard gunboat now got ready to destroy the target; the next shell from the cannon blew MV *God's Gift* to smithereens, and Abdul Wodood Chowdhury, his wife, and his sons were lost to the waters along with the trawler – only Asmantara was left alive, in Satkania. That evening, Asmantara heard the news on television about the sinking of a trawler and the watery graves of a gang of smugglers, and after that an employee of MV *Mother's Blessing* or one of their other trawlers telephoned from Gohira to convey the news that MV *God's Gift* had sunk, and that Wodood Chowdhury and his family had been on board the vessel; Asmantara's life came to a halt as it were, her father's world had been shattered to bits; three days later, Aibak, or Rabbit, arrived, he was the only survivor from MV *God's Gift*, perhaps he had managed to evade the coastguard's eyes and clutch a buoy or suchlike, or some piece of broken wood, and float away and thus save his life, and although it was astounding, something like that could definitely happen; Rabbit sat beside the semi-conscious Asmantara for the next three days, applying cold compresses on her forehead, so her condition improved slightly, and Rabbit wound up his affairs in Gohira and came away to Satkania. He began living in Satkania; Asmantara remained in Abdul Wodood's building, while Rabbit stayed in the tin shed; Asmantara stopped going to school, outsiders no longer saw her; perhaps Abdul Mabud then arrived from Dhaka, but he did not meet Asmantara, and Rabbit asked him to sit in the drawing room of the house and attended to him, and told him, 'She's not well,' and so Abdul Mabud returned with the three sacks of cash handed over to him by Rabbit, and never set foot in Satkania again; Rabbit then met Asmantara, but they did not converse, Rabbit instructed the maidservant to use the blender to make grape juice for her, and when the maidservant brought the juice, Asmantara drank it. Asiya Bua was looked for and found, and Rabbit put her on the job of caring for Asmantara constantly; then one day, Rabbit came into the house, all by himself, and Asmantara asked him, 'Aibak, why didn't you kill me?' Rabbit gazed at the girl's face, all the weeping had made her pale and weak, and when she attempted to rise from the bed and stand, she kept falling, so Rabbit cradled her in his arms like a child, while tears rolled down Asmantara's eyes, and she asked, 'Aibak, what are you going to do with me now?'

Perhaps Rabbit was at a loss for words, he knew that Asmantara would be well after a few days, she would be able to think clearly then, and she wouldn't say all these things, and so Asiya Bua made pomegranate juice for her, she made her chicken soup, but it took time for Asmantara to recover; Rabbit spoke to Abdul Wodood's employees in Chittagong city over the mobile phone, and he managed the work and activities in Gohira, but his sense of unease only grew and sleeplessness was observed; he sat and waited in the tin shed, but Asiya Bua didn't bring him any message of hope. Perhaps Asiya had a grudge against Rabbit, but her womanly heart quickly melted, she also felt sad for Rabbit, after all he hadn't forgotten her; and so she explained to Asmantara about Rabbit, hadn't Rabbit been dearer to her than her own life? Hadn't he? And Asmantara had no option but to agree, and so that night, Rabbit, who had escaped the coastguard, tied a rope around his neck and entered Asmantara's room, he sat on the floor near her bed and held out the free end of the rope to Asmantara, who was lying in bed with a sheet drawn up to her neck; Asmantara Hoore Jannat then smiled weakly, she took the rope in her hand and asked him, 'What shall I do? Where's the cage?'

Rabbit's cage, much the worse for wear now, after being exposed to sun and rain, was searched for and found on the bank of the pond, and brought to Asmantara's bedroom where it was placed along the wall, and Rabbit, aka Qutubuddin Aibak, transcended his helplessness and was once again transformed into Asmantara's rabbit. Then, that evening, or that night, Rabbit went and sat on the edge of Asmantara's bed, and after that he entered the cage, folded up his knees and lay down inside, curled up in a circle, he felt sleepy, and Asmantara locked the cage from outside, and that's when the incident took place; perhaps MV *Mother's Blessing* was on its way to Burma with cargo, perhaps Mozaffar was steering the trawler, and Rabbit then got Mozaffar's GP-to-GP call on his mobile, MV *Mother's Blessing* had been destroyed by the coastguard, and although it had crossed the maritime boundary of Bangladesh and entered Burmese waters, this time the sons-of-bastards followed them and sank MV *Mother's Blessing* with an artillery shell. While lying curled up inside the cage in Asmantara's room, or sitting near her bed with the rope around his neck, Rabbit pondered over the matter: So mother's blessing had sunk! It had been there all these days, now she was gone – who was his mother? And then he remembered two things: that his name was Mamun, and that his house was in Ghost Lane, in Narinda, Dhaka, so he slipped the rope off his neck, exited the cage and left for Dhaka, and Asmantara was stunned; perhaps Mrs Zobeida Rahman was also very upset, because she was confronted with an extremely difficult problem or mystery, and although she wanted to believe that all of it was Khoimon's doing, her trickery, she had to admit that hatching such a conspiracy was beyond her; so she kept gazing blankly with her cloudy eyes at Rabbit Mamun, who was standing before her, and then she said, 'Aibak, my dear, will you listen to me?'

'Why won't I listen? Tell me.'

Rabbit then sat in the outer room of Mamun's residence and listened to Mamun's Ma, and like Mamun's Ma, Mrs Zobeida Rahman, he too fell into bewilderment; 'What's this you're saying, I can't understand it,' and Mamun's Ma explained to him once again: What credence could one give to what a few stupid, ganja-addicted coolies at the sawmill said, was there any head or tail to what they uttered without knowing any facts whatsoever? There was no reason for there to be, who knows whose son they dispatched with the sawdust, and then they concluded it was so-and-so's son, perhaps Qutubuddin Aibak was someone else's son, someone else's boy, who was without a name or a home now; and so when Zobeida Begum, full of trepidation at the prospect of losing her son, Mamun, proffered a cup of tea to Rabbit Mamun, aka Qutubuddin Aibak, and said, 'Imagine I had another son, and you are that child of mine, I am your Ma, call me "Ma"'; Aibak sipped the hot tea and gazed at her, and then he wept, the human life of the adroit and brutal Rabbit aka Aibak broke down, and looking at his face there was no end to Zobeida Begum's anxiety, and then Aibak got up and left. That day, Aibak went to Hotel Arzoo on Bijoy Nagar Road and wept some more, and seeing his tears, his old servant, Abuilya, patted his head, and comforted him saying, 'Come now, don't cry, bhai, don't cry,' and then Rabbit stopped sobbing and said, 'Bring me a sack of cash.' Abul then made a GP-to-GP call to Chittagong and asked for a sack of cash to be sent on the night bus, and the following evening, Rabbit bought a reconditioned Lexus from Kakrail with half of the money, and he drove it personally and went to Mrs Zobeida Rahman's house and emptied out the remaining cash in front of her; 'I'm your son,' he said.

Rabbit thus gave rise to a great crisis for Mrs Zobeida Rahman, 'So much money here? Good God!' She just stared helplessly, 'Tell me what I should do.'

'*Apne shotyi kore bolen ami ki apner chele na?* Tell me the truth, am I not your son?'

What could Zobeida Rahman say then? Her maternal instinct surged, in front of her was Rabbit, deprived of love all his life, starving, looking at her dolefully, and at her feet, bundles of money lay strewn on the paved ground; couldn't she abandon Mamun ul Hye? Was Mamun ul Hye even her son? Or was it Rabbit who was her son, who perhaps had never returned after having gone to Nayabazar to buy sawdust; it was someone else who had returned, perhaps Mamun ul Hye was someone else and perhaps on account of some bustle they didn't notice that – wasn't something like that possible? But Mrs Zobeida Rahman didn't change her mind, the boy was wooing his teacher's daughter, he was in a very fragile state, he could not be abandoned at such moment, and so Mamun ul Hye was saved, and there was no hope for Rabbit; he said to Mrs Zobeida Rahman, 'Take this money, I brought it for you.'

'*Ei tyaka ami niya ki korum, ami ki pola bodlamu, ashchoirjo!* What will I do with this money? Will I exchange my son? Astounding!'

Perhaps Rabbit then wept again, he spoke over the mobile to Abuilya, who was waiting at Hotel Arzoo, 'Hey Uncle Abul, I'm coming, we'll leave today itself!'

But Rabbit Miya didn't depart, because Chan Miya perhaps spotted his shiny Lexus in front of the temple, and when Rabbit came out of Mamun's house, he could not find his car, he had parked it in front of the temple but now it was gone. It was Zobeida Begum and her family members who were more shocked and agitated over the theft of the car than Rabbit himself, Zobeida Rahman declared, 'Isn't Rabbit my son? What kind of thief would take my son's car?' They went with Rabbit to the Sutrapur police station, the officer-in-charge, or his junior, listened to everything and then asked, 'You said you arrived in Dhaka a day ago and bought a Lexus car, can you tell me what exactly you do?' Rabbit Miya was then in a crisis: What did he do? He took out a packet of Benson & Hedges from his pocket and held it out in front of the officer, but the intelligent officer didn't accept it, such cases were not resolved merely with Benson & Hedges, it was vital to know what the livelihood of a citizen like this one was, so he said, 'I don't smoke.'

'That's fine, please come this evening to Hotel Sagarika at the Moghbazar crossing.'

Sitting in Hotel Sagarika, Rabbit resolved the problem with the help of the officer from the Sutrapur police station, but the officer knew nothing about the possible car thief, and he declined to provide any specific assistance to Rabbit, he seemed to be saying, 'File a case if you like, we'll look into it later'; Rabbit then asked him, 'Do you know who stole it?'

'Why would I know a car thief?'

There was nothing Rabbit could do, so he said, 'All right, sir, I don't need a car, if you need something let me know,' and he gave up the idea of returning to Satkania, he moved out of his double-bedded room at Hotel Arzoo, and shifted to a large suite instead, and the next day he presented himself at Mamun's residence in Ghost Lane, and asked Mamun's Ma, 'Are you well, Amma?'

Mamun's Ma was overcome with joy when he greeted her, and eventually she told Rabbit in elaborate detail about Chan Miya and his monkey brigade; as Rabbit listened to Zobeida Rahman, he reflected that battling monkeys was no kind of pursuit at all, and the people of Dhaka were indeed very strange, they were concerned about monkeys, they were fighting monkeys – while he had confronted the coastguard, gunboats, machine guns and naval artillery! He assured Zobeida Begum, 'Don't worry, I have an Abul Kasem 47, once it's fired they're finished'; but when he climbed up to Mamun's roof and counted the number of monkeys there, and saw the monkey shit lying all around, he began to comprehend how frightening the situation was, and he realized that using a weapon like the Abul Kasem 47 in this narrow lane against as nimble a target as a monkey was perhaps not possible. But when Rabbit first said that he would use an Abul Kasem 47, Zobeida Rahman and her family members were beside themselves with hope and excitement, 'What's that, dear, Abul Kasem 47?'

'It's something very expensive.'

But when Rabbit later decided that he wouldn't use that thing, and that bringing it to Dhaka from Chittagong was also a problem, Zobeida Begum and her family members became despondent, '*Byabohar na korow, amago ekbaar dekhao, amra kunodin dekhinaika Abul Kasem 47, eita kemun amra dekhte chai.* All right, don't use it, but please show it to us once, we've never seen an Abul Kasem 47, we want to see what it looks like.'

'Okay, I'll show it to you!'

But Rabbit was a veteran of chases by the coastguard and the navy, so he knew that an army was a terrible thing, and if he had to find out about the car thief, he would have to find a solution to the monkey brigade as well; so he sat in Suite No. A-3 on the third floor of Hotel Arzoo and prepared his plans, he called a carpenter and got three or four 3' x 3' wooden traps made in the courtyard behind Mamun's house, and after that he and Mrs Zobeida Rahman's two sons took the traps to the roof and laid them there, jars of Horlicks were placed inside, but the roguish monkeys didn't touch them! Rabbit then spread a bait of some laddus mixed with poison on the roof, two or four rats ate the poisoned laddus and died, perhaps one or two crows as well, but the monkeys stayed out of Rabbit's reach, they observed all his shenanigans, perhaps they laughed, monkeys could laugh too, who knows, and perhaps they thought, 'All right, just you wait,' and so, on the evening of the day after the poison laddus were laid out, when Rabbit went up to the roof to survey the situation, the monkeys threw a half-piece of brick from the roof of the stairwell of the adjacent building at his forehead; the brick came flying, and before he could realize anything, it hit his head, *dhop*, and Rabbit fell in slow motion on the bed of monkey shit and passed out. However, it's difficult to say what really happened to Rabbit's Lexus, if Chan Miya had stolen it, once it entered Basumati Motor Garage Ltd in Gazipur, it had surely been digested, but a few days later, Chan Miya was spotted inside another car in front of the temple at the crossing of the lane, perhaps it was another Honda vehicle – perhaps an Accord, it could have been a Civic too – and he was sitting inside and eating bananas with his monkey friends. Ledu, the fat Fakhrul Alam Ledu, then arrived, and when he asked, 'Won't you take me for a ride in your car?', Chan Miya asked him in return, 'Where would you like to go?'

Ledu had no mischief in mind, he wasn't a wily boy like that, it is very difficult to have a wily mind when you are fat, and so after they emerged from Ghost Lane that day, they went past the Gour Math and the Christian cemetery and headed towards Hathkhola, perhaps they could have gone via Jatrabari and over the Postogola bridge for a long drive on the smooth highway, but after they passed Baldha Garden, Ledu said, 'Do you know who lives right here?'

'Teacher!'

'Come, let's go and meet her!'

Surprisingly, Chan Miya agreed, and then that evening or dusk, Chan Miya met Julie Florence at the lane housing the Women's Education Institute after almost two decades; Fakhrul Alam Ledu asked her, 'Recognize him?' And surprisingly Julie could. 'Chan Miya?'

'I'm Monkey Boy!'

Mrs Mary Clark was inside, lying in bed with her eyes shut, and when Chan Miya went and stood near her and said, '*Teacher, ami Chan Miya.* Teacher, I am Chan Miya,' perhaps Mary Joyce gazed at him and wondered, who's this boy? And when Julie gave her consent, his monkey friends were brought from the car downstairs to her room on the first floor; the wild monkeys jumped and pranced around and left Julie's room in a shambles, and Julie was overcome with fear and excitement; and because wherever there were monkeys there would be bananas, all of them consumed bananas inside the room, perhaps Chan Miya offered one or two bananas to Julie and said, 'Monkeys eat bananas, and so do humans, here, have it,' and Julie had to accept the bananas; she then remembered her mother's caution, 'Beware of…' but she thought that it was too late now, because hadn't Ledu told her that she had already accomplished the task of eating a banana given by Chan Miya when she was very small, so it was a case of 'it's too late' for Julie; she enjoyed eating the bananas with Chan Miya, Ledu and the monkeys, and because she had asked Chan Miya, 'Why don't you come to visit?', Chan Miya visited again; his car and the monkeys were downstairs, and he sat in Mrs Clark's drawing room and conversed with Julie, '*Ami Teacherke bhuli nai.* I did not forget Teacher.'

'What do you do now?'

'I steal cars!'

Julie was completely flabbergasted.

'What?'

'I steal cars and sell them, I'm a car thief; there's a car parked downstairs, a Toyota Sprinter, I stole it this morning!'

Perhaps Julie thought Chan Miya was definitely joking, and then Chan Miya got up and left; when Chan Miya returned after one, or two, or five days, Julie asked him, 'What car did you steal today, Mr Car Thief?'

'I don't have a car, I came by rickshaw.'

And then it seemed it was another Julie who stood before Chan Miya; she asked, 'Did you bring your monkey friends?'

'They can't travel without a car.'

'*Kola achhe pockete?* Do you have a banana in your pocket?'

Did Julie Florence do all this out of desperation? Why was she desperate? Chan Miya took out two sweet-as-sugar champa bananas and offered them to her, the way Fr Albert Charles D'Souza had offered bananas to Miss Bidyunmala Das or Miss Labanyaprabha Das a long time ago; Julie bit into the bananas carefully and ate them, and she observed that Chan Miya was almost invisible as he sat in the shadowy corner, she then asked him, 'Will you take me in your car one day, Chan Miya?' So he reflected: he was Monkey Boy, a car thief, he had no attachment to this girl, Julie; so he got ready for the hunt, he would stick the knife right into the heart, and he said, 'I'll take you if you want to go, I'll steal a BMW and bring it!'

Perhaps it was from Arfan Ali in Basumati Garage that Chan Miya first learnt about BMWs, and after his conversation with Julie, he found out more about this vehicle; Arfan Ali was a scholar of this trade, he told Chan Miya everything candidly, 'A Mercedes is good, better than that is a BMW, the car's made in Germany, it's terribly expensive, the price may be even more than ten million, there are a few in Dhaka, there may be a hundred or two hundred of them' – but Arfan Ali was unable to say who owned them. Chan Miya then said, 'I need one, Master, shall I get you one?'

Arfan Ali didn't show any enthusiasm, it was difficult to consume a BMW, and impossible to digest, there weren't any people who would buy it; in this trade, a Toyota was the best of all, it vanished very quickly, Arfan Ali could handle as many as two, or ten Toyotas a day. But finding a BMW became of vital importance for Chan Miya, if he were to go to Julie's residence now, he could not do so without a BMW, after all, he had given his word, so it was a question of his honour; besides, he couldn't take Julie out in a Toyota, or a Honda, or a Nissan, these were run-of-the-mill cars, and a Maruti Suzuki Esteem, or a Tata Indica, were out of the question – these weren't cars, they were just lumps of iron! Thereafter, Chan Miya was observed to be remiss as regards his main work, he was busy looking for a BMW; and one day, either at the Sheraton or at the Sonargaon, or at the Lake Shore or the Lake Castle in Gulshan, in Dhaka, he spotted a BMW; it was on a holiday, either a Friday or a Saturday; he saw one, no, an entire fleet of BMWs parked in a row, and then the colour-blind Chan Miya's grey world once again became real in front of him; he saw that one of the five cars was black, one was white, and one was blue, and the other two were grey- or ash-coloured, and so he chose the blue-coloured X-series model, an X-5. Be that as it may, perhaps the location was indeed Hotel Sonargaon, there were four cars in two rows under the almond tree in the parking area, two were parked bumper-to-bumper on one side, while the blue-coloured car was somewhat afar, all by itself; Chan Miya made that his target. He asked the security guard in the parking lot, 'Who's the owner of the BMWs, boss?' When the security guard, perhaps his name was Habibur Rahman, heard that, his hair stood on end, he retorted, 'Why do you need to know?' But coming to an agreement with Habibur Rahman was no problem at all, and he came to terms with the driver of the vehicle too; Chan Miya explained that there was no risk as far as Habibur Rahman was concerned, because the car wouldn't be lost, BMWs stolen in this country could not be resold, there were no customers, he said that he would take the car for perhaps ten or twelve hours, and after that he would definitely return it – the car would be standing in front of the Arunoday Gate of Ramna Park, near the beginning of Bailey Road. He told Habibur Rahman, 'If the police catch you, all you need to do is to get through twelve hours somehow, and then you're done with any problems – so whom do the cars belong to, boss?'

Perhaps Habibur Rahman knew who the owners of the cars were, if a BMW suddenly appeared within the crowd of Coronas and Corollas or Sunnys, how could Habibur Rahman fail to notice the owners? Perhaps Chan Miya put a Pran candy into his hand by way of expressing additional cordiality – 'Taste it, it's indigenous' – and it was observed that Habibur Rahman was a knowledgeable and experienced man, he had various opinions about the world, and so, after undoing the wrapper of the candy and putting it into his mouth, he described the owners: 'The white car belongs to Ghasir Bin Ahram, he has an airline company, he trafficks people to the Middle East; the arsehole Pakistani or Indian employees in the airports of Dubai or Dhahran or Jeddah address the trafficked folk of Bangladesh rudely, calling them "tui" – "*Aei, kidhar jata hai tu*"; the Arabian brothers don't speak to them either, but flying them is a very lucrative business; the owner of the black one is Andrew L. Bautop, his shop is called Vocal, he memorizes Bengali nonsense ditties, like "*Sultana bibiyana, saheb-babur boithokkhana*" and then he wails, "Doctor sa'ab, I can't get rid of the gas in my stomach, I'm dying"; the blue one belongs to Gandiv Bahta, his company is For Beauty, he has beauty all right, he's the crazy man behind the TV programme *In Search of Your Egg, Chicken*; the red car is Anwantry Tunabatne's, he's a loan shark, he lends money and takes it back, and if the government announces privatization of two or four banks, he'll swallow them up…' – Chan Miya couldn't see the red car, he thought that red was one of the shades of grey – 'and the ash-coloured car belongs to Kokil Chanda, his job is to feed people, spend your cash and go on eating, he's saving money to buy the Dhaka Sheraton at the appropriate time, and he copied his friends by buying a car, albeit a less expensive one, of the 3-series, just so that he can be a member of the BMW club.' And so, these five members of the BMW club in

Bangladesh were sitting and chatting at the poolside in Sonargaon, perhaps they were relaxing, taking it easy, stretching their limbs, taking a break – they were such busy folk, and that's why they needed rest! Ghasir Bin Ahram, from the desert land, was a newcomer in this country of moisture and rain, and he considered Gandiv Bahta – who seemed to have blended into the grass in the garden like a chameleon – his guide, so he had asked him, 'My master, what's the best scheme to expand my business?'

'Advertising and more advertising.'

'I'll advertise.'

There was no conflict of business interest between Ghasir and Gandiv, so the latter displayed utmost graciousness, 'Get hold of a good advertising company, that's very important in this country.'

'Tell me more.'

'The leaders of civil society of this country like to run advertising companies, just pay them and they will make everything acceptable.'

Habibur Rahman chewed on another Pran candy and said to Chan Miya, 'Go inside and take a look'; and Chan Miya walked towards the swimming pool and saw the five people, they sipped their glasses of martini, prepared with an ounce and a half of dry gin, half an ounce of dry vermouth and crushed ice, and a slice of lemon, and chewed on cashew nuts imported from Honolulu; Chan Miya went and hovered around them, they thought he was perhaps one of the hotel staff. Gandiv Bahta then said, 'They are associated with art and culture, I make donations and so on.'

'I'll do that too.'

'I sponsor programmes.'

'I'll do the same.'

But Anwantry's enthusiasm lay elsewhere, he said to Gandiv, 'I'm in a terribly "dry" state, do you get me!'

'Take someone tasty along and go for a holiday to Pattaya, or to Kota Kinabalu, five nights for a hundred thousand, you pay for travel, food and accommodation. I have the mobile number, I can give it to you if you want.'

Their thinking then converged, the inner differences and ambiguities between their respective words and sentences disappeared; Anwantry Tunabatne, Ghasir Bin Ahram, Andrew L. Bautop, Gandiv Bahta and Kokil Chand all spoke in the same language.

'The people in this country say that they have the cheapest labour in the world!'

'Probably, it's not a problem, we will use them, and we will make money.'

'They are the cheapest, yes, we will give them work, and they will sing to us!'

'Their women will!'

They then remembered Gandiv Bahta's television programme, 'In Search of Your Egg, Chicken' – they demanded of Gandiv, 'Come on, tell us what you're doing!'

'I've paid my advertising agency, they are handling it, no one can make any ruckus about it – we'll discover beauties!'

'And we will pick some of them, and build a little doll's house in … somewhere or the other!'

Gandiv added, 'On the Panthakunja … we will take it on lease from Mr Koka.'

Andrew L. Bautop then expressed his opinion, 'Governance is a problem in this country, there's a dearth of good governance,' and he asked, 'Can't something be done about that?'

'Of course it can! We can tell them, you run the administration, and give the finances to us, we'll handle that, Tata is coming, the Dhabi group is coming, bhai, after all it's a free-market economy!'

But Mr Bautop couldn't understand, he asked, 'What's that?'

Anwantry knew a bit of history, he was amazed, 'That will be excellent,' he said, and Gandiv Bahta thought that after three servings, the martini had perhaps started going to people's heads, so he declared, 'You are going too far, my friends!'

Sitting at a vacant table, Chan Miya listened to the conversation of the five members of Dhaka's BMW club, or maybe he didn't because he didn't know English, he only watched them as they applied their tongues and lips to the rims of their glasses and licked the white liquid inside, and he stole Gandiv Bahta's blue-coloured car. Perhaps

Julie then told Mamun that Chan Miya and Ledu had come to spend some time in her house, and Mamun then maintained a stony silence owing to his immense grief, he did not want to get into the subject of Chan Miya, so he asked about Costa instead, 'What news of your Costa saheb?' Perhaps Julie sympathized with Mamun, she realized that Mamun had fallen into a deep pit, and that he would fervently clutch at any straws he found, but Julie didn't throw any lifelines his way, she was heartless, and Mamun then said, 'Will you come to our house one day?'

'Why?'

'Just like that.'

'All right, I'll come one day.'

'Come today, right now.'

Julie did not agree, but she said that if Ledu Bhai also came along, she would go to Ghost Lane one day with Mamun.

'Promise?'

Perhaps Julie was pained, perhaps her heart wept for Mamun who was seated in front of the window with his head downcast, she said, 'I'll go.'

'Tell me about Costa.'

Julie didn't say anything, or perhaps she did, there was no news regarding Costa; actually it was when her mother, Mrs Mary Joyce Clark, had gone to visit Ms Rosalyn D'Costa at her residence that Ms D'Costa had suggested this marital alliance, and Mrs Clark could not object because Julie did need to get married, but where could she find a good groom who would marry her daughter? Costa was a fine boy, on what grounds could she demur, and why? Although she was anxious about what Julie might say, Julie too had no grounds to say no, and observing her mother's weary face, she said, 'Do whatever you think is best, Mom.' And so, Pius D'Costa returned to his campus in the American University in Ward Circle in Washington DC, taking the No. 32, or No. 34, or No. 36 bus after making a quick visit to a used-books store in M Street, and when his roommate in Centennial Hall, the Indonesian undergraduate student Hotomo informed him, 'Your mother called,' Costa thought that his mother was troubling him unnecessarily, she was making things difficult for him; it was on Hotomo's urging that they had installed the National Bell company's telephone in their room, it was Hotomo who had gone to the Sears store in Tenleytown and bought the handset, and it was he who used it night and day, paying a bill of a hundred and fifty or two hundred dollars every month, but Costa never received any phone calls, and then one day his mother Rosalyn phoned him and spoke to him for the first time about Julie, 'She's a nice girl, think about it.'

He thought about it, he had a jurisprudence class at five-thirty in the evening, at Myers Building, on the subject of justice research; after finishing the class that day, he walked beside Binder Library and returned to his hall which lay in semi-darkness, he had taken two subjects with six credit hours this fall semester, the trees in Washington DC began shedding their leaves soon after October, melancholy, dry leaves of oak and maple rustled under his feet as he walked, and because his mother had called, he called her back the next morning, she received the call and asked him, 'What time is it now over there?'

'It's ten in the morning.'

'It's eight o'clock at night here, we are watching television,' Rosalyn D'Costa said, and then Pius D'Costa was observed to be restless, he exited the campus and walked absently down Nebraska Avenue and Loughborough Road in the autumn sun, he arrived at the bank of the Potomac – a lot of fat women were jogging along the man-made C&O Canal beside the river – and when he went to the chain bridge over the Potomac, near Little Falls, and sat down there, gazing at the water, the sun turned fierce and intense. When his mother phoned again at night, he said, 'Julie is indeed a nice girl, but she hasn't completed her studies, who knows when she'll finish!'

Rosalyn explained to him, 'She'll finish her studies, don't worry, how much longer will you stay this way, aren't you getting older?'; and just then, sitting in her residence, Julie was conversing with the failed fox Mamun, 'Why do you want to take me to your house?' Mamun was dumbfounded when he heard her say that, is this who the girl really is? There was no point pretending so much; did she really not understand why Mamun said all this? And so, Mamun was quiet, and it was Julie who had to break the silence again, 'It looks like Ledu Bhai isn't coming!'.

'Come to my house, it'll be an outing for you!'

'I'll go on Eid, I'll go at the end of the fasting month and have semai.'

'Eid is very far away, Julie, you know that!'

Julie then said that D'Costa had phoned her from Washington, but Mamun wasn't really interested, nevertheless Julie spun tales regarding Pius D'Costa, perhaps D'Costa had told her all this on the phone, or perhaps he hadn't, but nonetheless Julie narrated it to Mamun; perhaps it pleased her to say it, or perhaps she talked about her probable husband in order to pour cold water on Mamun's fond hopes, and Mamun Miya realized that there was no end to the girl's intelligence!

'Why do I need to hear about D'Costa?'

'What's the harm? Don't be like this, listen – we'll live close to the Tenleytown metro station, either on Veness Street, or Albemarle Street, or at a slight distance, on Macomb Street, D'Costa's university is within walking distance, there's also a shuttle-bus service, perhaps we'll be able to find a room in a basement for two hundred and fifty or three hundred dollars a month; the grocery store called Joint is almost within arm's reach from Macomb Street, it's no hassle at all, and there's a convenience store called GC Murphy right next to that, perhaps I can work at the sales counter there if I want, I'll have to work until D'Costa completes his studies, perhaps we'll buy some second-hand hotel furniture and make do with that, there's a warehouse on King Street, in Alexandria, where nice second-hand furniture is available, D'Costa can bring it home in a U-Haul van, perhaps I can also work in the evening in Cactus Restaurant and Bar at the corner of Macomb, working in a bar pays more, and when we have some money – there's a store right nearby, in Langley Center, it's called Samsar – perhaps I'll buy a new dressing table, that's what I'd like, I'll also buy a new baby cot from there when I have a baby, perhaps baby cots aren't available in the warehouse in Alexandria, so I'll buy a new one; very close to our residence on Macomb Street, at the corner of Wisconsin Avenue and Massachusetts Avenue, is the Washington Cathedral, it's very beautiful, with Gothic architecture, if I'm not working on Sundays, perhaps I can join the prayer service there, perhaps I'll go for an outing somewhere sometimes, to the mall area on Capitol Hill, or the National Zoo in Woodley Park, or to Arlington Cemetery, a bit further away, I'll visit President Kennedy's grave, or go to Crystal City, or Pentagon City, or to New York itself by Greyhound bus, and if there's a winter sale on at Woodward & Lothrop or JCPenney, I'll stand in queue, and perhaps buy a turtleneck jumper for D'Costa, I might also buy two pairs of gloves, lined with wool inside, and that's how it will be; you know, Mamun Bhai, life is terribly short, there won't be any problem.' Perhaps Julie had made Mamun weep inwardly by saying all these things, but when Chan Miya arrived, she told him, 'I want to ride in a car stolen by you!'

'I'll take you!'

'When?'

Perhaps that was before Chan Miya found Gandiv Bahta's car; he had told her that he was trying to find a nice car for her, that after all, he couldn't take her out in any ordinary car because she was Teacher's daughter, and since she had expressed her wish to ride in a stolen car, a nice car had to be found, or else Teacher's dignity would be sullied, her daughter's dignity would be sullied, Chan Miya's as well! Julie then exclaimed, 'You steal cars, you don't think twice about doing that, but just because I said I want a ride, you now pin the blame on me!'

'I never said that I took that amiss, I am Monkey Boy, I am not offended by anything!'

'Why do you talk like that? Why are you like this, Chan Miya?'

What could Chan Miya say in response to that? Nothing; so Julie said, 'I'm going away to America, I'm getting married to Pius D'Costa, do you remember D'Costa? He was one or two years senior to you all.' Perhaps Chan Miya could not remember D'Costa, or perhaps he did, but he couldn't find a nice, appropriate car, and so when he visited Julie again, she then told him that she no longer wanted to go for a ride in his car, 'Why don't you just get a Subaru instead, or else even a Maruti Suzuki, I'll go to Mamun's house in your car!'

'Why?'

'Mamun's insisting I visit his place.'

And then Julie again mentioned her marriage, 'Did I tell you that I am getting married?' Chan Miya was at a loss to understand why Julie was doing this, he remained submerged in the shadows inside the sitting room; Julie then went and fetched a book given by Steven Arnold, the title of the book was *Innocent Eréndira and Other Stories*, the author was Gabriel García Márquez, and she said, 'Take the book, there's a story in it called "Death Constant Beyond Love", do read that.'

'I can't read such difficult English.'

Julie then said, 'It's a wonderful story, there's an elderly senator, probably in Colombia, named Onesimo Sanchez, who falls in love with a young girl and desires her, and the girl's scoundrel of a father surmises that, so he schemes in order to obtain some benefit through the opportunity, the girl's name is Laura Farina, her father then puts a chastity belt on her, keeps the key with himself, and sends the girl to the senator. After that, the senator discovers that the girl is under lock and key, and he asks her, "Where's the key?" And the girl replies, "My dad has it."' Chan Miya heard this tale, and he remarked, 'What kind of story is this? I couldn't understand anything,' because while the five members of Dhaka's BMW club were conversing in Hotel Sonargaon then, they got the news of Gandiv Bahta's car having been stolen, perhaps the bell captain came and informed them, perhaps the customer service manager himself came with the news, Gandiv Bahta's local Bengali driver wept and wailed a bit too loudly, 'Sir, I just went to the bathroom, and when I returned I saw the car was gone,' and the parking security guard, Habibur Rahman, too narrated the story he had made up, 'I didn't notice anything, I thought the driver was in the car, I didn't realize the driver had left the car unattended and gone somewhere,' perhaps they had thought that they would somehow get through the hours before being released, and that Chan Miya would phone the hotel, or the police station, and inform them of the whereabouts of the car; but things weren't quite so simple, because policemen from the Ramna police station arrived there very quickly, the case involved CIPs (Commercially Important Persons)-cum-Foreign Investors, it was a question of the image of the country, if they could not be provided security, investments worth billions of dollars would fail to materialize and go to China or Vietnam instead, that would be appalling, and so there was no option, if there were any slip-ups perhaps the Home Minister himself would drive a bamboo pole up your arse – the policemen tied up Habibur Rahman and Gandiv Bahta's Bengali driver and took them to Ramna police station. Perhaps Ghasir Bin Ahram then gave a lift to Gandiv Bahta in his white BMW – 'Come along, now that I've got the chance, let me drop you' – and Ghasir was very amused, he remarked, 'So, not only do they have cheap labour, they also have car thieves!'

'Yes. Actually we forget about one class, who would probably not be totally under our control!'

'Who? Car thieves?'

'Yes, we are foreign investors, how dare they steal our property!'

Perhaps Chan Miya had thought there wouldn't be much of a ruckus, but as soon as two lashes landed on their backsides at Ramna police station, they blurted out everything to the police, and so plainclothes officers were dispatched to keep watch near the Arunoday Gate of Ramna Park. The Rapid Action Battalion, or RAB, of the police was speedily attached to the case, RAB-2 scanned their database and found the profiles of three possible car thieves, and within two hours of the theft they landed up at Khoimon's house on No. 36 in Ghost Lane and found a blue-coloured BMW parked at the corner of the temple, and when Chan Miya got word about the RAB, he abandoned the idea of taking Julie for a long drive and fled; Khoimon told the RAB that the car did not belong to her son, the moholla folk too feigned ignorance, no, they hadn't seen anything, they didn't know anything either, and so the owner of the car could not be traced. Gandiv Bahta was overjoyed to get his car back within two hours, he said, 'Very good! Thank you! But you must catch the thief, I want to see him!' And so, perhaps for the first time in her life, Khoimon broke down thinking how things had turned out for her sweet boy, she recalled that she'd had suspicions right from the beginning, but she had never imagined that Chan Miya would become a full-fledged car thief. Khoimon then went to Nurani Bilkis's house and wept, and Nurani Bilkis Upoma consoled her, 'What can you do, you spent your whole life caring for your son – forget about him now, beseech Allah, start praying and fasting.'

Khoimon began covering herself with a cloth, she didn't have to buy it, Nurani Bilkis had given her an old, brown-coloured covering cloth, Khoimon wound that around the upper part of her body and went about her chores; and then Nurani Bilkis told her about religion.

'You'll be asked at the grave, *"Man Rabbuka?"*, what will you reply?'

'What does it mean?'

'Who is your Lord?'

Khoimon said, 'I'll say, Allah is my Lord,' and she made paper packets and went to Thatari Bazar to sell them.

Nurani Bilkis said, 'You'll be asked at the grave, *"Maa Dinooka?"*'

'What does it mean?'

'What's your religion?'

Khoimon said, 'I'll say my religion is Islam,' and she went to Thatari Bazar to collect the money from the sale of paper packets.

Nurani Bilkis then said, 'You'll be asked at the grave, "*Man Nabiyyuka?*"'

'What does it mean?'

'Who is your Prophet?'

Khoimon replied, 'I'll say my Prophet is Mohammad,' and she got Nurani Bilkis's wheat ground in Banagram.

Then one day, on returning home, Khoimon found Chan Miya lying in bed and playing with monkeys, one monkey had inserted a finger inside his ear and was tickling him, and when he made to push it away, the monkeys scooted; seeing Chan Miya at home, Khoimon's very life seemed to depart her body out of fear, '*Tawre RAB dhorbo, krusfayar koira maira faelaibo, tui bhaiga ja, Chan Miya!* The RAB will catch you, they'll kill you and claim you were caught in the crossfire, run away from here, Chan Miya!'

'Where will I go?'

Then on another day, Khoimon came upon the book *Innocent Eréndira,* and she saw on the cover of the book a half-naked woman reclining on a blue bed, she had a tiny, lacy skirt at her waist, the exposed breasts between her arms hung down like a pair of small gourds, and near the bed, sat an old woman, wearing a loose, green-coloured cloak, with her head buried in her bosom; Khoimon said to Nurani Bilkis Upoma, '*Ghore lyangta mayaloker chobiawla boi loya achhe, kawnto ki kori?* He's sitting at home with a book that has a picture of a naked woman, tell me what I ought to do?'

Nurani Bilkis listened to her and was shocked, she exclaimed, 'What are you saying!' And so Khoimon asked Chan Miya, 'Where did you get the book with the picture of a naked woman?'

'Teacher's daughter gave it to me.'

'Who gave it?'

'Julie.'

Khoimon remembered Chan Miya's teacher, she pondered over the matter, she lamented the trajectory her fatherless boy's life had taken; the RAB was after him, and here was Julie giving him a book like this one! And when she asked, '*Tui ki taile gari churi korochh?* So do you steal cars?', Chan Miya was silent.

'What did you do with the money?'

'I haven't got the money yet, but I will.'

Khoimon burst into tears before her son, 'Run away, my dear!' There was nothing Chan Miya could say, after all, where was he to go? Chan Miya then sought Arfan Ali's help, he sought Sergeant Rafiq's help, they too told him to flee, but where did Chan Miya have the time to flee then? Moreover, it was not merely the RAB that was after him, Rabbit was pursuing him too. Rabbit was laid up for a few days after he was hit with a stone by a monkey while on the roof of Mamun's house, and then he was up and about, he bought a red-coloured Nissan Sunny and he parked it in such a way at the corner of the lane beside the temple that it seemed the car had been abandoned; a day went by, two days went by, but no one touched his car, Rabbit bided his time sitting or lying down in Mamun's house, but nothing happened, and then on the evening of the third or the fourth day, while returning to Hotel Arzoo, he observed that a row of monkeys was sitting on a wall near the temple, he was scared, and angry too, if he had been carrying a weapon he could have shot the whole lot of them with a sweeping motion, and when he approached the car and opened the door, he broke out in profanity, 'Sons of whores, the lot of them,' and then with the speed of lightning, one of the monkeys sitting on the wall flung a stone the size of a two-kilo iron weight at him, the stone hit Rabbit above his ear, *bang*, and he collapsed on the dirt in the street in front of the temple. One thing became crystal clear to Rabbit Mamun, a final settlement was called for, and so he made a GP-to-GP call to Satkania and instructed his trusted servant, or legman, or assistant, Abu Jafar, to send an Abul Kasem 47, 'Hey Jafariya, how many Abul Kasems do you have?' Abu Jafar then made the arrangements, following Rabbit's instructions: from Satkania to Chittagong in Rabbit's Toyota car, and from there to Dhaka on the Greenline Company's night coach; either Chhowor or George would go with the Abul Kasem

47, perhaps both of them would go, they would deliver it to Rabbit and return – it was most urgent. And before they left in the evening, when the maidservant served them dinner, Asmantara noticed it, and when Asiya told her that Rabbit had called, and that Chhowor and George were leaving for Dhaka, Asmantara Hoore Jannat packed a bag and got ready – as Chhowor and George were about to climb into the car, they saw Asmantara inside, so they asked, 'Where are you going?'

'I'm going to Dhaka!'

There was nothing Rabbit's servants could do, because after all, Rabbit's servants were also Asmantara's servants, and Rabbit too was her servant; Asmantara rebuked them, 'Hey Chhowor, don't try to argue with me, I said I'm going and I'm going!'

Caught in that melee, Abu Jafar tried to get Rabbit on his mobile phone, but he couldn't get through, and that continued, and so the car left, carrying Asmantara as well, and when Abu Jafar finally managed to reach Rabbit after midnight, it was too late, Asmantara and her two companions had already left Chittagong on the Greenline Transport AC bus. Rabbit then called Chhowor in the bus, 'Where are you people now?'

'We haven't reached Feni yet.'

'Where's Asmantara?'

'She's sleeping?'

Chhowor assured him that everything was fine, there was no problem; but that was not what happened, because intelligence of an Abul Kasem making its way to Dhaka on the Greenline Transport AC bus had reached the ears of Lt Col. Anwarul Azim, the commanding officer of RAB-7 in Chittagong, and the source had informed him that a disassembled Abul Kasem would be found inside a bundled-up mattress. Rocked by the motion of the bus, Asmantara remained fast asleep throughout the journey; and when the bus gathered speed after they passed Moynamoti cantonment, and thinking that perhaps there were no more dangers ahead, Abdus Chhowor and George Miya also dozed off, and just then, a patrol squad of the RAB on the Cumilla bypass received a wireless message and they stopped the bus. While the RAB folk unloaded the rolled-up mattress that had a rope tied around it from the hold under the bus, how Chhowor and George managed to get off and vanish into the darkness was indeed something incredible, and when the RAB team sought to find the owner of the mattress, they got to Asmantara, and she made a GP-to-GP call to Rabbit while she was in RAB custody, but Rabbit had already learnt about the incident from Chhowor, and so he knew why Asmantara was calling him; he asked, 'Where's the RAB?'

Asmantara replied that she was sitting in the RAB vehicle, and when Captain Mujibar of the RAB squad spoke to Rabbit on Asmantara's GP-to-GP phone, Rabbit straightaway offered to surrender, 'I am in Suite No. A-3 at Hotel Arzoo, if you find me here, you must release Asmantara'; Captain Mujibar agreed to the proposal, what wouldn't a man do for a woman, even a great smuggler turned soft when it came to his lover, and he then remembered Rita, and wondered what Rita was doing now. Perhaps she was sleeping, perhaps she was curled up in bed, senseless. Captain Mujib agreed, after all it was Rabbit that they were after, they had no need for Asmantara, so they communicated with the RAB-2 headquarters in Dhaka, a RAB-2 squad went at once to Hotel Arzoo and discovered that Rabbit Mamun, aka Aibak, aka Qutubuddin Aibak, and his servant, Abul Hussain, aka Abuilya, had fled; Major Shahiduzzaman, the deputy commander of RAB-2, made Asmantara call him again, and Rabbit asked her, 'How are you?'

Asmantara replied, 'I'm all right, don't worry, where are you?'

'I can't tell you where!'

'Just run away!'

When Asmantara asked him, 'How are you?', Rabbit was unable to tell her how he was, and Khoimon then interrogated Chan Miya about the book given by Julie, and thus Chan Miya remembered the story in the book, and he went to the lane housing the Women's Education Institute and sat in the shadows in Mrs Clark's drawing room on the first floor – Julie looked at him – Chan Miya was the spitting image of his father, Moyna Miya, tall and with an aquiline nose, high hip bones on his backside, black eyes like deep pools, the muscles on his arm taut like ropes wound around them – and this man was a car thief! Chan Miya told Julie that he had got hold of a BMW for her, but because the police were after him, he was unable to give her a ride; Julie then retorted, '*Tumi ki mone kawro je tomar churi kora garite chorar jonyo ami more jachchhi?* Do you think I'm dying to get into your stolen car?'

Chan Miya was at his wits' end – *e kemun maiyalok,* what kind of girl was this, he wondered – and Julie told him that she had got engaged to Pius D'Costa, and that they would get married when Pius visited in a month or two.

Julie then asked him, 'Did you read the book? But, of course, you can't read English!'

Chan Miya was silent.

'Why didn't you continue your education, Chan Miya? Tell me why you didn't! My mother was so fond of you, you brought her grief!'

Perhaps Chan Miya wondered, what on earth is all this? Julie said, 'I gave you a book, I'm sad that you couldn't read it or understand it!'

Although Chan Miya was sitting amidst shadows, his eyes lit up, he told Julie that he wanted to get a dress made and present it to her, perhaps he'd give it to her for her upcoming wedding, and so he needed to know her waist measurement, 'Can you give me your waist measurement?', he asked Julie, and she gave him a panty of hers in a paper packet; Chan Miya did all this eluding the RAB and Rabbit, he took Julie's flowery nylon panty and gave it to a blacksmith in Jinjira, and in accordance with Chan Miya's instructions and the panty measurement, the blacksmith made a chastity belt of steel foil, with a hinge – there was an arrangement below for emitting bodily waste. Perhaps a month before Pius's planned visit to the country, Chan Miya waited in a jerky yellow cab he took from near the Elysium Rest House in Tikatuli, and when he spotted Julie walking home, Chan Miya opened the door and stepped out, grabbed Julie's hand, dragged her and bundled her into the cab, and as Julie sat inside, she asked, 'What are you doing?'

Julie was missing for two days, and after that she returned to her residence in the lane housing the Women's Education Institute, and when she rang the doorbell, she was worried about whether she would even find her mother alive! But Mrs Clark opened the door, and asked her, 'Where were you?'

'Chan Miya kidnapped me!'

Perhaps Mrs Clark went back to her room and lay in bed for a long time, and after that Julie prepared supper, called her mother and made her sit at the dining table, she combed her unkempt, grey hair and knotted it using a rubber band, 'Nothing's happened to me, Mom,' she said, 'after all, you know Chan Miya, he loves you, he didn't do anything to me, Mom!' But when Mrs D'Costa came to fix the date of the wedding, Julie made several pretexts, 'Not right now, let's wait for a few more days to pass,' and that night, as her mother, Mary, was having the vegetable soup Julie had prepared, she said, 'Please don't do this to me, I am tired, Julie, you should know that,' Julie Florence then held her sick mother's hand and told her that she wanted to become a nun and go away to Shripur, and Mrs Clark left her bowl of soup on the table and went and lay down on her bed; perhaps Julie was anxious about her mother, she came and sat by the bed and said, 'There's nothing I can do, Mom, I cannot marry D'Costa!'

'But why? Why are you doing this?'

Julie took her mother's hand and placed it at her waist, and through the cloth of Julie's long skirt, Mrs Mary Joyce could feel the shape of a medium-sized padlock, she was visibly terrified, 'What's this?'

'A chastity belt!'

'What are you saying?'

Julie said, 'I can't marry D'Costa in this situation, I want to become a nun, Mom!'

'Where's the key to the lock?'

'With Chan Miya!'

Mrs Clark then broke into tears – 'Oh my God, you are only punishing me … All right, let Chan Miya come' – warm tears rolled down her old, weary cheeks, and having failed to nab Rabbit, Major Shahid of RAB-2 was furious, he didn't let Asmantara go, he took her to the court on behalf of the Ramna police station, and obtained further remand, but no sign of fear or discomfiture was observed in Asmantara, she did whatever Major Shahid or Captain Anis of the RAB, told her to; but there was no trace of Rabbit – he was entirely busy plotting Chan Miya's punishment. Perhaps after stealing the Lexus, Chan Miya had found out about Rabbit, perhaps Sergeant Rafiq told him that Rabbit was probably some big-time thief or robber, or even a smuggler, 'He seems to be a dangerous man, don't lay hands on his things,' and Chan Miya didn't lay his hands any more, he didn't touch Rabbit's second car, even though Rabbit had deliberately left it lying for three or four days in front of the lane beside the temple; of course, his monkey brigade couldn't tolerate such barbarous behaviour, these grey monkeys of Bangladesh knew the value of friendship, their hearts wept for their friend, and so one of them threw a stone and broke Rabbit's head.

Rabbit was aware that perhaps the RAB would keep an eye on the red car he had seemingly cast away, but Chan Miya just didn't touch it, and then one night the car disappeared, come morning it was discovered that it was no longer parked at the corner of the lane beside the temple; Major Shahid swore at his men, 'What on earth were you doing, you useless lot!' Perhaps it was Rabbit who removed the car from the corner of the lane beside the temple, and after he found out about Chan Miya's lover, on Thursday night, he parked his red Nissan Sunny at the corner of the lane housing the Women's Education Institute, and he also parked a second Nissan Sunny of the same colour there – this was like tethering two mice on the route frequented by a cat – and then Major Shahid of RAB-2 got word from his source that the red Nissan had been found, and a squad from RAB-2 went to the spot and found two identical cars matching the description! They were confused, but on checking the number plates, they realized that one of them belonged to Rabbit, and they took up positions nearby and began keeping a watch on the car; then on Friday, Chan Miya had his lunch after the Jumma community prayer, took a nap in their secret attic, and left for Julie's residence once he woke up. Perhaps Rabbit too went somewhere to meet Abuilya, 'We won't stay in Dhaka any longer, let's go,' he said, and thought about meeting Asmantara; and then in the late afternoon or in the evening, he entered Hotel Arzoo in the guise of a sweeper, the hotel staff were busy attending to the customers and watching the cricket match on television, they did not notice the sweeper. Rabbit entered the hotel without encountering any hindrance, went up to Suite No. A-3 on the third floor and knocked on the door, and Asmantara opened the door and saw a bearded sweeper clad in a lungi and a vest standing outside with a broom in his hand, and she said, 'My room doesn't need to be cleaned,' the sweeper with a long beard untied the gamchha around his waist, wiped his face, and said, 'I'm Rabbit'; Asmantara made way for him, and Rabbit went inside and sat down, and saw to his amazement that the old wooden cage was placed beside a wall inside the room; seeing the cage, Rabbit became very excited, he was overwhelmed, and he asked, 'Where did you get the cage from?'

'I got it from Satkania!'

Asmantara said that Abu Jafar had brought the cage on a truck, and Rabbit, clad in gamchha-and-lungi as part of his disguise, perhaps thought he ought to try lying down inside, and he went cheerily and lay down curled up inside the cage; after being pursued by the RAB, and having become weary sleeping in the attic in Mrs Zobeida Rahman's house that stank of monkey shit, perhaps Rabbit shut his eyes in comfort, and then Asmantara went and locked the cage.

'Why are you doing this!'

After that, when Asmantara told the captive Rabbit, 'Come, let's return to Satkania,' Chan Miya went in the late afternoon, following the Jumma prayers, to Julie's residence, stood beside Mrs Clark's bed, and said, '*Teacher, ami Chan Miya.* Teacher, I am Chan Miya,' and Mrs Mary Joyce Clark then removed her hands from her eyes, where they had lain all day, she opened her eyes and looked, and said, 'Chan Miya, take Julie!'

Chan Miya replied, '*Ami ashbo, Teacher.* I'll be back, Teacher,' and as he left Julie's residence, he spotted two grey-coloured Nissan Sunny cars parked at the corner of the lane – the colour-blind boy didn't realize that both of them were red-coloured vehicles – the car thief instincts within him awakened, he was seized by the fervent longing to plunder someone's goods and inside the cage, Rabbit then placed his hands on the two sides of his head and shut his eyes, and it seemed that he curled himself up like a foetus in his mother's womb in preparation for another birth – the cage was his mother.

SHAHIDUL ZAHIR (1953–2008) completed his post-graduation at the University of Dhaka and the American University, Washington, D.C., and joined the civil services in Bangladesh. He is best known for his novella, *Jibon O Rajnoitik Bastobota*. Shahidul Zahir's oeuvre includes the short story collections *Parapar*, *Dumurkheko Manush O Onyanno Golpo*, and *Dolu Nodir Haowa O Onyanno Golpo*, the novels *Shey Raate Purnima Chhilo* and *Mukher Dike Dekhi*, and the novella *Abu Ibrahimer Mrityu*.

V. RAMASWAMY has translated Subimal Misra's *The Golden Gandhi Statue from America: Early Stories*, *Wild Animals Prohibited: Stories, Anti-Stories*, and *This Could Have Become Ramayan Chamar's Tale: Two Anti-Novels*, Manoranjan Byapari's novels *The Runaway Boy* and *The Nemesis*, and *Memories of Arrival: A Voice from the Margins* by Adhir Biswas. His translations of Shahidul Zahir's *Life and Political Reality: Two Novellas* (co-translated with Shahroza Nahrin) and *Why There Are No Noyontara Flowers in Agargaon Colony: Stories* were published in 2022.

30 Years *of*

HarperCollins *Publishers* India

At HarperCollins, we believe in telling the best stories and finding the widest possible readership for our books in every format possible. We started publishing 30 years ago; a great deal has changed since then, but what has remained constant is the passion with which our authors write their books, the love with which readers receive them, and the sheer joy and excitement that we as publishers feel in being a part of the publishing process.

Over the years, we've had the pleasure of publishing some of the finest writing from the subcontinent and around the world, and some of the biggest bestsellers in India's publishing history. Our books and authors have won a phenomenal range of awards, and we ourselves have been named Publisher of the Year the greatest number of times. But nothing has meant more to us than the fact that millions of people have read the books we published, and somewhere, a book of ours might have made a difference.

As we step into our fourth decade, we go back to that one word – a word which has been a driving force for us all these years.

Read.

Harper Collins · 4th · HARPER PERENNIAL · HARPER BUSINESS · HARPER BLACK · हार्पर हिन्दी

HarperCollins *Children's Books* · HARPER DESIGN · HARPER VANTAGE · Harper Sport